SEARCH FOR THE MEDALLION

THE WIZARD ACADEMIES
BOOK 2

MIKE SHELTON

Search for the Medallion

Library of Congress Control Number: 2020906085
ISBN: 978-1-7335104-6-2

Salem, Oregon

Sign up for my email list to get further news and information on my books and giveaways at:
http://www.michaelsheltonbooks.com

Cover Illustration by Gordon Napier

Map by Robert Altbauer

ACKNOWLEDGEMENTS

I love all the support I have received throughout the years from my wife, family, editors, friends, and very importantly my readers. Thanks for letting me keep writing and telling the stories that are in my head!

-Mike

Books by Mike Shelton

WESTERN CONTINENT BOOKS:

The Cremelino Prophecy:
The Path Of Destiny
The Path Of Decisions
The Path Of Peace
The Blade and the Bow (A prequel novella to The Cremelino Prophecy)

The Alaris Chronicles:
The Dragon Orb
The Dragon Rider
The Dragon King
Prophecy Of The Dragon (A prequel novella to The Alaris Chronicles)

The Dragon Artifacts:
The Golden Dragon
The Golden Scepter
The Golden Empire

The Wizard Academies:
The Mark of the Medallion
The Search for the Medallion
The Power of the Medallion

GEMSTONES OF WAYLAND BOOKS:

The TruthSeer Archives:
TruthStone
TruthSpell
TruthSeer
The Stones of Power (A prequel novella to The TruthSeer Archives)

MAPS

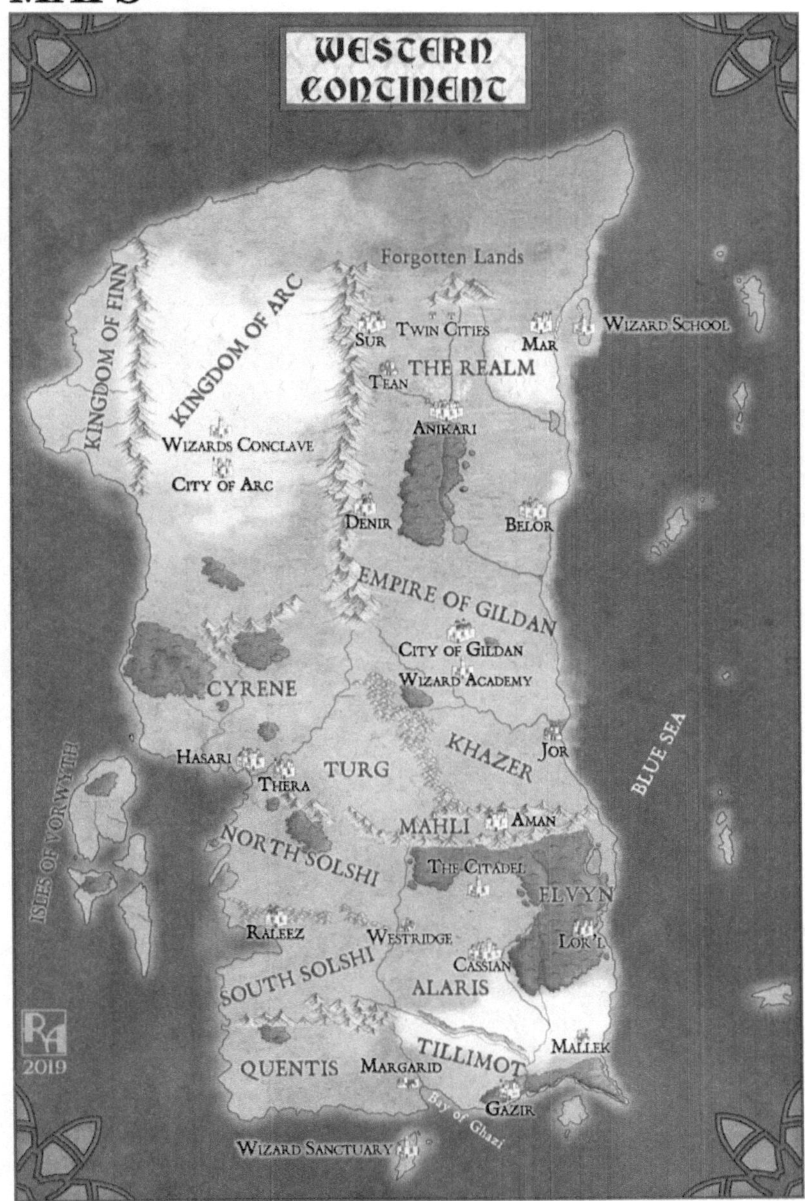
WESTERN CONTINENT
Forgotten Lands
KINGDOM OF FINN
KINGDOM OF ARC
SUR
TWIN CITIES
MAR
WIZARD SCHOOL
THE REALM
TEAN
ANIKARI
WIZARDS CONCLAVE
CITY OF ARC
DENIR
BELOR
EMPIRE OF GILDAN
CITY OF GILDAN
WIZARD ACADEMY
CYRENE
KHAZER
JOR
BLUE SEA
HASARI
TURG
THERA
ISLES OF VORWYTH
MAHLI
AMAN
NORTH SOLSHI
THE CITADEL
ELVYN
RALEEZ
WESTRIDGE
LOR'L
CASSIAN
SOUTH SOLSHI
ALARIS
RA
2019
TILLIMOT
MALLEK
QUENTIS
MARGARID
Bay of Ghazi
GAZIR
WIZARD SANCTUARY

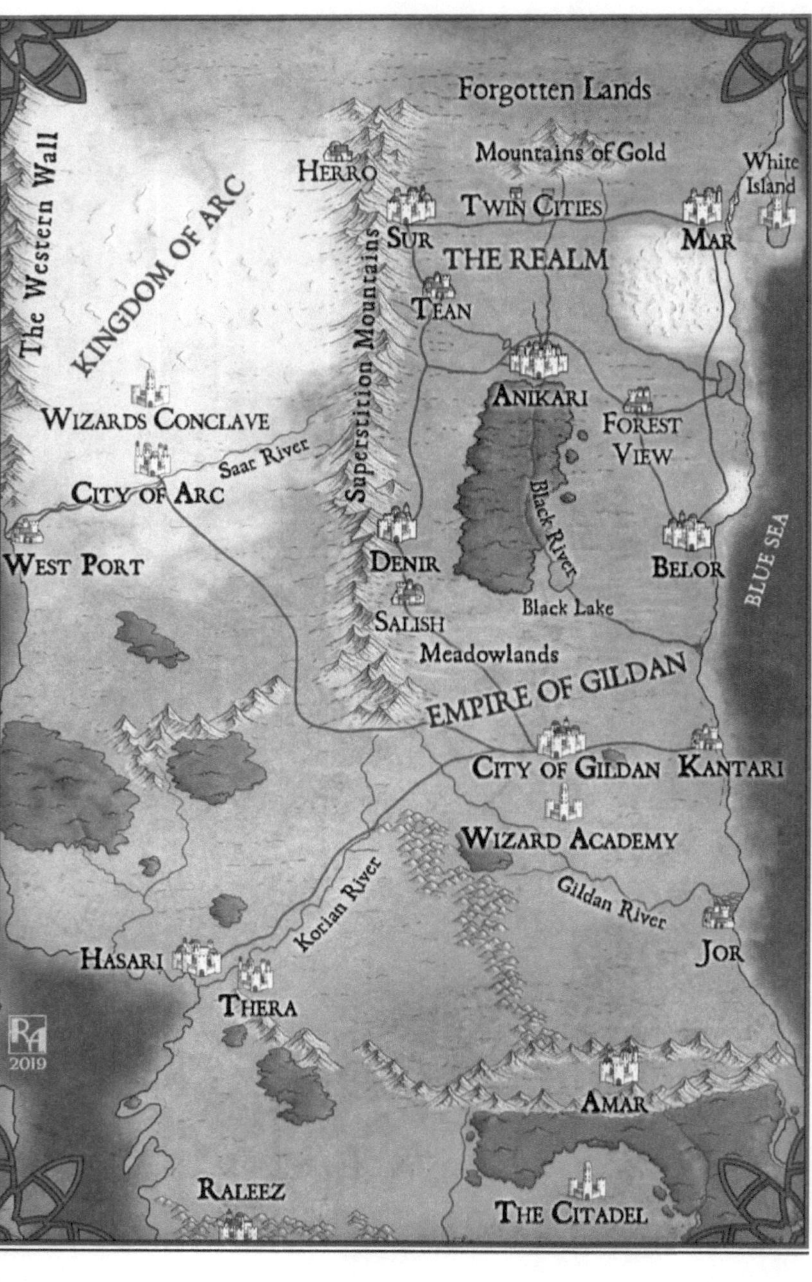

Forgotten Lands
Mountains of Gold
The Western Wall
Kingdom of Arc
Herro
Twin Cities
White Island
Sur
The Realm
Mar
Superstition Mountains
Tean
Anikari
Wizards Conclave
Forest View
Saar River
City of Arc
Black River
West Port
Denir
Belor
Blue Sea
Black Lake
Salish
Meadowlands
Empire of Gildan
City of Gildan
Kantari
Wizard Academy
Korian River
Gildan River
Hasari
Jor
Thera
RA
2019
Amar
Raleez
The Citadel

CHAPTER ONE

Kyril leaned over and vomited, and Joelle immediately tried to jump out of the way. Bumping into a bookshelf, she steadied herself and tried not to get sick. That was the first time she had ever transported and she shook her head to clear away a bit of disorientation.

"That's gross, Kyril," Sylvie called out from the other side.

"Sorry," Kyril mumbled. He heaved once again and then stood up. Apparently his stomach was now empty.

The stench of the vomit immediately reached Joelle's nose and she tried not to breathe in too deeply.

"Why did you bring us here to the library?" Joelle asked. "Do you always get sick when you transport? Are you doing all right now? I can take you to the healers' room if you need to lie down. I…"

"Joelle," Sylvie snapped at her, shaking her head.

Ah, not the time for questions, it seemed. Joelle glanced around the library of the Wizard Academy in Gildan and then back at her two friends. Sylvonna Hickory and Kyril Siravan were wizards like herself—Kyril had just been promoted from an apprentice a few moments before by the Emperor of Gildan himself, although a more public ceremony would be held later.

The three couldn't have been more different. Joelle herself, a wizard of the heart with an affinity for healing, was from Belor, a city in the southeast corner of the Realm, the kingdom just north of Gildan. Slender with long red, unruly hair and green eyes, she was quite the opposite of Sylvie who was from the Kingdom of Arc, and had short blonde hair, blue eyes, and was already a powerful wizard of the earth. Sylvie tended to jump into things while Joelle was more cautious of adventure in general.

Kyril groaned and plopped down on a chair. He was the only one of the three from Gildan itself. After being raised in Haran, a small town in the meadowlands just east of the Superstition Mountains, he had been taken to the Wizard Academy when the rest of his family had died in a tragic fire. Kyril had the brown skin and dark hair common of those from the Empire of Gildan. At fifteen, he was a year younger than Joelle and Sylvie. Even for his age he wasn't very tall, and until recently was a relatively weak wizard.

But that had all changed the previous day. Kyril had embraced the power of the medallion and saved the emperor and his son. After which the emperor himself raised Kyril from an apprentice to a full wizard. And now, even though their backgrounds and wizard disciplines were varied, they had a common cause.

"Joelle," croaked Kyril, still pale, "you asked why I brought you here. To defeat Gamal and find the other two medallions before he does, we need to do more research. I figured this was the best place to start."

Joelle glanced at the gold medallion hanging from a chain around his neck. Now that they were done transporting the initial glow it had let off was subsiding. She took a few steps toward him, keeping an eye on the mess on the floor, and put her hand on his forehead. It was clammy and warm. Closing her eyes for a moment to concentrate on the task, she used her healing abilities to calm his racing heart and still his stomach.

"Thanks.," Kyril smiled up at her. "You're great to have around."

Joelle rolled her eyes and Sylvie snorted at his joke.

"We could have been around you helping more if you hadn't shoved us away," Sylvie said. Her right hand rested stubbornly on her hip as she frowned at Kyril.

"I know." Kyril hung his head. "But I couldn't tell you what I was doing with Targon…" His voice fell away.

Joelle patted him on the shoulder. She knew he was still reeling from having to betray his mentor Targon Quereshi—an influential wizard that had had grand plans to set himself up as a ruler of Gildan. During a battle at the palace, they had figured out that it was really his scribe, Gamal, a short balding man with a birthmark on his forehead, that had been the evil influence behind Targon. And now Gamal had escaped.

"What in the emperor's name happened here?" said a woman coming around the corner.

All three flinched and Kyril jumped to his feet.

"Joelle! Sylvie!" said the man next to the head librarian.

"Hi, Hasani," Joelle said, not really even aware of the smile that was spreading on her face. Hasani was a wizard apprentice of the mind from Mahli, a kingdom to the south of Gildan and was an apprentice to the librarian to finish his training.

"Hasani?" the librarian said with a glance to her apprentice and then at the mess on the floor.

"Oh no!" Hasani shook his head, his long braids swinging around his dark-skinned face. "I'm a librarian, not a custodian."

"You're my apprentice," the librarian said with a flash of anger across her face. "At least for a few more days."

Hasani groaned loudly as he turned and left to get supplies to clean up the mess.

At first the librarian gazed steadily at the three young wizards then raised her brows at their fancy cloaks. With her eyes going wide she eventually focused on the gold medallion that hung down from Kyril's neck.

"Where did you three come from?" the librarian said with hands on her hips and her eyes returning to their faces. "This is not a place for games."

Joelle glanced at Kyril and then turned toward her best friend, then opened her mouth to explain.

"It's a long story," Sylvie jumped in instead.

"I'm not going anywhere," said the librarian. She tapped her toe and continued to glare at the three young wizards. She was a kind woman who had been very patient with them over the past week. She ran a tight, neat, and quiet library—but since the three of them had shown up, her apprentice Hasani had been kidnapped, thieves had stolen a rare book from the basement rooms, and secret whispers had replaced serious studies. Her patience had apparently run thin.

"Last night Kyril saved Emperor Alrishitar and his son, Prince Zaidan from an attack," Joelle said to the surprise of the librarian. "The Palace was so amazing. It just glows with power. And everyone was so beautiful. The music and the food…" She trailed off as Sylvie grabbed her attention with a shallow cough. "Oh yes, well—we have just returned from a meeting with the emperor where he thanked us for our help."

"But how?" The librarian glanced around with a puzzled expression on her wrinkled face. "How did you get here? I didn't see you come in."

Kyril reached his hand up to the medallion around his neck. It had three concentric circles. Six lines came from the center; three went all the way to the edge of the ancient relic where three small half-circles stuck out from the mostly round medallion. As Kyril clutched the relic, Joelle noticed it began to once again glow. "I transported us here," Kyril said with a shy grin. "Sorry about the mess. I get sick every time I transport."

"Every time?" The librarian put a hand on the edge of the table to steady her obvious nerves. "But an apprentice has never done that before," the librarian said.

"But Kyril is no longer an apprentice," Joelle said. "Oh, you should have seen him last night when he told his handler—Bale! Can you believe that? He always teased Kyril, and then they had to work together. Well, he told him about Wizard Targon and then Kyril tricked them all. Targon had taken the prince and proclaimed himself governor of Gildan when Kyril foiled his plans. Then Gamal attacked all of us—you see, he has a black medallion, an evil one of sorts. But Kyril saved the emperor and his son. Then Gamal got away."

Joelle had to take a deep breath and was just about to continue when the librarian put her hand up for Joelle to stop.

"I think you went a bit fast, Joelle." Sylvie smiled.

"Sorry," Joelle said. She could feel her cheeks heat up. She did have a way of rattling on when she was excited.

"What happened to Wizard Targon?" said Hasani who had just shown up with a mop, bucket, and towel. "I never did trust that man."

A streak of sadness ran across Kyril's face. He had been taken in and cared for by Targon, even when other students teased him. It had been a hard thing for Kyril to turn him in, but it was the right thing.

"He died trying to protect me," Kyril said, his voice barely more than a whisper.

Hasani's dark eyes opened wide in surprise, but he said nothing more and instead bent over to begin cleaning up the mess.

"Hasani," Sylvie said, putting her arm out to move him aside. "Let me get this."

With a quick wave of her hand, the mop left Hasani's hand and the bucket tipped slightly. Some water spilled out and the mop seemingly on its own accord swept over the vomit. After a few mop-overs, she brought the towel out and finished wiping up the mess. All without any of them having to lift a hand.

As an earth wizard, Sylvie received her powers from the earth itself—its trees, rocks, wood, even forces of nature. At sixteen, the same age as Joelle, she was a very powerful wizard already. However, what she did now was more of a gesture than using any real amount of power.

"Thank you, Sylvonna," Hasani said with a deep bow. "I wish my own powers could do such things."

"We all have different ways to help," Sylvie said, waving away the compliment with a slight blush to her pale cheeks. "Your scholar abilities that allow you to absorb and understand all of this"—she waved her arms around the library—"are truly amazing."

Hasani beamed, and the librarian offered her own chuckle at her apprentice's reaction.

"And that's why we are here today," said Kyril. "We need to see more of the books in the basement. We need to find out all we can about the medallions and their ancient magic."

The librarian sighed. "I suppose the prince or even the emperor now has sanctioned this?"

Joelle smiled, reached inside her green cloak, and pulled out a scroll. "The emperor has given Sylvie and I permission to study any book in Gildan, and…" She pointed to her side. "Wizard Kyril has taken on a special task."

"How exciting," Hasani said. "And you are a full wizard now?"

Kyril appeared a bit nervous but a big smile covered his face. "Yes, though I must admit I'm not very good and don't know a lot."

"But with the medallion he's able to do things no one else can do," Sylvie said.

"Like transport to the middle of my library," the librarian said, warming up a bit more to the young wizards around her.

"Sorry again," Kyril said. "It was the only place I could think of on a moment's notice."

"We made quite a dramatic exit leaving the emperor," Joelle said with a light giggle. "The look on Bale's face was priceless."

The group joined in Joelle's laughter. Bale was a noble from Gildan without any wizarding powers who had bullied many wizard apprentices; Kyril had received the brunt of his latest attacks. But along with Joelle and her friends, Bale had performed his duties as a new handler for the spymaster, and had also received accommodations from the emperor.

The librarian gestured toward the basement door. "Well, let's go and see what we can find for you." Turning toward her apprentice she raised her dark eyebrows. "And Hasani, could you please get rid of that bucket before it stinks up the entire library?"

Hasani pouted but did as she asked.

Turning to Joelle on their way to the basement, the librarian asked, "Now I think I got the gist of your story, but what happened to Scribe Gamal?"

Joelle turned to Kyril.

"He got away with a black medallion," Kyril said. "Our task is to find him and stop him from discovering the location of the remaining silver and bronze medallions. Together the three medallions bring balance to magic. A balance that Gamal, with his black medallion and aspirations for more, is threatening. We must stop him." He brought a hand up and over his own gold medallion and a bright light shone out from it as if to give him comfort.

"That's a tall order for three young wizards," the librarian said.

"Yes, it is," Kyril said seriously. "It really is."

CHAPTER TWO

After two days leafing through books in the Wizard Academy library, Joelle El'San slammed Ancient Relics of Magic closed and pushed her fists into her eyes. Having attended the wizard school on White Island in the Realm, she had endured her years of studying, but she still didn't like the quiet that always ensued around it.

"I'm not made for all this studying," Joelle complained to Kyril. "How do you wizards of the mind handle all of this?"

"It's our minds that drive us," Kyril said with a smile. "The more knowledge we have, the greater our ability to use our powers is."

"I'd rather just *do* something," said Joelle with a huff. "I'm feeling more and more useless here. Since Gamal left there have been less injuries to heal, and graduation is tomorrow.

Sylvie stood up, her short hair swishing around her head. "I agree with Joelle. I can't stand sitting here anymore. We're not going to find the medallions in the library. We need to be doing something, Kyril."

The two women stood up and glared down at Kyril.

"Why are you staring at me like that?" Kyril said.

"Because you're the one with the medallion," Joelle said. "It was your idea to find Gamal and the other medallions—but for all we know they don't even exist anymore."

"They do," Kyril said with a quick nod of his head. "I saw them."

"You saw them once *in a vision.*" Sylvie let out a puff of air. "That was over four hundred years ago. They could be anywhere now."

"Anyway, what makes you think we can find them?" asked Joelle. "Maybe they've been lost or stolen or destroyed. Are we just supposed to traipse around the continent until they pop into our hands?" Joelle watched Kyril close his eyes in what she thought was a move to ignore them.

Wizards of the mind could be so infuriating at times with their need to think and reason things out. As a wizard of the heart, Joelle was used to her emotions driving her need. She didn't have to think about it, she just did it. Like with her healing. She felt compassion and needed to help those that were hurt. She didn't think about how she was going to do it, she just felt along the way.

"Kyril Siravan," Sylvie slammed a hand down on the table. "Are you listening to us?"

Kyril jumped and was on his feet with his eyes wide open. "What'd you do that for? I was thinking!"

Joelle slammed her own palm to her forehead. "We're not going to find anything else in these books. The time for thinking is done."

"You're right," Kyril said with a sly grin. He pushed a few stay strands of black hair out of his brown eyes. "It's time to leave Gildan and search for the medallions."

"Who put him in charge?" Joelle said to Sylvie, but a grin began to light up her face with thoughts of actually doing something besides leafing through old books.

"And to think, Kyril was only an apprentice wizard a few days ago." Sylvie tossed her head and laughed. "And now he thinks he can tell us all what to do."

"No. No, I didn't mean…It's just that…" Kyril stammered as his cheeks reddened. "You two have much more experience than me…"

Both women laughed and Joelle put a hand on Kyril's arm. "We're just teasing you, Kyril. But you are right, we do have more experience."

Kyril looked like he didn't know whether Joelle was chiding him or not.

"But you have the power of the medallion," Sylvie said. "That means something."

As Joelle dropped her hand from Kyril's arm, Sylvie reached over and softly took his left hand and turned it so his palm was facing up. She traced her finger around the heavy scar there—a mark that was in the shape of the medallion he wore around his neck. A mark that he had received from grabbing the medallion in the fire that had taken his family. The medallion was a precious heirloom that had been his mother's. He had lost it in the fire, but a recent trip back home had brought it to him once again.

His palm began to glow softly and he moved it away from Sylvie's hand.

"Does it hurt?" Joelle said, feeling some compassion for Kyril. Before saving the emperor's life he had been a lonely apprentice that had little power or friends. She had always felt a bit sorry for him. But he was a good man.

"No." Kyril shook his head. "I can feel it warm up when the light comes, but it doesn't hurt."

"Fascinating," Joelle murmured. "It would be interesting to study from a medical perspective."

"I thought you were done with studying," Kyril said with a grin. "Anyway, I'm fine. I really am."

An uncomfortable silence stretched for several seconds, and then Kyril turned to gather up the books they had been studying and began to put them back on the shelves.

"You don't have to go with me," Kyril said softly. "Neither of you owe me anything. I'm the one who told the emperor I would find Gamal. I just assumed…"

Joelle glanced at Sylvie who was moving in front of her with a handful of books herself as Kyril's voice trailed off. He turned back around, his eyes downcast, as he stared at the table between them.

"I'm game," Joelle blurted out in the silence. "One of the medallions may be in the Realm. If so, I can help you find it."

Kyril turned his eyes up at her and nodded his head. She smiled back at him.

Kyril and Joelle turned and toward Sylvie. The wizard of the earth appeared to be deep in thought. She took a few moments and then nodded her head as if deciding on something on her own.

"Yes, you're right, Kyril," Sylvie said. "We need to find the medallions and if there is one in Gildan and one in the Realm, I suspect the other one is in my home kingdom of Arc. The High Wizard of the Wizard Conclave there may be able to help us."

Joelle rushed over and squeezed Sylvie with a quick hug. "Oh, how fun! I can take you to Belor to meet my family. My parents will love you. But will we be all right traveling alone?"

"You're squeezing me to death, Joelle." Sylvie laughed as she untangled herself out of Joelle's embrace. "We'll be fine."

Joelle glanced at the knife that hung at Sylvie's waist. She had been wearing the weapon ever since the night of the Prince's party—the night of the attack. Sylvie was right; she could take care of herself. For a young wizard she was very adept in her abilities, and as a wizard of the earth, she was trained to be a weapon herself. There wasn't much that Sylvie couldn't do, Joelle supposed. It was the rest of them she was worried about.

"I would feel better with you there, Sylvie," Kyril said. "You can protect us, and Joelle can heal us."

"Just remember, Kyril, the medallion isn't your only power. You have to keep studying your other abilities. They have to become natural to you."

"Spoken like one of our instructors," Kyril laughed.

"Guest instructor," Sylvie said, and then joined him in laughter.

They all three grinned at each other for a moment, all taking in the adventure that awaited them. Before anyone said anything else, Hasani, the apprentice librarian, came into the room. Upon noticing that the books were all re-shelved he grinned at them, even winking at Joelle. She knew she blushed under his stare, but he just threw back his head and laughed, his bright white teeth shining in contrast to his dark skin.

"Thank you for cleaning up," Hasani said. "I'll be able to get out of here on time and not miss the curfew bell."

"That's one advantage to being a wizard now," Kyril grinned. "No more curfew."

"Hmmph," Hasani grunted. "Just one more day and I'll be joining your ranks."

Sylvie's eyes went wide. "Oh, how wonderful, Hasani! And then what are you doing for the remainder of the summer break? Are you going back to Mahli?"

Hasani's face grew more serious. "I don't know. It's a long way away, and there is not much for me to do there. I'd rather spend more time up here in the northern kingdoms. They're fascinating. So much to learn. But…"

Joelle had a sudden flash of an idea. It burst through her with so much force that it came out before she had a chance to think any more on it.

"Come with us!" Joelle said.

The three others in the room looked at her in surprise. But she didn't care. She could feel the rightness of it. "It's perfect, Hasani. You can see more of the northern kingdoms and help us find the medallions. You remember everything you've read. It'll be like having our own library with us."

Joelle's positive emotion was so strong that the other three swayed on their feet for a moment. Kyril placed a hand on a table and Sylvie and Hasani on a chair to steady themselves.

"Joelle!" Sylvie exclaimed with a broad smile and a giggle. "Is that you making us feel this way?"

Joelle nodded her head and then tried to tone down her feelings. Sometimes she forgot how influential a wizard of the heart could be. Their ability to manipulate others' feelings was both useful and dangerous, depending on the wizard's intentions. It was a continual conscious effort to keep her emotions contained.

"I'm sorry, sometimes I get so excited I forget to rein it in."

"A great ability you have as a wizard of the heart, Joelle El' San," said Hasani with a small bow of appreciation. "The joy you spread is as beautiful as you are."

Joelle's face heated up and she was sure she appeared as bright as a tomato after Hasani's compliment. She ran a hand down her long red hair and with a last giggle herself, brought the emotion under control, leaving the others with only their own thoughts.

"Well?" Joelle asked the group.

Kyril nodded his head in agreement.

"Sounds wonderful," Sylvie says.

The three of them waited for Hasani's answer.

"So where are we going, Kyril?" Joelle asked. "What grand place will we start searching for the medallions? The Black Forest? The Superstition Mountains? Elvyn? Oh this is going to be so exciting."

Sylvie laughed. "You're not usually one for adventure, Joelle. I would think you would want to be more careful—this could be dangerous."

Joelle agreed with Sylvie's assessment. She wasn't usually one to search out excitement. But the thought of finding one of the fabled medallions had invited a new sense of energy into her heart. She knew it could lead her someplace dangerous and mysterious, but she didn't care.

Kyril was silent for a moment, then a broad smile spread across his face.

"Where, Kyril?" Joelle bounced on the balls of her feet.

"The Wizard School on White Island," Kyril said with a gleam in his eyes.

"What?" Joelle said in disbelief. She had spent years there already, studying to become a wizard. "Why would you want to go there? There's nothing exciting, mysterious, or dangerous there...and certainly no medallion. It's just a school."

Before Kyril could answer, Hasani's mouth opened wide and he laughed. "Because that's the nearest other great wizard library."

"We're going to read more books?" Sylvie asked, slapping her forehead in what Joelle felt assured was in response to the same frustration she herself felt.

"Sounds fun!" Hasani said.

CHAPTER THREE

Sylvie watched Hasani walk away with a bounce in his step. He was definitely excited to visit the library of another wizard school. Even though she was looking forward to getting out of the school for a while, she had to admit to herself that she felt some elation about visiting the Realm—a place that, although it bordered the Kingdom of Arc and the Empire of Gildan, she had never been before. The wizard school there, the newest on the continent, had only been around a bit longer than she had been alive.

"Kyril," Joelle shouted a little too loudly and other students in the library turned her way. She quieted her voice and continued on. "Why are we going to another library? We've been looking here for days. We need to find the medallions and Gamal. He's not going to be at the library reading a book. Nothing ever happens there. I've spent years of my life there. I do have fond memories, but…"

Kyril put his hand on Joelle's arm and she stopped talking. Sylvie suppressed a grin. Her friend could definitely talk up a storm when she was excited. It was very obvious she had been expecting to go somewhere else.

"We have to study this out, Joelle," Kyril said. "Gamal and his black medallion are dangerous. We're just a bunch of young wizards. He has years of learning on us, and he must have other followers, too. We need more information and they might have something different there."

Joelle let out a loud puff of air. "All right. But it'll take quite a while to get there. We have to ride east to Kantori on the coast and then take a ship north to White Island. I…" She paused with downcast eyes. "I was hoping I would get to go to Belor and see my family."

Now Sylvie understood her friend's outburst. She didn't dislike the wizard school; she was just homesick.

"She has a good point, Kyril," Sylvie said. "Traveling all the way to White Island just for the chance of finding a bit of information that could help us, while Gamal is traipsing around. Shouldn't we try finding him first or going someplace closer? This could take us two weeks or more depending on the weather."

Kyril's lips opened to an enormous grin and his brown eyes sparkled as if holding in a secret. As she gazed at him, Sylvie realized how much he had changed in the past few weeks. She had befriended him a year ago when she had first come to the Wizard Academy as a guest instructor. He didn't have a lot of friends and was picked on quite a bit. The newfound confidence he'd found with both Targon's attention and the power of the medallion had definitely altered him. His ability to think more clearly and take control of a situation were only two ways he had matured.

"It won't take us that long," Kyril said.

Both Sylvie and Joelle waited for him to continue. Before he said anything more he motioned them outside the library and down the hallway toward the external door. About two-thirds of the way there, Bale and two others approached them in the hallway. Sylvie could feel Kyril stiffen up next to her. They hadn't seen Bale—the newest member of the spymaster's organization—since they had left the emperor's office a few days before.

"Well." Bale's grin grew wide. "What are you three up to, Wizard Sylvonna?"

"Don't worry about them, Bale," said Gabriel, one of Bale's followers. "The twig and her friends are not worth our time."

"Shut it, Gabriel," said Bale with his arm held out to the side. "Have some respect for the wizards."

Sylvie was surprised by Bale's actions. He had actually used her full name. Previously the man had taken every opportunity to taunt Kyril and herself. Joelle had seemed immune to his teasing for some reason. Maybe it had to do with her ability to heal.

"Wizards?" asked Mikal, Bale's other companion. He glanced around the hallway. A few other apprentices preparing for graduation activities passed them by. "I only see two wizards here…and one pathetic apprentice."

"Kyril was raised to a full wizard by the emperor," Sylvie said.

Mikal and Gabriel's jaws dropped in surprise. They turned and waited for Bale's response, who obviously was the leader. Their eyes held questions.

"It is true," Bale said, and then he cleared his throat and addressed the three wizards again. "Do you three need help with anything?"

"Bale!" Mikal said. "What's gotten into you? Let's leave these strays to themselves."

"Show some respect," Bale said, again to the surprise of Sylvie and her friends. "They have performed a great deed in Gildan."

Mikal hit Gabriel softly in the arm. "Let's get out of here, Gabe. Bale's been acting strange lately. You'd think he's forgotten his place in one of the noble families."

Sylvie could see that Bale held his anger in check. His two friends left him standing alone with the three of them.

"Thank you," Sylvie said.

Bale, jaw clenched, nodded his head a few times as if still convincing himself of what he was doing, then he took a step closer and with a quick glance around lowered his voice. "If you need anything from the spymaster's office for your quest, please let me know. I…uh…" He stumbled a bit on his words. "I respect your actions of saving the emperor and Prince Zaidan."

"Why, Bale Nabhani, that must be hard for your noble blood to admit," Sylvie said, but followed it up with a smile that showed she was teasing.

"Don't push it, Sylvie," Bale said, then turned to Joelle. "Nice to see you again, Healer. Thank you for helping with the aftermath of the attack."

Joelle nodded her head and for once kept the babble to a minimum. "My pleasure, Bale. Be careful, there still may be those intending harm in the city. If you need healing, let me know…" Then she looked at the others. "Well, at least over the next few days or so. We will be leaving soon."

Bale nodded his head in understanding. He had been in the emperor's office when Kyril had said he was going to go in search of the other medallions and stop Gamal.

Kyril and Bale still hadn't said anything to each other and it didn't appear that they had any plans to do so. Kyril took a step toward the door and motioned for Sylvie and Joelle to follow.

"Kyril," Bale called out.

Kyril turned his head, and his expression hardened, obviously steeling himself for a familiar insult. But Bale surprised them all.

"Good luck," Bale continued with a short nod of respect.

Kyril's eyes opened wide but all he did was nod back, turn, and continue walking. Sylvie gave a shrug to Bale and followed Kyril, with Joelle a few steps behind.

Once outside, Sylvie had a hard time keeping up with Kyril. He headed around the side of the school toward a small private garden area by the back wall before stopping.

"Kyril!" Sylvie said. "Be nice to Bale; he's changed too."

Kyril only blew out a puff of air. "I have a hard time believing that."

After a short awkward silence, Joelle spoke up. "Why are we here? What does this have to do with getting to the Realm quicker?" She pushed back a strand of her long red hair—hair that Sylvie found herself just a bit jealous about at times. Her own short hair was cut in the style of Danijela Anwar, the High Wizard of the Wizard Conclave in Arc. But next to Joelle she felt a little too simple and unattractive.

"We're going to transport there," Kyril blurted out.

Sylvie and Joelle stared at him for a few seconds before they both started talking at once, asking a lot of questions and telling him together how stupid of a plan that was.

Kyril put up his hand. "Just listen to me." He waited until he was sure he had their attention.

Sylvie waved a hand at him to go ahead and explain.

"I know all the arguments you are making," Kyril started explaining. "Believe me, I've thought of them all. I get sick each time I do it."

"And—" Joelle tried to jump in, but Kyril kept talking.

"And I know that I thought I could only transport places I've been before. But remember when I went with Targon into the basement of the library to search for books?"

Sylvie nodded her head. "And you found Hasani and me."

"Yes," Kyril said. "Well, I've been thinking about it. I had never been to the library basement before. Targon had explained it to me, and with the help of what I can only suppose was either his black medallion or his own substantial wizard powers, I transported him there."

Sylvie's mind raced. She opened her mouth once, but didn't actually know what she would say. Glancing at Joelle sideways, Sylvie saw she appeared as shocked as she was at the possibilities.

"Joelle, nothing to say?" Kyril chided with a smile.

Joelle blushed but only shook her head, definitely a clear sign that Kyril's words had not been what either of them had expected.

"You've been to the wizard school on White Island in the Realm," Kyril said to Joelle. "With your direction, the power of the medallion, and all our wizard abilities, I think we could do it."

"Transport all the way to another kingdom?" Sylvie said softly. "I can't believe…" She paused a minute before saying her biggest concern. "But what if something goes wrong? What if it doesn't work and we get hurt, or stuck somewhere?"

"Well, we would need a bit of practice," Kyril said. "That's why I brought you out here. I have thought this through, Sylvie. It isn't a whim. We have to find a way to get ahead of Gamal. First we'll go to the wizard school in the Realm and then to the Wizard Conclave in Arc. Once we gather all the information that we need, hopefully we can find some clues to where the other medallions are."

Joelle laughed out loud and Sylvie knew what she was thinking.

"What?" Kyril said.

"You've changed, Kyril," Sylvie said.

"It's the medallion," Joelle added. "Your wizard of the mind abilities are definitely growing."

Kyril smiled. "Well they couldn't have gotten any worse. Are you two up for some experimenting?"

CHAPTER FOUR

Joelle held on to Kyril's hand after they had discussed a few scenarios. It was a bit awkward at first and she had felt her face heat up. Kyril was a fine enough man and all, but she wasn't interested in him any more than a friend would be. Sylvie grinned at her red face and she turned away to ignore her.

"All right, Joelle," Kyril said with a bit of nervousness to his voice. "I want you to think of a place in the city that you've been to, but I haven't."

"Why don't we try something a bit closer?" Joelle said hesitantly. She wasn't sure this was going to work and she didn't want to be left somewhere strange in the city. "What about someplace on the academy grounds?"

"Fine," Kyril said. "But where have you been that I haven't?"

"The women's lavatory?" Sylvie said with a laugh.

"Oh, no, no, no." Kyril shook his head vigorously.

"My room," Joelle said. She willed herself not to blush again. A man had never been to her room and she didn't want people to get any ideas, but if they just popped in for a moment no one would know.

Kyril nodded his head. "Close your eyes and picture your room and then tell me about it. Where it is, what it looks like, anything you can think of. Then open up your mind to me and I'll take you there."

Joelle began explaining the small room as her left hand held Kyril's right hand. She knew that he planned to grip the medallion around his neck with his left hand—the hand with the mark on it.

"The room is in the center of the women's hall. The walls are gray stone. I have one piece of artwork on the walls—a rendering of the Blue Sea. In the center of the room is a small sitting area with two chairs and a table on top of a worn rug. My bed is on the far wall under a window that looks out on a back lawn."

"You have a window?" Kyril asked.

"Focus, Kyril," Sylvie said. She wasn't going to be transferring with Joelle or Kyril this first time.

"Think harder, Joelle," Kyril added.

She did. She had lived in the room by herself for a year now. Apprentices had to share rooms, but as a full wizard she was given her own—though not as large or lavish as the older wizards. As a young wizard, although she was very talented at healing, she was still treated almost like a student by many of the older instructors and adult wizards at the wizard academy.

"Picture it in your mind now and open yourself up."

Joelle did as he asked…and felt another presence in her mind.

"I think I can see it," Kyril said from her side. "Are you ready?"

Joelle nodded and opened her eyes a bit. A golden glow surrounded Kyril's medallion. She continued to think about her room. Perhaps this would work after all.

The glow expanded and Joelle readied herself. And then her stomach growled and her attention shifted for a brief moment to the next meal.

With no warning she found herself falling to a floor—not in her bedroom, but in the academy cafeteria instead. She rolled and came up under the edge of a counter, knocking over a bowl of gravy left over from the last meal. She turned away, but not before she received a splattering of the brown liquid down the side of her neck and arm. A loud noise next to her caused her to turn her head.

"Joelle!" yelled Kyril. "What did you do?" He rolled on the floor and into a chair, knocking it over into another chair, sending both scattering across the hard floor.

At least he doesn't have gravy on him.

Joelle had let go of Kyril's hand upon hitting the floor, and now tried to stand up. When she did she noticed three young apprentices in the back of the cafeteria with eyes as round as saucers. She was glad the rest of the cafeteria was empty.

The sounds of Kyril gagging took Joelle's attention back from the three bystanders. She rushed to his side, ignoring the thick gravy sliding down her arm.

"I'm so sorry," Joelle apologized. "I was thinking of my room, but then all of a sudden my stomach growled and I thought about food—it was only for a moment."

Kyril stood up, rubbing the side of his head. He winced at a spot on the back. He scowled at her for a moment, but then his lips turned up into a grin instead and he barked out a laugh.

Joelle relaxed. He didn't seem too upset.

"You're a mess!"

"Thanks for letting me know," Joelle said with a sarcastic smile of her own. She grabbed a nearby towel and wiped the gravy off the best she could, but it had stained her green cloak.

"I saw your room, Joelle," Kyril said. "I saw it in my mind and directed myself there, but at the last moment the intrusion of the cafeteria was too strong and we tumbled here instead."

"But you still don't know if it would have worked, because you've been here before," Joelle said, disappointed that she had ruined the experiment.

"Let's try it again," Kyril said, his eyes sparkling.

"What about this?" Joelle pointed to the gravy stain.

Kyril shrugged, clearly not as worried about her appearance as he was excited to try again. His excitement was infectious.

"Are you sure you want to try again? Do you feel all right? What about the apprentices over there? Oh, this is a big mess and it's all my fault." Joelle cursed herself once again for messing it up.

"I'm fine," Kyril said. Then with a bigger grin he repeated himself. "I'm really fine. I didn't get as sick this time; only a bit of gagging."

"Well, then, where to now?" Joelle asked, trying to redeem herself.

"Sylvie's room," Kyril said with a sly smile.

"Oh, no," Joelle said. "She won't like that."

Kyril gave her a longing look and she sighed and took his hand once again. This time it didn't feel so strange. She knew Sylvie's room almost as well as her own. Having arrived at the wizard academy in Gildan within a week of each other and both being foreigners, they had become quick friends.

"Concentrate, Joelle," Kyril chided.

Joelle thought about Sylvie's room. It was much like hers. However, the comforter on the bed was different colors and her chairs were arranged differently. The room came into focus in her mind and she heard Kyril shifting his feet beside her. She took a deep breath and tried to concentrate on Sylvie's room.

She opened her eyes and the light flashed around Kyril again.

"I got it." Kyril grinned broadly.

In the next moment they began to transport. Even though it should have been instantaneous, Joelle had a moment to think about the gravy she had wiped off her hair, neck, and arm, and looked forward to taking a good bath.

When the flash of light cleared she stumbled a bit but stayed upright this time. She peered around, expecting to see Sylvie's room. But instead she heard a horrified gasp from Kyril.

"Joelle!" he screamed, his voice echoing around the tiled room. "I'm in the girl's washroom."

Joelle stood speechless and her eyes frantically searched the room for anyone else. Luckily, they were the only two there. Before she could say anything or apologize again, Kyril grabbed her hand.

"Don't think of anything," said Kyril, his face full of frustration.

In the next instant they were once again standing next to Sylvie. Kyril leaned over with his hands on his knees and took deep breaths but once again didn't get sick. Joelle put a hand against a tree to steady herself. She had transported three times in the last two minutes and was feeling a bit disoriented.

"Did it work?" Sylvie asked while bouncing on the tips of her toes.

Joelle and Kyril eyed each other for a moment then both burst out laughing.

"What?" Sylvie asked. "What happened? Did it work?"

"Yes, yes, it worked," Kyril said between fits of laughter.

"Joelle, what's so funny?"

Joelle tried to explain to her friend, but the entire experience had left her a bit lightheaded and she couldn't stop laughing. She thought of Kyril standing in the women's washroom with his eyes darting around in horror, and she started snickering again, finishing with a loud snort.

"Will you tell me what happened?" Sylvie's blue eyes flashed angrily and she stood facing them with her hands on her hips.

Things quieted down for a brief moment and Kyril opened his mouth to explain, but upon seeing Joelle's grin he burst out in laughter once again. And she joined him.

CHAPTER FIVE

Later that day, Sylvie took a few minutes to make sure that she dressed her best. Smoothing down her finest blue cloak, she finished preparing to go to the graduation ceremony. As a guest instructor at the Wizard Academy she would be seated on the stand next to Joelle.

Thinking about her friend she chuckled a bit at their afternoon excursions. After Joelle and Kyril had finally settled down and told Sylvie what had happened, they'd decided that maybe Joelle's thoughts jumped around a bit much for practice. Encouraged by the fact that the transporting had actually worked, they continued to practice with Sylvie instead.

After a brief transport across the academy grounds they moved farther out into the city. By the end of the afternoon they had gone to a dozen places around Gildan. Kyril was pleased by their progress.

Opening her door, she found Joelle standing there, just about to knock. They walked together toward the sizable assembly hall and took their places on a raised stage. She spied Kyril out in the crowd. Even though he'd already been raised to a wizard by the emperor, he would still participate in the public graduation ceremony. Peering down the row toward the center of the room she saw Prince Zaidan there representing the emperor for this event. He leaned over, nodded his head, and smiled at her.

Sylvie smiled back. The prince had helped her in recent weeks to find the concentration she needed to break through to a higher level of wizard powers.

Feeling a knock against her elbow, she turned to Joelle.

"I think the prince likes you," Joelle said in a whisper, her green eyes sparkling bright against her silk green cloak.

Sylvie rolled her eyes at her friend's audacity, but felt her pale cheeks heat in response to her words. "We're friends, Joelle, that's all. He is the prince."

Joelle just shrugged and looked like she was going to say more, but Commander Brashir, the headmaster of the Wizard School of Gildan, took the stage and the room quieted down.

"Students, faculty, visiting guests, and distinguished rulers," he began, "we welcome you to Gildan's Wizard Academy graduation ceremony. Today we will add eighteen new wizards to our ranks. These apprentices have worked hard here at the academy for years…" His voice trailed off a bit as he looked in Kyril's direction. "Or less time for some, it seems."

The headmaster did not appear completely pleased with Kyril's early promotion to the ranks of wizards, but Sylvie knew that he didn't dare question the emperor's actions.

"It pleases me that we have graduates from all three magic disciplines today," the headmaster continued. "It's important to keep balance in magic and among the powers of the kingdoms."

Sylvie caught Kyril's eyes. She knew that once, he had seen a vision of all three medallions being given to ancient wizards with a charge to protect the balance of magic in their kingdoms.

Sylvie wasn't sure if that balance was only among the three kingdoms of Gildan, Arc, and the Realm, or if it included all those on the western continent. She supposed if trouble happened here, it would spill over into the other smaller kingdoms to the south.

Commander Brashir ended his formal speech and the heads of each magic discipline came forward.

"Earth," he called out. "Wizards of the earth are known for their ability to draw their power from the earth and are trained in many kingdoms as battle wizards and assigned to keep the peace among us. Today we have six new wizards of the earth."

Everyone applauded and each of the graduates walked forward and received a diploma, a new blue cloak, and handshakes from the head of their discipline, the Commander, and Prince Zaidan. Sylvie thought back to her own graduation over a year earlier. The Wizard Conclave in Arc was much smaller and there had only been two other wizards graduating with her. They had been two and three years her senior.

"Heart," Commander Brashir called out. "Wizards of the heart are known for their ability to draw power from their emotions, whether in love or hate. They make the best counselors and healers. Today we have four new wizards of the heart."

Sylvie caught some movement at the back of the room and cranked her head to see better. Bale stood at the doorway and caught her eye for a moment. With a few hand signals from him, Sylvie saw others spreading around the room as if expecting a disturbance to the proceedings.

"Joelle," Sylvie whispered with a nod of her head toward Bale and the other guards. "Watch out for trouble."

Joelle only nodded and sat up straighter in her chair.

The crowd finished applauding the wizards of the heart and they retook their seats.

"Mind," Commander Brashir said loudly. "Wizards of the mind are known for their ability to draw power from their minds. The ability to think things out methodically and efficiently make them great scholars, engineers, and leaders. Today I'm happy to add eight new wizards of the mind."

The Headmaster's smile was broader now. He himself was a wizard of the mind. Sylvie watched as both Hasani and Kyril approached the stage. Hasani beamed broadly, and bouncing on his toes, he looked happier than she had ever seen him.

Kyril, on the other hand, walked more stoically, though Sylvie knew him enough to see a slight sparkle in his eyes. He wasn't one for the limelight and only wanted to get back to work finding the other medallions. He was last to reach the stage of the eight new wizards—and suddenly he tripped and pitched forward, hitting his head hard on the edge of the stage. Laughter rippled through the first few rows.

Sylvie jumped from her seat, and Joelle quickly followed. Sylvie caught some movement at the back of the room. Bale had signaled to someone and even before the laughter died down, a guard grabbed a student from the end seat of the second row and began to escort him out of the room. Joelle pushed Sylvie out of the way and kneeled down next to Kyril who was now sitting on the floor with his head in his hands. A trickle of blood leaked out between his fingers.

Others started to come forward when Sylvie's attention was drawn to a new ruckus in the back of the grand hall. She turned around and saw people running down a hallway toward the exterior of the academy.

"Fire!" someone yelled at the same time that Sylvie deciphered a strange smell in the air.

Multiple things suddenly happened at once, and Sylvie stood still for a moment trying to figure out where she would best be needed.

"Get the prince," Bale's clear deep voice rang out above the ensuing din. "Get him out of here."

Within moments a group of guards escorted Prince Zaidan to a side door. His eyes caught Sylvie's for a moment. They were angry and dark about having to leave, but he was born to duty and went with the guards for his own protection.

Commander Brashir stood up to address the room, only for his words to get lost in the shuffle of people standing up and running out to see what was happening.

Sylvie bent down to help Joelle and Kyril.

"Go," Joelle said. "I can take care of him."

Before Sylvie could answer back, Joelle had already turned her attention away from the rest of the room and had focused on healing Kyril.

Sylvie tried pushing through the riotous group of people—wizards, apprentices, and families who had gathered for the ceremony. She was tall for her age but not tall enough to see over the crowd clearly—but she was thin, and so was able to squeeze between groups until she emerged out into the hallway. Using her wizard ability to reach out she pulled the power of the earth into her. Fighting the crowds running against her she pushed her way toward the library—where the smell of smoke was the strongest.

Getting closer, she saw that guards were trying to coordinate people leaving. Off to the side with eyes darting around the crowd was Bale.

"Sylvie, you shouldn't be here," he said. "The library's caught fire."

"How bad is it?" she asked.

He shook his head. "It's hard to tell. It started in the back by a stairwell and quickly began spreading."

Screams grew louder inside the library and a group of apprentices came running out. Sylvie glanced back the way she had come and saw the headmaster stop and turn at the shouting of one of his senior wizards at the other end of the hallway.

"But why are you here?" she said quietly to Bale.

"Fires don't start by themselves," Bale said with a slight sneer. "I'm here to investigate. This was deliberate."

Before Sylvie could comment, a blast of wizard power shook the hallway behind them. It was hard to tell what was happening amidst all the smoke that surrounded her, but she saw four men with hoods appear from a side hallway. They seemed to throw the senior wizards to the ground before turning and grabbing the headmaster.

"It's a diversion," Sylvie yelled out turning her attention back and forth between the burning library and the confrontation in the hallway. "This fire was a diversion."

Bale's eyes narrowed and his teeth clenched as he nodded his agreement. "Go do what you can in the library, Sylvie," Bale said, pointing toward it. "I'm going to try and help the headmaster fight off the attackers."

CHAPTER SIX

Sylvie paused. She wanted to help the headmaster, Commander Brashir, but she realized the bigger threat might actually be the loss of knowledge in the library, so she did as Bale bade her—though it grated on her nerves to have him command her like that. With a quick wave of her hands in front of her she pushed the smoke and fire to the side as she ran into the burning room.

"We need to stop the fire without damaging any more books," called out the head librarian who was pushing past Sylvie.

"Wait," Sylvie said trying to grab the old lady. "You can't go in there."

She stopped and turned around. Tears ran down her cheeks. "My books! The fire can't survive without oxygen. Quick, we need to suck the air out of the room."

Sylvie was surprised at how quickly the librarian had come up with a solution. She understood what needed to be done. Another wizard, not much older than Sylvie, broke one of the thick windows out at the other end of the room and with magic they began pushing the air away from the fire. Sylvie began to feel lightheaded from both the remaining smoke and lack of oxygen in the room. They couldn't keep this up for long.

The fire was beginning to die down near them, but then there was a large crash and a spark of fire flared up again farther into the room. A window on the far side had broken, allowing more oxygen back into the room, and the flames received new fuel and raced down the shelves in another direction.

Sylvie thought she saw a shadow with a dark hood move from the back of the library and toward the hallway. The apparition turned and looked at her and she gasped. Even through the smoke, the dark red birthmark on his forehead was visible.

"Gamal!"

As she took a step toward the fleeing character she heard another noise. Suddenly, a door at the bottom of a stairway opened as if on its own and the fire jumped in that direction toward the new fresh air.

"The basement!" Sylvie called out. It was where all the more protected and valuable books were held. She couldn't let them be destroyed.

Running toward the stairs, she ignored the calls of the other wizards to stay back. She made it to the stairs ahead of the flames and began running down them, but now she was trapped between the basement door and the raging fire. When she pushed air up and against the fire, it only sent the flames racing closer to the other wizards and the rest of the library. She had to do something better.

Remembering her lesson with the prince on becoming one with her powers, she closed her eyes to help her concentrate better. The heat of the room brought sweat running down her face but she tried to put it from her mind. She needed water to douse the fire.

Rather than work with real rocks like in her lessons, she imagined three large rocks in front of her and how she could make them smooth and mold them with water. She let everything else disappear and became one with the imaginary rocks. She felt the cool water falling over her, rounding her edges and polishing the stone that she had become.

A storm had rolled through Gildan the night before, and even though it had left, the humid air lingered—and there was water in that air. But would it be enough?

A loud crash sounded to her right and she imagined a shelf of books falling to the ground.

"Wizard Sylvonna!" a wizard yelled out in the far recesses of her mind. "We can't get to you."

She pushed the thoughts away while trying to ignore the growing heat in front of her. She heard another window burst and more oxygen fed the spreading fire, but also more moisture from the outside became available to Sylvie.

As soon as the humid air entered the room, though, the fire licked it up. Sylvie would have to gather it from farther away. Digging deeper into the earth, she pulled upon the power of the rocks, the building around her, the air, and commanded each water droplet to come to her aid. She was the stone in the water. First it was a trickle, then a stream, then a river in her mind.

She slowly opened her eyes to find the fire coming down the stairwell toward her. Her face was burning and she backed down as far as she could go. With her back to the door she heard someone banging on the other side.

"Help!" a voice called out.

Sylvie groaned. If she opened the door, the new air from below would pull the flames toward her and the basement, engulfing them at once. The person was much safer down below behind the door.

"I can't breathe!" the male voice said. "The smoke is coming in under the door."

A crackling on the stairs turned her attention back to the fire and she threw her hands up in front of her. A gust of air pushed the fire back up a few feet, but caught an additional shelf up above on fire. She groaned at the impossible situation she was in.

Could she open the door and pull the person out in time before the fire was drawn down upon them? She didn't know. But she couldn't doom someone to die of smoke inhalation, just to save some books.

With one final push of air away from her she turned back around and pulled open the door. Expecting to find one of the apprentice students there, she was surprised when instead a fist came directly toward her face.

Saved only by her quick reflexes and current connection to her powers, Sylvie swerved to the side and the man's fist grazed only her shoulder. But it was hard enough to knock her off-balance. With a loud *whoosh,* the flames rushed down the stairs to feed on the new oxygen that the basement door allowed to enter the library. Wrestling to get away from the attacker, she used her earth powers to slam the door back shut behind him, but in so doing the heat of the fire above her became almost more than she could bear.

"Help!" Sylvie yelled out to anyone that could hear. But it was clear that she would not get any assistance. "Help me!"

Through the roaring fire she saw the silhouette of a man trying to get past the flames, but there was no room and it was too hot. The attacker lunged at her again.

"You will die in the fire, wizard," the man spat as he tried to grab her around the waist. "And the headmaster will die."

Sylvie couldn't spare the time to think about the headmaster. She kicked out with her legs while trying to keep the fire at bay with her outstretched hands. But it wasn't going to work. She was losing her grip on her power. She needed to concentrate more and bring the water back. But doing so would take her attention away from the attacker.

A loud crack drew both of their attentions for a brief moment. A nearby bookshelf crashed to the ground and sparks splashed down the stairwell and over her blue cloak. Patting out the burning embers, she had an idea.

In a surprise move she pulled off her cloak. When the man came at her again she raised the cloak up and wrapped it around his head, spinning him around as she did so. He screamed that he couldn't breathe but she didn't care at the moment and kicked him hard in the back forcing him to the ground.

Sylvie knew she only had a few moments before the angry assailant would unwrap himself from the cloak, so she used it to concentrate again on the moisture in the air. She closed her eyes and tried to pick up where she had left off earlier. She was the rocks in the ground, the stone in the walls, and she envisioned a giant stream running over her. The stream was the water she pulled from the air and the ground outside the academy walls. She built it first in her mind and then she became one with the torrent and brought it into being. Water rushed from the grounds and coalesced together from the humid air and began to pour through the outside doors and windows of the library.

She opened her eyes and directed the newly created stream of water through the air and toward the largest parts of the fire, and had a small portion to come to her aid on the stairs.

Steam and white smoke filled the room as the fire began to dissipate. A wind picked up in the room—the doing of one of the other wizards—to blow out the remaining flames now. It was working. The fire was going out. They could save the library!

Without warning, Sylvie was hit in the back and fell forward against the hard steps. Her knees cracked against the stone and she screeched in pain. She scrambled to crawl back up the steps to the main floor as the fire now had allowed her a way out, but her legs would hardly move. She was exhausted, but had to keep going.

A man came running through the smoke to help her, but with her eyes stinging from the smoke she couldn't tell who it was. He kept having to dodge burning embers and fallen shelves. With steam and smoke rising around her and water flowing along the floor she tried to be strong and keep going, but her power faltered and she collapsed at the top step.

The water on the floor began to recede back outside and she hoped she had done enough to let the others finish putting out the fire because she had nothing left. Echoes of the prince's warning a few weeks earlier about being careful not to burn out flashed across the back of her mind. She had been practicing moving rocks and he had instructed her on how to reach her full potential by becoming one with the objects she was trying to move. It was dangerous and a wizard of the earth had to be careful. However, she didn't feel she had burned out—this was only extreme exhaustion.

Sylvie felt hands on her back pulling her away from the steps and she tried to twist around, but she didn't have enough energy or strength to do so. Instead, out of the corner of her eye she watched a meaty fist hit her in the side of the head knocking her against the stone stairwell.

It was the last thing she remembered.

CHAPTER SEVEN

After Joelle told Sylvie to go and see what was happening she turned back to Kyril. He sat on the ground and cradled his arm—the same one he had hurt before when he had foolishly tried to jump off a wall and fly. Joelle tried to reach for him to heal him but at that moment a rush of people from the graduation ceremony began to run by them. A contingent of guards had already taken Prince Zaidan out a side door, but the others ran out of the room with Commander Brashir in the lead.

Apprentices and wizards alike yelled and darted toward the nearest doors with no regard for anyone else. A foot kicked the side of Joelle's leg and she winced in pain.

"Come on, Kyril, we need to get out of here. Your arm will have to wait."

Kyril nodded his agreement and stood up with a wince of pain. He glanced around the room as if searching for someone.

"They're gone," Joelle said as she pulled him by his good arm toward a door. "I think it was Mikal that tripped you. Don't worry about them. You are a wizard now—this was just a formality, right? I mean, the medallion makes you more important than any of them."

"I'm not important," Kyril grunted. "They still tease me."

"But Bale is better than he used to be," Joelle said.

"He is at that," Kyril flashed her a lopsided grin. An older wizard bumped into his arm from the other side and his grin turned to a wince of pain. "At least he's tolerable. More so toward you and Sylvie than me."

Joelle only shrugged. She tried to stay out of the petty squabbles that appeared to be as prevalent in the Wizard Academy of Gildan as in the Wizard School on White Island where she had trained. She remembered with a grimace a few at her school that had thought themselves better than others.

A loud sound brought her back to the present. They stood at the crossroads in the hallway of the academy, looking toward the library, from where the sound and subsequent crash had come. A few dozen apprentices came running from that direction while only a few ran toward the smoke and obvious fire. She was sure that was the way Sylvie had gone. Her powers would be useful there.

"Joelle!" Kyril shouted, pushing her aside. Running past them were three senior wizards.

"Commander!" one of them yelled up ahead.

In the growing smoke and din, the headmaster, Commander Brashir turned around to see who had called him. As he did so four people in dark hooded cloaks came at him from one of the other hallways. Joelle saw the commander's eyes open wide as he tried to get away.

The wizards that had pushed past Joelle and Kyril thrust their hands out in front of them to stop the others. But one of the four hooded individuals waved a hand out in front of him and black tendrils snaked out and grabbed the wrists of those trying to help the commander. They were flung to the floor.

"It's a diversion," a voice yelled from the entrance to the library. Joelle thought it was Sylvie's, but in the smoky hallway it was hard to tell.

Kyril took off down the hall toward the fight and Joelle ran to keep up with him. Three of the hooded figures grabbed the commander and began to drag him away. The fourth man swung his hand around in a half circle, dark fire blazing from his fingertips until it reached Joelle.

"Kyril!" Joelle screamed out in warning.

Kyril's medallion flared to life and spread golden light down the hallway, meeting the dark wizard's fire head-on. An explosion of sound rocked the walls when the two powers collided.

"It's him," Kyril said, his voice quivering in anger. "It's Gamal."

At the sound of his name, Gamal stopped and glared down the hallway at them. Even in the smoke and pandemonium, Joelle recognized him for his beady eyes and red birthmark on his forehead. She began backing away but Kyril started forward.

"No, Kyril!" Joelle screamed, and tried to grab at him. She grabbed his hurt arm and he bellowed in pain and staggered.

It was enough of a diversion for Gamal. He turned and joined his fellow companions with Commander Brashir. Kyril picked up his pace and fled forward with a yell of anguish and frustration. At the same time Bale raced from the other side. Joelle wished she had her bow staff with her. Not usually one to join a fight and absent the only weapon she was comfortable using, she simply stood and watched.

"Kyril, let me handle this," Bale said, rushing closer to the hooded men.

"It's Gamal!" Kyril said as he skidded to a stop in front of the man that used to be the scribe of his mentor.

Gamal threw his hood off his bald head and laughed at Kyril. He stood a few inches taller than Kyril but was much more broad-shouldered. A black medallion hung around his neck and Kyril felt the pull of his own to offset the evil swirling around it.

"What are you going to do, Apprentice Kyril?" Gamal spat.

"I'm a wizard now," Kyril said.

Joelle winced at how pathetic the comeback had sounded and started to walk closer to the melee.

"Ah, the power of the medallion," Gamal said. "That's why they made you a wizard. The emperor won't let you out of his sight now. They want to control the power."

"You're wrong," Kyril said. "You were always the one pushing Targon and planning the prince's assassination. You are the one trying to gain control. Targon is dead because of you."

"Oh no, Kyril," Gamal sneered. "You did that all on your own. You betrayed your mentor."

Bale moved closer to Gamal and one of Gamal's men jumped to intervene. The young noble brought his sword out in front of him and tried to hold his own. But it was difficult to compete with a wizard and he had to jump back from flashes of fire too often to do any real harm.

"Kyril, get away from him!" Joelle called out. "He's dangerous!"

"Yes, listen to your friend," Gamal said, turning to meet Bale who had somehow gotten around the other hooded man. "I am dangerous and powerful, and soon will have all three medallions in my grasp."

"No!" Kyril leaped forward and his medallion flared to life.

Joelle reached for Kyril's good arm to pull him away, but at the same time, Kyril reached out and touched Gamal's back, while Gamal took a hold of Bale's shoulder. For a brief instant, Joelle felt conflicting surges of power run through her—Kyril's gold medallion and Gamal's black one. She screamed. Suddenly they were all surrounded by a bright light, and then all four crashed to the ground inside of Joelle's room. Bale, Kyril, and Gamal appeared momentarily stunned, and Joelle spied her staff leaning against the wall. Leaping toward it, she then took it in both hands and spun around to smash it into Gamal—but suddenly Bale stood up, and she couldn't stop her forward momentum. She winced at the sound of her wooden staff cracking into Bale's skull.

He stayed standing but put a hand up to where Joelle was sure bump would be forming.

Bale shoved her aside and glanced around. "How did we get here?"

On the ground, Gamal was untangling himself from Kyril. He placed his hand over his black medallion and a darkness spread through the room.

"You have no idea of the power I have," Gamal said. "I will find you and those medallions, no matter where you try to hide. I will be a shadow lurking behind your every corner."

Kyril moaned on the floor, lying on top of his injured arm. Bale jumped forward and grabbed onto Gamal, and they both winked out of existence before Joelle or Kyril could do anything to help.

Joelle leaned down to Kyril and softly tried to turn him over.

Kyril let out a groan, but eventually stood up. His face was pale and he looked like he was going to pass out at any moment.

"We need to get you to the healers' room," Joelle said, taking hold of his good arm. "Can you walk?"

Kyril's only reply was a groan but he took a few steps toward the door. With one hand still grasping her staff and the other guiding Kyril, Joelle dragged him down the hallway. She hoped they made it there before he collapsed.

Screams and yells echoed through the hallways of the wizard academy and twice they had to stop to allow a group of wizards and apprentices to pass by them. People were running in all directions. Joelle just hoped that Bale was all right and wondered where Gamal had taken him.

Before turning toward the healers' rooms, Joelle glanced toward a loud ruckus in the main corridor. Gamal was back with his other hooded men and Commander Bashir was now slumped over between two of them. Bale was behind them and running back toward the library, which now had clouds of white smoke pouring from its doors.

Kyril took that moment to stumble and fall to the ground. Pulling him to the side of the hallway, Joelle guessed she would have to heal him here; at least enough to get him back on his feet. Taking a deep breath she brought forth her powers of the heart and bent over Kyril.

CHAPTER EIGHT

Sylvie opened her eyes with a groan and then closed them again. A few moments later she succeeded in peeking out at the brightness surrounding her. She was in the healers' room. For a moment she glanced around the room expecting to see Joelle, but then she remembered that she had separated from her and Kyril during the chaos. She hoped they were doing all right.

Someone next to her cleared his throat and she turned her head, surprised to find Bale standing next to her.

"The library?" Sylvie croaked, her mouth dry.

"The fire got some of it," Bale said slowly, as if not wanting to say the rest, "but your heroics saved the most valuable books."

"Is that a compliment, Bale Nabhani?" Sylvie grinned and let out a small laugh. But the laughing brought on coughing instead.

There was still defiance in the young noble's eyes but it had softened. "You took in a lot of smoke. You need to rest."

"But what happened?" Sylvie asked. "How did I get here?"

As she spoke, one of the older senior healers joined them. "By all accounts, our young noble here ran into the thick smoke, fought off your attacker, picked you up, and carried you out just before a weakened shelf crashed over the stairs where you had been."

Sylvie's eyes opened wide in surprise as she glanced first at the tired healer, and then at Bale, who had a red tint on his dark cheeks. He looked away with a groan.

Reaching a hand out, Sylvie touched Bale's arm and his attention returned to her. "Thank you, Bale. Thank you."

She meant it. She had taken on so much power there at the end trying to save the library, and had thought in doing so she had doomed herself to her attacker.

"Does anyone know who tried to attack me?" she asked.

"Later," Bale said with a pat to her hand.

The healer came forward and put his hand on Sylvie's forehead. His brow furrowed in apparent worry and Sylvie wanted to ask more questions, but soon felt herself drifting back to sleep.

***

"Water," Sylvie croaked, her throat raw and dry.

Joelle rushed toward her, but out of the corner of her eye she watched as Bale beat her to a pitcher of water. He filled up a small cup and brought it to her lips.

"How long have I been asleep?" Sylvie asked Bale.

"Since last night," Bale said, concern in his voice.

He still hadn't changed his clothes; they were singed and full of soot and his eyes now were sunken and hollow. His short black hair still held flakes of ash in it. Sylvie marveled that he was still upright and awake.

"He hasn't slept all night," Joelle said with a nod of her head toward Bale.

Sylvie handed Bale the cup of water and tried to thank him, but instead began coughing.

"You need to be careful," Joelle said. "You took in a lot of smoke. We healed you the best we could, but your body still needs rest. As strong as your powers are, you'll heal quickly I'm sure."

"Kyril?" Sylvie whispered and peered around with concern.

Bale's eyes flashed in anger and he held his jaw tight. "Off getting food or taking a nap, I surmise. If it wasn't for him, Commander Bashir might still be here."

"What's this about the commander?" Sylvie asked.

"It wasn't his fault, Bale," Joelle said. "He tried to stop Gamal."

"It wasn't his place." Bale said.

"Well, it wasn't Kyril's fault. He was trying to help," Joelle continued.

"He's barely a wizard at all." Bale interrupted. "He had no right to…"

"No right to what, Bale Nabhani?" came an older, more commanding voice from the doorway. A small golden crown sat atop his dark, clean-cut hair. His royal blue robes swirled around him as he approached the small group.

All three turned their heads and Bale's eyes grew round. He offered a short bow.

"Emperor Alrishitar, what are you doing here?" Bale said. "It might not be safe for you."

"Don't worry about me," the emperor said. "I can handle myself. I came to see how our formidable wizard Sylvonna Hickory is faring."

"Sire," Joelle said as the emperor walked by. Mezar Alrishitar had been emperor for over fifteen years now. He was renowned as one of the most powerful wizards on the western continent. Regardless, his even temper and good nature earned him more respect among his people than his magical abilities.

"And I hear I have much to thank you for also, healer. Your services here in Gildan will be sorely missed when you are away."

'Thank you," Joelle stuttered and Sylvie watched her friend's face heat up with the attention. She unconsciously reached her hand up to her hair and tried to comb her fingers through the unruly waves of red.

"And how are you faring, Bale?" the emperor asked.

"He hasn't moved from her side all night long," Joelle said. "I told him he needed healing himself, but he wouldn't hear of it. He said to treat her and the others first."

The remark brought Bale's hand to his head and he winced a bit.

Joelle blushed once again. "I kind of hit him with my staff last night."

When the emperor and Sylvie gave her confused looks, she tried to explain. "Well, it wasn't on purpose. You see, Kyril had been hurt and we were trying to get away from the fire when we saw Gamal…"

"So it really was him?" the emperor's voice interrupted her. "He's the one that kidnapped the headmaster?"

"*Kidnapped* Commander Bashir?" Sylvie said, and tried to sit up. "I saw him in the library too. He must have set the fire."

Bale moved closer to her side and put an arm around her back to help her. Sylvie caught a brief smile from Joelle but shot her a warning glance.

"Yes, Kyril…" Bale jumped in.

"Yes, Kyril, what?" came Kyril's voice from the doorway. He walked in with Hasani. The young man from Mahli only smiled, his teeth shining brightly and his braids swinging around his head. Kyril, on the other hand, was not smiling, but was instead scowling at Bale. "From what I saw, Bale, you did nothing to stop him either."

"Enough!" Emperor Alrishitar said firmly, and they all stopped talking.

Joelle opened her mouth to defend Kyril, but with a shake of her head, Sylvie warned her to stay quiet. She knew that was sometimes hard for her friend to do, but instead of speaking, she let out a puff of air.

"These are dangerous times," the emperor said. "I'm not sure what Gamal's endgame is. I hadn't thought him brave enough to kidnap the headmaster of our Wizard Academy."

"His plan is to gather all the medallions," Kyril said, holding his hand over his own, "and wreak havoc on the kingdom. I'm afraid he wants to be able to control all the magic and through the medallions have access to the powers of a wizard of the mind, heart, and earth."

"But I thought the medallions brought balance?" Sylvie asked, and immediately had to lay her head back against a pillow. She didn't know why she felt so weak.

The emperor shook his head. "I don't understand it all. But I would surmise if they were all held by one person, there would be trouble." He looked at Kyril. "What have you found in the library?"

Kyril shrugged. "I'm not sure much of anything that actually helps us at this point. I do believe each of the other medallions are in the Realm and the Kingdom of Arc—at least originally. I'm…" He glanced around. "Well, *we* are planning to go to the Wizard School at White Island and see what else we can learn there."

"You must hurry, Kyril," the emperor said. "I understand that as a wizard of the mind your desire to learn everything first and to study it out—remember, I am one also." He smiled before continuing. "But sometimes those of the heart have the right idea and we need to act. I'm afraid we must do so quickly now."

Kyril glanced back at Joelle, and then at Sylvie in the bed. "I had hoped to leave today originally, but possibly tomorrow would be better given the current circumstances. We were going to transport there." Kyril paused and his face grew more serious.

"We saw what happened last time he transported," Bale said under his breath. "Took Gamal and me with him. He has no control."

Emperor Alrishitar raised his voice and gave Bale a dark look. "Bale, leave magic to the wizards."

Sylvie was surprised at the verbal slap, but then the emperor softened his tone and continued speaking to them all. "Magic is difficult to control sometimes—especially when it is something we don't know much about. You have different skills, Bale. Thank you for giving the orders to get my son to safety and for saving Wizard Sylvonna. Both you and Kyril tried to apprehend Gamal, but we have all underestimated him, it seems." He paused for a moment before continuing. "I guess I have all of you to thank once again. This seems to be becoming a habit."

The five stood quiet for a moment, and then the emperor moved to dismiss himself. "I must see to the library."

Hasani, Bale, Kyril, and Joelle bowed to the emperor as he left the room, while Sylvie only nodded her head from bed.

"Don't think that just because I am a noble I don't appreciate what wizards do," Bale said for all to hear, but primarily to Sylvie. "I work for the Empire of Gildan and stand with the emperor."

Sylvie nodded. Even though his past insults and bullying were immature and mean, she had never doubted his loyalty to Gildan. "Thank you again, Bale."

Bale looked uncomfortable at the praise but then gave a rare smile. "I need to talk to the spymaster. We need to find Gamal and those that were helping him. We need to find the headmaster."

With those words he turned, then stopped abruptly in front of Kyril. Kyril didn't move and his jaw was held tight. The two seemed to square off for a moment and Sylvie thought it may come to blows. But then Bale gave a short nod of his head and walked around Kyril.

She sighed and shook her head. Bale was definitely a complicated man to understand. His preconceived notions of how he fit into the world around him had sorely been tested this past week. And…he had actually *complimented* her.

Kyril let out a long breath.

"Well, that man's come a long way in the past week," Joelle said with a laugh that lightened the room.

Kyril only grunted, but Sylvie saw a brief smile splay across his lips.

"Sylvie needs her rest," Joelle said to Kyril and Hasani. Kyril moved to join her as she walked out of the room, but Hasani stayed behind.

"Sylvonna," Hasani said. "Are you really all right? I tried to visit you, but each time I meant to they called me back to help in the library. I guess I am only one of a few that can remember most of the books and can help to re-catalog what was destroyed."

"Oh, Hasani," Sylvie said as she reached out and patted his arm. "I'm so sorry. This is devastating for you. I wish I could have done more."

"*More*?" Hasani said loudly, but quickly lowered his voice. "You are a hero around here. The way you saved the books in the basement and brought in water to stop the fire…Gildan will be in your debt forever. I'm not sure how you did it…"

Sylvie didn't know for sure either and could hardly remember anything from the night before. "It was something Prince Zaidan taught me. I became one with my powers."

"But it is one thing to think it in your head, quite another thing to bring water from your thoughts to the library itself," Hasani said with a shake of his head.

"Have you read anything about anyone doing that before?" Sylvie asked.

Hasani pursed his lips and seemed about to speak a few times, but each time closed his mouth once again. He was obviously running his mind through the catalog of books he had read. “I could do a bit of research, but it is not in my recollection. As you know, there are abilities of moving things through the magic stream—done by the strongest wizards like Emperor Alrishitar, the Dragon King, and possibly the King of the Realm, but not in the way you have done.”

“I’ll have to ask my High Wizard in Arc,” Sylvie said. “She may know.”

“Aaah, I had forgotten about High Wizard Danijela Anwar,” said Hasani with a nod of his head. “My apologies. She too is a very mighty wizard.”

Sylvie smiled at the memory of her mentor, the High Wizard. It would be nice to see her again. She yawned and felt her eyes growing heavy.

Hasani gave a short bow and began to move away. “I'd better get back to the library.”

Sylvie put her hand out and touched Hasani’s arm. “About our journey?”

Hasani’s face fell a bit. “I’m sorry Sylvonna. I really am. But I need to stay here and help out. It would be selfish for me to leave right now just to satisfy my cravings to see more of the world.”

It was as Sylvie expected. She knew his love for the library and its knowledge. “I understand. I will see you before we leave.”

“Of course,” Hasani said, and then excused himself.

CHAPTER NINE

In the middle of the afternoon the next day, Joelle stood next to Kyril in a small deserted room in the wizard academy. Taking a deep breath and letting it out again she tried to relax her mind and clear away all thoughts of her surroundings, the recent events, and the current state of her best friend.

Sylvie had slept better that night and her cough was improving, but she was still weak. There didn't seem to be anything that Joelle could do for it because the problem was magical, not physical. Sylvie had pulled too much power into herself, something that was common among wizards of the earth. Joelle and the other healers thought she would be fine, but her body apparently needed more rest to replenish her magical reserves.

"I wish Sylvie was here," Joelle said.

Kyril nodded his head in agreement. "Me too. But she needs to get better before she comes with us. You and I can transport to the wizard school on White Island and see what we can find. By the time we get back in a few days she'll be better."

That was the plan, anyway. They had all discussed it together only an hour ago. Butterflies churned in Joelle's stomach thinking about just popping into the wizard school on White Island. She wasn't sure it was the best idea to suddenly appear there out of nowhere. But Kyril, feeling pressure from the emperor, said they had to hurry.

"Now, you must concentrate, Joelle," Kyril said. "We can't afford a mistake this time. Where are we going in the school?"

Joelle shook her head again trying to clear away everything but the school. "I'm not sure. Should we just show up in the library there, or maybe the healers' room? Maybe it would be better to find a quiet place in the garden. But what if someone is there? Perhaps we should go to the town first, then walk to the school—then we won't be noticed so much."

"Joelle!" Kyril said, grabbing her hand. "This isn't the time to prattle on. Concentrate."

Joelle frowned in response and then closed her eyes and pictured a favorite spot in the gardens of the wizard school on White Island. It was on a bluff and overlooked the blue sea. This time of year, there would be dahlias beginning to bloom, petunias, and possibly even gladiolas soon. She loved the smell of flowers in the summertime.

The air seemed to shimmer around them and Kyril gripped her hand tighter. She could almost feel the breeze blowing off the sea. The salty scent reminded her of growing up in Belor.

No. No. No. I'm not supposed to think of home.

Without warning Kyril pulled his hand away and Joelle opened her eyes. They now stood on a rocky outcropping. Joelle stumbled a bit but stayed upright. The scent of the sea tickled her nose and she took in a deep breath. However, as she raised her eyes up higher she noticed buildings in the near distance and her stomach fell.

"Uh, Kyril?"

"Hmm?" Kyril said, doubled over with his hands on his knees. His mouth was held tight and his face was pale.

"Oh, are you all right?" Joelle put her hand on his forehead and drew on her healing powers. "You did better. No gagging."

Kyril's face lit up as Joelle's healing brought him back to full health. "And to think we just traveled from the middle of Gildan to the northeast portion of the Realm."

"About that…" Joelle grimaced. "We didn't quite make it to the wizard school."

"Joelle?" Kyril said, turning around. "What did you do?"

"It wasn't my fault," she stammered. "Well maybe it was, but I didn't mean to. I was thinking of the flowers at the school. They have beautiful gardens there. You should see them sometime. Oh, I guess we will, since that's where we are going. Well, I was thinking of those…and then the beautiful Blue Sea…"

"Where are we?" Kyril interrupted her.

A wave splashed against the rock they were standing on and Joelle pulled Kyril back closer to the shore. As they moved away from the sea the sounds of the nearby docks began to fill their ears. She pointed over them and toward the grand domed buildings behind the ancient city wall. Kyril followed her gaze and then with a squint of his eyes and a shake of his head turned back to her.

"Joelle?" Kyril begged an answer once again.

"Belor," Joelle squeaked out with a timid laugh. "We're in Belor, Kyril."

Kyril let out a long breath but words were long in coming.

"We could transport again," Joelle offered.

"Oh, no!" Kyril threw his hands up in the air. "I thought you could concentrate for once, Joelle. How do you do it while healing?"

"But…Well…" Joelle tried to argue. She knew she could do better. She couldn't take the look of disappointment on Kyril's face. If she had only had more time to practice.

Before anything else could be said, however, a loud horn sounded off toward the docks. Two short blasts were followed by one long blow.

"A ship!" Joelle pulled Kyril along. "A ship going north is heading out soon. We should be able to secure passage."

Kyril gave her a look but still said nothing.

"You don't believe me?" Joelle frowned. "This is my hometown. A ship departs every few days north and south and the type of horn blasts signifies which direction it will go. They blow it one hour before departure. You'll see. It'll be great. It's only a few days to White Island by ship. It will do us good to relax a bit. We can make plans and…"

Joelle stopped talking before Kyril said anything.

She really was trying to do better at rattling on. She pulled Kyril's hand harder and they made their way into the busy port district.

The seaside port was only a short walk northeast from the city walls of Belor. In reality, the city had outgrown its walls long ago, and the sprawl from the city walls to the docks themselves was filled with homes, offices, storage buildings, merchants, and ship builders. More centralized and mild weather than the northern port around Mar, Belor had recently become the main port for the Kingdom of the Realm. Most goods from the southern cities to the families in the capital city of Anikari came through Belor.

Growing up, Joelle had always enjoyed sneaking away from home and watching the bustling crowds. Merchants hawking their wares, sailors unloading goods, and businessmen making deals captivated her attention. All that, along with citizens from virtually every kingdom on the eastern coast of the Blue Sea. She especially enjoyed spotting the occasional elf up from the Elvyn Kingdom.

"What about provisions for the trip?" Kyril asked, pulling Joelle out of her daydreaming. "We didn't bring much with us. It was supposed to be a quick trip."

She ignored his quip, stopped, and stood on her tiptoes and looked around. "There," she said, pointing at a shop not too far away. "I'll get us some provisions and you go and secure us passage."

Kyril gave Joelle an uncertain look and she smiled softly at him, putting her hand on his arm. With all that had happened recently she tended to forget that he had been a somewhat timid young man with not much experience in the world. "You'll be fine, Kyril."

He sighed and nodded his head. "All right. Just don't spend too much of our money."

Joelle laughed and leaned in closer. "Not like you can't get more."

"We need to be careful, Joelle. The emperor has been very generous."

Indeed he has, Joelle thought. The emperor had been very open to the fact that money would be no hindrance to their search for the other medallions and Gamal. Besides a few bags of gold and silver they had attached to their bodies, they also carried certificates that would allow them favors from practically any kingdom on the western continent—at least any kingdom that wanted to maintain a friendship with Gildan, which was all of them.

A loud ruckus caught their attention down the road. They ducked together into a small doorway and watched two men ride recklessly by on horses. Both had cowls over their heads and cloaks that fluttered in the breeze behind them.

As they rode past, one slowed down and glanced over at Joelle, his eyes holding hers for a moment longer than a casual look. It was hard to tell his age and Joelle felt her cheeks redden at his attention.

"Kaldar, come," said a voice from the front horse without turning around. "We must hurry if you want to make the next ship north."

Kaldar stiffened for a moment, raised his eyebrows at Joelle, and then kicked his horse in the sides to catch up with the other rider.

Joelle let out a sigh at his good looks and brief attention, but was interrupted by Kyril.

"Joelle, what was that all about?"

She giggled and patted his arm. "Don't worry Kyril. My honor is intact. It was only a glance."

"They were riding recklessly," Kyril mumbled.

A loud, long horn blast sounded, followed by a short blast.

"We have to hurry," Joelle said. "The ship is leaving soon. Go on and secure passage for us and I'll meet you on the ship after I buy our supplies."

After making sure Kyril got on his way she headed toward the shop she had seen. Before entering she turned her head back around toward where the two men had ridden. They were long gone down the street by now.

"I wonder if I'll see him again," she mumbled to herself as she pushed the door open.

"Welcome, my dear," came the deep voice of a merchant. "How may I help you today?"

CHAPTER TEN

Kyril picked up his pace and headed toward the docks. The scowl on his face sent those in his path scurrying away. When the man had called out Kaldar's name, Kyril had been sure that his medallion had grown warm against his chest. However he didn't dare take it out now and look at it. He didn't trust this new city.

After a few wrong turns he saw a sign up ahead that signified the place to buy a spot on the passenger ships. As he made his way through the crowd he caught another glimpse of the two horsemen. They were walking out of the building that he was heading to.

"I'll see you on the ship," said the second man to Kaldar, his height was average, his hair was dark and his beady eyes glanced around him nervously. "I'll introduce you to the others."

Kaldar waved back and continued walking toward a supply store while the other man with a quick look around hurried toward the side of anther building. Something in Kyril made him suspicious of the man and he followed.

Kyril moved into a slow jog and ran toward the side of the building where the man had gone. The man stood whispering to someone else that Kyril couldn't see well in the shadows of the small alleyway—a dark black cowl covered his head. After a few minutes the man Kyril had been following turned to leave and Kyril had to duck out of the way behind a pile of stone. The man exited a small alley and turned toward the passenger ship.

Kyril waited a few moments and then turned back to the alley where the man had come from. A brief flash of fading light caught his attention for a moment but he passed it off as a trick of the sun. There was no one to be seen. The man in the covered cowl had disappeared into the shadows.

As if in reaction to what he had seen, Kyril's medallion grew warm on his chest. A fleeting feeling of danger overcame him. It was familiar to him but he couldn't quite place it. He stood and thought for a moment, then spun around, surveying the scene once again.

"Gamal," he whispered. At least it might have been. He shook his head at being so paranoid. There was magic all over the western continent, and holders of good and evil intent existed everywhere. It *couldn't* have been Gamal.

Another horn sounded and he saw people begin to scramble toward a docked ship. He ran into the local office hoping he wasn't too late. Racing up to a long counter with three redheaded people standing behind it he blurted out his need.

"Two tickets north please, to White Island," Kyril gasped.

Two shook their head, with one lending his voice. "You're too late, young sir. They are boarding now."

"I can make it," Kyril said. "I will get on the ship in time."

"But how? The line is already dwindling and they are pulling the ropes off the ship."

"Trust me," Kyril said more firmly and brought up his hand out in front of him. With hardly a moment's thought now—much easier than it used to be—he let a blue glow push out in front of him.

The third man at the counter coughed with surprise and motioned Kyril over.

"Two tickets, sir," he said as he handed them to Kyril, "but it'll cost you extra."

Kyril didn't have time to haggle and didn't know how much he should pay anyway, so he thrust two gold pieces at him and grabbed the tickets from the man's hand.

"You've given me too much, sir," said the surprised man at the counter before Kyril left.

"Let him be, man," said one of the other two. "He's one of those wizards, can't you see?"

It was a short distance to transport, and Kyril tried to picture the ship he had seen outside clearly in his head. Bringing out the medallion and encircling it with his hand, he willed himself to transport and a bright light erupted around him.

As Kyril transported out of the office he heard the man say, "The missus will love getting a few extra trinkets today."

Kyril bumped into a railing and grabbed on tightly, barely holding himself upright.

"Hey you there!" yelled one of the sailors. "What are you doing up on the deck? This is not for passengers. Get below."

Kyril moved toward where he saw the last passengers entering the ship. A man stood accepting tickets and stuck out his hand for Kyril's.

Kyril glanced around for Joelle. "I'm waiting for a friend," he told the man.

"If she's not on the ship yet, she's not going," the sailor said. "We're just about to push away."

Suddenly, Kyril heard someone calling his name and he spun around. Running up the dock was Joelle. A man was trotting next to her loaded down with supplies. The ship began to separate from the shore and the man grabbed her hand and yelled for her to jump. Both Joelle and the man sailed through the air and landed with a thud on the edge of the ship where the gangplank had just been pulled in-- the contents of the supplies spewing across the deck.

Joelle untangled herself from the man's cloak and Kyril helped her up. He gave her a questioning glance about all the supplies scattered across the deck.

"I didn't know we were going for a week," Kyril said with a smile.

Joelle blushed and then jutted out her chin at him. "The merchant might have taken advantage of me a bit. Everything looked so wonderful!"

Kyril laughed and reached down to help pick up the supplies.

"You do have to be careful around merchants, they will say anything to make a sale," said the man in the dark cloak.

"I wish I could tell what people's intentions were," Joelle said. "That would make things so much better."

The man stopped in his tracks as he handed Joelle a box from the deck floor. "Aaah, the age-old wish for a woman to understand a man's intentions," said the man with a flourishing bow. "Allow me to introduce myself," he continued. "I am Kaldar, but you can call me Kal."

Joelle blushed again as she gathered up the last of the supplies. They were not very organized anymore but she and Kyril had their hands full.

With light brown hair, a sloped nose, and an oblong face that seemed to hold a balance of mirth and sophistication, Kaldar appeared to Kyril a bit younger than he had first supposed when he and the other rider had almost run them over in the street. Now he appeared to be only a year or two older than Joelle.

Joelle giggled at Kaldar's exuberant behavior, while Kyril only rolled his eyes at her. The ship lurched and a nearby sailor scolded them and told them to get below.

Walking close to Joelle, Kyril bobbed his head toward the door to the passenger apartment. "We need to get settled in."

She scowled at him and then turned her head toward Kaldar. "Thank you for your help, sir Kal. Maybe we will see you at mealtime."

"Joelle!" Kyril pushed her through the door and down a small flight of stairs.

"Be nice, Kyril," she said from in front of him. "He was only trying to help."

"I don't like him," Kyril grumbled, not quite knowing why.

Already something didn't feel right on this ship. Someone had magic on board. Powerful magic that he did not readily recognize.

CHAPTER ELEVEN

A few hours later, Joelle walked in front of Kyril down a narrow hallway on the way to the evening meal. Pushing a heavy wooden door open, she peered around the dining room, surprised by how bright it was. Candles stuck in holders adorned the walls, and a small glowing ornamental stone sat in the middle of each table. Joelle and Kyril looked at each other with questioning eyes. Apparently Kyril didn't know what they were either.

The galley was off to her right and she could see men and women scurrying around trying to ready the meal for their patrons. It seemed they had boarded quite an upper-class ship.

"How much did you pay for this, anyway?" Joelle asked Kyril.

He shrugged and his brown cheeks reddened slightly.

"Seems I wasn't the only one to be taken," Joelle laughed.

They made their way to a small table at the back of the room, passing about a dozen tables on the way there. The walls were whitewashed with picturesque sea paintings attached. Two small round windows sat on the outside wall adding to the brightness.

The dining room was about half full. What appeared to be a few merchants discussing business sat at a larger table, and a few nicely-dressed women were at another. A loud laugh ensued, and Joelle turned and spotted four young people in their early- to mid-teens, most likely going to the Wizard School at White Island. At another table two other men sat with drinks in their hands. A head turned and she stifled a gasp.

Next to her Kyril let out a small groan and elbowed her to sit down. But she took a moment longer to smile at Kal before she did so, feeling her cheeks heat up. The man with him only frowned and turned back to his drink. Joelle scooted around the table so she had a view of Kal.

"Joelle, you need to focus on the mission," Kyril chided her.

"Lighten up Kyril," she said in a hushed tone. "We have two days on this boat with nothing much else to do. Did you know that I've made this trip about ten times, back and forth between Belor and White Island? But I've never been on a ship so nice. Those students over there must be from noble families. I wonder if I know any of their families.

Kyril nodded his head to the steward who now stood next to them, ready to assist them.

"Oh, sorry," Joelle said. She had let her mouth wander off again.

"We have roasted pork, fresh vegetables, and bread," the steward informed them. "Will that do for the two of you?"

Kyril's eyes opened wide and Joelle saw him almost salivating. *Boys! Always hungry!*

"Yes, sir," said Joelle, and the man turned crisply and walked away. "I've never eaten this well on a ship before," she whispered to Kyril. "We're very lucky to have found this."

"I've never been on a ship before at all," Kyril said, putting a hand on his stomach as the ship lurched a bit.

"You'll get used to it." She smiled, remembering the first time she had been on a ship. "I got sick my first time."

Kyril looked relieved. "How old were you?"

"Three," Joelle said. "It's one of my first memories. I spewed food all over the deck."

"Oh great!" Kyril moaned. "Just great."

"Let's take your mind off it," Joelle ventured. "Can I ask you something?"

Kyril nodded.

"Do you know how or why your mother had the medallion?" Joelle began. "Was she a wizard? Were her parents wizards? Did they find it or know who had it first? Did she know it was a magic artifact? Did…"

"Joelle!" Kyril finally spoke, a small grin spreading across his face. "One question at a time, please."

"Sorry," Joelle said with a grimace. "I talk when I get excited."

"You must get excited a lot," Kyril said, a full smile now covering his face. Apparently he had gotten over his anger at her for transporting them to Belor instead of White Island. She would have to be more careful next time.

Joelle noticed how his deep dark brown eyes twinkled with mirth. Ever since coming into his magic with the medallion and saving Emperor Alrishitar and his son Zaidan, Kyril had changed. He was more mature and comfortable around people. He was still naïve to the things of the world, but his mission to find the other medallions and keep Gamal away had given him focus. And it showed in his face.

She allowed herself an exhale of breath and then joined in with his laughter. It felt good and relieved some of the stress she had been feeling. She turned her head a bit and caught the dark eyes of Kal, watching her. He was a handsome man. From his looks and speech she couldn't tell where he was from. His skin was not as pale as those from Belor, but not as brown as those from Gildan—his heritage was hard to place.

She realized she had been staring at him. He grinned and she turned back to Kyril, a bit flustered.

"In answer to your many questions," Kyril said clearing his throat, "I don't know a lot. I knew my mother kept the medallion in a special wooden box up on a shelf. I saw her look at it a few times. But only once did I see her put it on. It was a stormy day—we got a lot of those at the foot of the Superstition Mountains, and my father had been out for longer than he should have been. The wind and rain had picked up and by evening he still hadn't returned. She took the medallion out and then told my sister and I that she would be back soon. I remember watching out the window, and…" Kyril stopped for a moment as if in deep thought.

The ship lurched to the side, and they grabbed the edge of the table. A soft curse came from the merchant table as a plate slipped to the ground, throwing uneaten vegetables across the floor.

Kyril groaned, but seemed to get a hold of himself.

"Sorry," Joelle said softly. "What were you saying?"

Kyril took a moment to take a deep breath before continuing.

"I just remembered that as I watched my mother leave that day I saw a bright light in the yard. At the time I thought it was lightning or some other trick of the storm, but now I wonder if it was the light from the medallion itself. She returned later with my father, who had been hurt when his cart had overturned. They never spoke about how she had saved him, and when she got back home she reverently took off the medallion and put it back in the box."

"Wow," Joelle said. "Do you think she was a wizard? Do you know all the things the medallion can do?"

Kyril gave her a look, and she stopped asking questions.

"I don't think she was a wizard," Kyril said. "But maybe there is a separate connection to the medallion outside of being a wizard. She said it was handed down through her family. It must have come down from the first wizard that King Anikari gave it to when he distributed the three medallions to help keep balance in magic."

"So the fact that you're a wizard may not matter?" Joelle asked. It was hard to think of the ability to do magic without being a wizard. That's the way it always had been. Well, in her kingdom of Alaris, being a wizard had not always been accepted. In the past, certain wizards, both in groups and as individuals had grown in power and tried to take over the kingdom more than a few times. Their current king, Darius DarSan Williams, was the first king to be a wizard in a long time. Magic had been looked down upon in the Realm for many decades, but now after almost twenty years it was accepted by many and at least tolerated by most.

Their food arrived and they took a break in the conversation to take a few bites. Well, Joelle took a few bites; Kyril seemed intent on shoveling it in his mouth all at once.

"Kyril!" Joelle whispered to get his attention.

He was hunched over his bowl and glanced up with his fork almost to his mouth. "What?" he said, his mouth still full.

"Slow down," Joelle said. "It's not going anywhere."

Kyril seemed to remember where he was and glanced around the room nervously, hoping no one had seen him. She didn't think anyone had—except Kal, who was once again looking their way. She tried to ignore him and took a few bites herself.

"I'm not much of a wizard," Kyril said with a frown as he sat back let a bit of his food digest. "So the fact that I can do much of anything at all with my powers means that most of it is coming from the medallion at this point."

"And the mark on your hand?" Joelle moved her attention to his left hand while Kyril opened it up on the table in front of them. "You had some of the power of the medallion even before you had the actual artifact."

Kyril shrugged. "I'm not sure how it all works. I wish I could have asked my mother."

"I'm sorry about your family," she said, knowing that Kyril didn't like to talk about it, but wanting him to know she did care.

He took her words well and smiled his thanks before going back to eating.

"You were able to transport a bit before you had the medallion," Joelle said.

Kyril nodded his head and laughed. "Somehow. Who knows how this all works?"

Indeed, Joelle thought. She knew how her healing powers worked, but it had taken a lot of studying and practicing at the Wizard School to get to where she was. But there was no one to teach Kyril about the magic of the medallion.

They continued eating in silence for the remainder of the meal, both in their own thoughts until across the room two others entered and sat down at the table with Kaldar and his traveling companion. Kaldar soon excused himself and smiled at Joelle before leaving the room. The remaining three at the other table put their heads close together and began whispering in soft tones.

Something didn't feel right about them. Joelle wished she knew their intentions.

CHAPTER TWELVE

Joelle leaned against a railing on the port side of the ship, staff by her side, and watched the shadowy land speed by as they moved up the coast. Clouds covered the setting sun and she squinted in the glare. The wind had recently died down and she wondered how many rowers it took down in the hull of the ship to keep them going at their present speed.

"Hey, watch where you're going," slurred a young man only a bit older than her.

Joelle put one hand on the railing to balance herself, and with the other brought her staff roundabout in an arc. She stood facing the unexpected intruder on her thoughts.

"No need for that, sweetie," the man said, putting a hand up toward her. But in doing so he almost fell over when the boat lurched. "Stupid rowers."

Joelle didn't know what to make of the man. He was dressed in blue velvet finery and hosen, and with a bottle of wine in his hand, stumbled haphazardly across the deck. His light brown hair hung lifelessly, partially covering his blue eyes.

"Curse this weather. We'll never make it in time," the man rambled on. "Should have brought one of those weather witches with us."

"Excuse me?" Joelle asked, still not understanding the man's mumbles.

He turned toward her and gave a mock bow, almost tripping as he did.

Joelle stifled a laugh. The man was surely drunk.

"You should be getting down below to your quarters, sir," Joelle offered. "It's not safe up here for you."

The man took a step closer and squinted his eyes as if to see her better. "Who are you? I don't remember inviting you on this ship."

"I'm Joelle El'San. We're on our way to the wizard school at White Island."

"Ahhh." The man waved a hand in the air. "One of those witches. Why don't you do anything about this weather, then? My father and I are expected in Mar for important business."

"I am definitely not a witch, sir," Joelle began to explain, her anger rising up. "You see, I am a wizard of the heart, my specialty is healing. Kyril, he's a wizard of the mind. He's very smart and remembers things, but doesn't think he's a powerful wizard. But I think he's stronger than he knows. Now, my friend Sylvie, she's from the Kingdom of Arc, but right now she is in Gildan. She got hurt and…well…" She paused, trying to figure out how to shorten her story. "She is a wizard of the earth and could help bring up a wind, I am sure. She is very powerful. But she's not here."

The man shook his head back and forth in quick motions, almost as if experiencing tremors. "Why, why, why are you telling me this? I have no use for a healer," he spat on the ground. The movement brought his wine bottle down lower and it began to spill onto the deck. "Now look what you've done."

He reached his other hand down to his side and tried to pull out his sword. He finally succeeded on the third attempt.

"Maybe you should put that away," Joelle tried to calm down the drunk man. "You might hurt yourself."

He held it up in front of him and twisted it around in his hand. Then with a growl lunged toward Joelle. At that moment, numerous things happened at the same time.

Joelle stepped to the side, instinctively bringing her staff round and smacking him on the back of his calves. The last rays of sunlight suddenly burst out over the tops of the trees on the shoreline, and the momentarily brightness caused the man to bring the hand with the wine bottle up to shade his eyes. At that exact moment, the ship suddenly slowed, sending both of them skidding toward the edge. Joelle grabbed hold of the railing with her empty hand and stayed upright. But the other man, with both hands full, and apparently not wanting to drop his wine bottle or his sword, hit the railing hard in his gut and with hardly a moment to comprehend what was happening, was flipped over the side of the ship and into the water.

Joelle stood stunned for only a moment and then cried out for help. Soon Kaldar and his dinner companion came rushing forward, two other sailors only a few steps behind.

"A man fell overboard," Joelle screamed, pointing down.

A quick look of surprise crossed Kaldar's face but then he jumped into action. He grabbed a rope that was tied to the railing with a flotation device on the end, brought it up and over his head, and threw it out into the water as far as he could.

"Tell the men to stop," Kaldar instructed one of the sailors, who immediately took off running.

The other sailor grabbed onto the rope with Kaldar, and all three peered down into the water.

Soon they saw the man's head bobbing close to the ship.

"Figures," muttered the sailor. "It's Maddox."

Joelle didn't have time to ask what that meant.

"Grab the rope!" shouted Kaldar. But Maddox missed it and the ship began to move past him.

Joelle could hear a loud wail and wondered what she could do. The ship slowed again, but still moved faster than the man could keep up. Then, from the far side of the ship she saw a blue glow float out and down toward Maddox. It appeared to tether Maddox to the ship magically, allowing him to keep up with it.

"It's Kyril," Joelle explained.

The man with Kaldar stood up straight and stared down the ship toward Kyril, while Kaldar's eyes flashed in quick aggravation, almost immediately turning into a nod and smile to Joelle. He pulled the rope up a little higher, then swung it with all his might and threw it out again toward Maddox. The flotation device on the end landed right next to him.

"Grab it!" Joelle screamed down at him.

Maddox sputtered as water continued to splash into his face, but he managed to get both hands wrapped around the device.

Kaldar, with help from the sailor and two more that had recently joined, began pulling up the rope. The blue glow from Kyril's medallion settled around Maddox and kept him still until he came up to the deck of the ship.

Two men reached over the rail and pulled Maddox up and onto the deck of the ship. At that point Joelle thought she heard words of anger and a thud, but moments later the captain and another man, dressed in similar fashion to Maddox, joined the small group.

Maddox groaned, then began coughing violently. Joelle leaned down next to him to see what healing needed to be done.

"What have you done to my son?" shouted the man with the captain. His hefty frame shook with anger and his lips tightened under a bushy mustache. "Do not touch him."

Joelle glanced up with surprise.

"Sir Patrick Hughes, a wealthy merchant from Khazer," whispered Kaldar in Joelle's ear as he grabbed her arm and brought her back up to her feet. "He's a very powerful man."

Joelle pulled her arm away from Kaldar with a glare. "I don't care who he is, his son swallowed a lot of water."

A hiss of surprise slipped from Sir Hughes' lips. "Captain, please take this girl away from my son."

The captain appeared undecided for a moment, but catering to the wealth and privilege of the merchant, shook his head for a sailor to take her. However, before the sailor could take more than a step, Maddox began shaking and moaning.

"Joelle!" called out Kyril from behind the group of men.

Everyone turned to look at the newcomer. The golden medallion hung from his neck, still emitting bright flares of power from the magic he had used to help Maddox.

Joelle knelt down once again. She could feel Kaldar reach for her, but he stopped just short of touching her again.

"Captain!" bellowed Sir Hughes. "I don't trust wizards. Get these two young people away from my son."

"He took in too much water," Joelle cried out. "He'll die if I don't help him."

Sir Hughes glared at Joelle, but then Kyril stepped forward and his attention moved to him. Kyril understood what Joelle needed and placed himself between Joelle and the rest of the crowd. Joelle glanced around quickly and noticed the man that had been with Kaldar at first was nowhere to be seen now. Come to think of it he had disappeared before sir Hughes had arrived. Before turning to help Maddox, Joelle saw Sir Hughes' hand move toward a knife at his side and his eyes appeared fixated on Kyril's chest where his medallion hung.

Sir Hughes came forward, motioning sailors to join him, but Kyril held his space. Joelle smiled despite the situation. Kyril certainly would not have done something so brave even a few weeks before. The medallion certainly had changed him. She heard a shuffle of feet next to her and as she reached out to turn Maddox onto his side, she saw Kaldar move into place next to Kyril.

He winked at Joelle, his lips spreading into a small grin as he did so.

"Men!" huffed Joelle as she turned back to the task at hand. With her hands on Maddox, she dove into his body with her healing powers. She pushed the water out of his lungs, causing a flow of sickening fluid to erupt from his mouth, and violent spasms to engulf his body. She closed her mind to the scuffle that began around her.

She moved along the flow of his organs and veins, checking for long-term damage. His liver was already weak, most likely from too much alcohol in his young body. She shook her head at the lifestyle some bought with their money. So much good could come from it instead. She took a few moments to infuse his body with healing. It would take a few weeks but should get back to normal soon.

Maddox coughed a few times and spit up blood. Joelle dove deeper and saw an ulcer in his stomach lining. She healed that as well, dissipating the remaining alcohol, continued on to strengthen his lungs, then finally emerging from her healing ten minutes or so later. She sat back on the deck for a moment and took a few deep breaths.

Sir Hughes burst through the crowd and dropped his hefty frame down next to his son. "What have you done to him? You've killed him!"

"She's healed him, sir," said Kaldar. "Look."

Maddox began to stir and his eyes fluttered open. He took a few deep breaths, and with the help of his father sat up. He glared around at everyone, and then his eyes narrowed at the sight of Joelle next to him. Without any words he stood up and appeared to be thinking for a moment.

"She pushed me overboard," Maddox said to his father, while pointing at Joelle. He clearly was trying to push the blame for his condition to someone else. "And that man there"—he now pointed a finger at Kyril—"tried to kill me with magic."

"I did nothing of the sort," Joelle said, shocked. "You were drunk and came at me."

Sir Hughes stood back up and kept his attention on Kyril. "Quite a special talisman there, son." He took a step closer to Kyril and reached his hands forward. The man's eyes grew dark. "Are you sure you are trained to use it? Maybe we could come to an agreement of sorts. A trade?"

Kyril's eyes flicked toward Joelle, but she only shrugged.

"Or perhaps I could buy it from you," Sir Hughes said.

The man seemed to be suddenly more enthralled and interested in the medallion than his son.

"Father, why would you want a magic artifact?" said Maddox, his eyebrows furrowing at everyone around him. "Magic is evil, you taught me to despise it. It's unnatural. Why would you want it?"

Sir Hughes whipped his head around to his son and Joelle noticed his pupils were dilated. "You have no idea of the power in this medallion." He spun around looking at the rest of the crowd. "None of you do!"

Kyril took a step back and Joelle tightened her hand on her staff. Sir Hughes seemed to be a bit obsessed with the magic of the medallion. He took another step toward Kyril but Kaldar stepped between them.

"And who are you?" Sir Hughes said with a flourish of his hand. "Get out of my way."

"I'm, uh, no one of importance," he mumbled, losing some of his earlier bravado at all the sudden attention. "No one at all. Just taking a sightseeing trip. But I think these two did help your son and you should take him below to rest."

Sir Hughes glared at Kaldar, then smiled broadly. "Very well," he said, then he turned toward the captain. "I will hold you personally responsible for the treatment of my son and myself aboard your vessel."

"Sir," Joelle said, "Your son had a bad liver and stomach ulcers. He would have been dead within a year."

Sir Hughes didn't seem to care much about the news but instead took another step toward Kyril his eyes once again fixated on the medallion.

"Father," Maddox said joining his father. "What's wrong with you?" He turned his father and began walking back toward the cabins.

"I'll have that medallion," Joelle heard sir Hughes mutter before they rounded a corner.

She gave a worried glance in Kyril's direction, but he shook his head to stop her from saying anything more on the subject.

"Back down below," ordered the captain. "All of you. It's getting dark and dinner will be served soon."

"Thanks for your help, Kal," Joelle said.

Kyril eyed him suspiciously, but nodded his head in thanks anyway.

"Joelle is quite amazing, isn't she?" Kaldar said with a smooth smile to Kyril. "I mean, as a healer, of course."

Joelle rolled her eyes and motioned for all of them to walk back downstairs. "I need to rest for a bit," she said. "I'll see you both at dinner?"

Kyril and Kaldar kept their distance from each other as they walked. Apparently neither one liked the other very much. Joelle couldn't understand why. Kaldar had been a perfect gentleman.

CHAPTER THIRTEEN

"It's beautiful isn't it, Sylvonna?" Prince Zaidan Alrishitar motioned ahead of him.

Sylvie shaded her eyes with a hand and peered down a small rise and across the Gildan River at the western edge of Gildan. Its waters were turquoise with white frothy caps. Lush green trees grew along the river's edge and a sturdy wooden bridge had been built across it.

It was cooler near the river and Sylvie let herself revel in the breeze for a moment before responding to Zaidan. When she did she noticed his dark brown eyes sparkling at her. Zaidan was the second child and only son of Emperor Mezar Alrishitar. He was a brilliant wizard of the mind, having been tutored since he was young. He had short dark hair and a thin face and stood almost as tall as Sylvie even though he was two years younger. More jovial than many Gildanians were—at least compared to Bale, who sat beside him—he had befriended Sylvie a few weeks earlier when he had helped her with her wizard abilities, and then had asked her to help watch for trouble at the academy.

"Yes it is," Sylvie said. "I've never seen a river this color before."

"It's from the snow and glacier melt high up in the Superstition Mountains," Zaidan informed her—but then his eyes grew sad. "I'm afraid this is as far as I go with you,

Sylvonna. It wouldn't do for me to cross over into the kingdoms of Turg or Cyrene. I hope you understand."

"Of course I do, Zaidan." Sylvie smiled at him. "You didn't need to come with me even this far. I do have Bale to watch over me." She said the last with a smirk. With her growing powers she sure didn't need any watching over, but ever since the fire in the library, Bale had been strangely protective of her.

Bale only grunted and moved his horse forward toward the bridge.

Sylvie had rested for three days after Kyril and Joelle had left. Though it was not as long as some of the healers would have liked, it was longer than Sylvie wanted. She didn't know what was taking Kyril and Joelle so long, but she was anxious to return to her kingdom and help Kyril in his research on the medallion. She would have liked to take Hasani with her as his ability to remember things would have been extremely helpful, but she understood his ties and affection to the library in Gildan.

The emperor had insisted on an escort for her and had assigned Bale. Zaidan had volunteered himself and three guards to ride with her to the border of the Gildanian Empire. From there she would ride with only Bale as her companion down the southwest road to the city of Hasari on the coast. There she would take a ship to West Port up in Arc.

"Are you coming, Wizard?" Bale called back to her with some irritation in his voice.

Sylvie sighed. She guessed his good mood was already wearing thin. But she wasn't going to let him goad her. She was excited to get home. Even though Gildan was beautiful and full of wizards, she missed the Wizard Conclave and her family.

"Please let me know if you hear anything from Kyril and Joelle," Sylvie said to the prince.

Zaidan nodded his head. "I will send a letter if there is any news. I'm sure they are fine."

Sylvie didn't know if she agreed with his assessment. Gamal could be anywhere. She certainly didn't want to run into him, but she didn't want her friends to, either.

"Thank you for the company," Sylvie said.

Zaiden moved his horse closer to Sylvie and reached out his hand. Sylvie shook it.

"Good luck, Sylvonna Hickory," Zaidan said with a short bow of his head. "For all our sakes, may you find the medallion and rejoin with the others before Gamal and his followers cause any more problems."

"Thank you Zaidan." Sylvie nodded her head back to him. "And thank your father for me once more. He has been more than gracious in his help and resources."

"You, Kyril, and Joelle did an immense service for Gildan and we will never forget it." Zaidan said with a quick glance toward the bridge. "As has Bale." His eyes twinkled in apparent amusement.

"I'll try and keep him in line," Sylvie snickered.

"I heard that," Bale called out, and Sylvie felt her face grow warm.

Zaidan chuckled and motioned his guards to follow him back east toward Gildan.

Sylvie rode to the bridge and joined Bale. He wore a beige cloak with a dark shirt and pants. She noticed new black stubble growing on his chin and tried to suppress a giggle but didn't totally succeed.

Bale glared at her for a moment but then shrugged his shoulders, and with the go-ahead from two guards, led her across the tall bridge. In the middle she turned around for a moment. She had a sudden feeling that her life was about to change once again. She watched Zaidan and his men ride off until she could hardly see them, then turned back and continued trotting over the bridge behind Bale.

Three guards from the Kingdom of Turg stood on the other side of the bridge, and while ignoring Bale asked Sylvie for their papers, which she produced. Their eyes grew wide when they saw they included the seal of the emperor of Gildan. He was widely known throughout the kingdoms as a powerful wizard and a fair and likable leader. The need for papers was a relatively new thing among the smaller kingdoms of Turg and Cyrene. Most likely due to new leaders in those nations who were both young. Of course, those with evil designs figured ways to cross borders anyway, so it appeared to be more of a formality than anything at this point.

The two low level guards motioned the two to ride forward.

When Bale took the lead, one of the guards gasped and jumped out to block them.

"Sir, the wizard needs to go first," the guard said.

"What?" Bale's dark eyes flashed in anger. "I am her escort."

"Be that as it is," the guard continued, as if put out about having to instruct a foreigner on their protocol, "in Turg the most powerful always goes first."

"And how do you know I'm not more powerful?" Bale asked.

Sylvie could see his neck muscles tighten and was afraid he would cause a scene. She rode up next to him, reached over and touched his arm before taking the lead. Her blue wizard cloak floated in the breeze behind her.

"Come on Bale," Sylvie said. "You've studied Cyrene as much as I have. You know their affinity for wizards and magic users."

The three guards bowed low as Sylvie passed them by. With a small groan Bale fell in behind her, and they rode off the bridge and into the northern tip of the Kingdom of Turg.

As soon as they were out of sight of the bridge and the guards, Bale's horse trotted up beside her. He glared at her for a moment.

"Bale, you need to let it go," Sylvie said. "It's just the way things are here. We'll be out of Turg and into Cyrene after we cross the Korlan River in a few days. Just think of it as part of your spymaster training."

Her words seem to perk him up a bit and the scowl left his face. "What do you mean?"

Sylvie laughed. "Isn't a spymaster all about being incognito and going unnoticed? Blending in with the environment?"

"Yes…" Bale was now actually grinning. "You're right, Sylvie. I can pretend you're my better…it's all part of the ploy right? Mighty wizard with lowly escort." Bale laughed, then added, "But we both know who should be out in front. I am from a noble house in Gildan after all and you…." He shrugged his shoulders to show that he didn't think much of her upbringing.

With those words, Bale jumped out in front of her and urged his horse forward faster.

"Bale Nabhani!" Sylvie called out. "You're horrible!" She picked up her pace and followed behind Bale for now. There was no one watching and it didn't matter to her who rode out in front.

Bale was from a noble family who had connections to the wife of the emperor. He was from southern Gildan, a relatively weak political area in the empire, but Bale obviously had high expectations for himself. He had grown a bit from the experience of helping to save the emperor and his son, Zaidan, but he still placed too much worth on his station rather than his actions. Sylvie had seen some cracks in his shell—and guessed he cared more than he pretended.

Bale had even cordially said his farewells to Kyril. She knew Kyril was still suspicious of his motives—the merciless teasing and bullying he had received from Bale and his friends was still a fresh wound in his mind. Sylvie, however, had seen a maturing in Bale over the past week—not unlike what she had noticed in Kyril. But sometimes Bale's haughtiness and *nobles are better than anyone else's* attitude still spilled over. Someday, she hoped, he would learn to put the needs of others before his own.

They passed by a few trade caravans that day, and each time, Bale slowed down and let Sylvie take the lead. Those from Gildan would nod their hellos, but those from Turg or even Cyrene would stop for a moment and bow low in their seats or saddles to Sylvie.

They would have a good two days of hard riding before they reached the Korlan River. After crossing it, they would continue on the road for another two-three days—depending on the weather, until they reached the coast.

CHAPTER FOURTEEN

Joelle stretched her arms high overhead, basking in the early morning summer sun. Her unruly red hair cascaded down her back, more frizzy than she would have liked. The crests of the waves sparkled in an iridescent turquoise and a thin mist filled the air around her at the bow of the ship. It was going to be a fantastic day.

"See the White Cliffs?" Joelle said to Kyril as she pointed toward the mainland. "And Mar is there in the distance. But I wouldn't want to go to Mar this time of year. It's hot. I don't mean hot and humid like it gets in Gildan. There are trees and grass there at least, but in Mar it's all desert and dry. Strange, don't you think? I mean it's this close to the sea and it's *dry*. I've never understood that."

"Joelle," Kyril said softly to get her attention back to his original question.

"Oh yes—we will be docking on White Island first, so we won't really be going to Mar," she said apologetically. "I guess you didn't need to know all about the desert."

But she was just so excited. She loved the wizard school at White Island. She had made many friends there among both the students and the teachers.

"Wait until you see a Cremelino!" Joelle squealed. They are the most beautiful and magical horses ever."

"You mean they are real?" said a voice from behind her. Kaldar joined the two as the docks of White Island grew larger in front of them. He looked a bit more unsure of himself than before and appeared to keep one eye on Kyril.

"Oh, yes," Joelle said. "This is where the herd is raised and kept for the king of the Realm. Their magic is similar to dragons. Have you ever seen a dragon? Maybe we'll be lucky and Dragon Rider Liam will come and visit while we are here."

"So much power," murmured Kaldar.

"Oh, yes, the Cremelinos and the dragons have very strong magic—the power of the spirit," Joelle said.

When Kaldar didn't say anything she looked over and caught him eyeing Kyril. The medallion was tucked inside his shirt, but she was sure that Kaldar was looking right at the spot where it hung. She realized that he hadn't heard her statement about the Cremelinos and dragons. Oh well, those that didn't have magic tended to get all excited about wizard powers, and would totally be fixating on such a powerful object as the medallion. Kaldar was no different from anyone else. She studied him for a moment. Nice sloped nose, high cheekbones, and hair styled just right. He was a handsome man.

He turned and caught her looking and she felt her cheeks heat up. He chuckled a bit but turned to Kyril instead.

"So what brings you to White Island?"

The question caught Kyril by surprise and he sputtered for a moment before Joelle came to his rescue.

"I used to attend school here. We are on our summer break from the Wizard Academy in Gildan and Kyril wanted to visit so I told him I would take him," she said with a quick lie.

Kyril gave her a short nod of thanks while Kaldar watched her.

"Hmmm," Kaldar said as if in thought. "Then why did you leave from Belor and not from Kantari in Gildan? I would have thought you would have sailed straight from there."

Joelle felt her heart rate quicken and she glanced at Kyril, who looked as troubled as she felt. It was hard to keep lies under control.

"We could ask the same questions of you. What are you doing here?" Kyril turned the question back to Kaldar. "You are obviously not from the Realm. Why are you visiting White Island?"

Joelle didn't feel that Kaldar deserved such stinging words from Kyril and was just about to say something when Kaldar smiled.

Kaldar shrugged. "Just a short sightseeing trip. I'll just be here a day, it won't take me much longer than that; then I'll be off to Mar. I've heard it's much more exciting there."

A loud horn sounded, signaling that they would be entering the small port soon.

"I'm going to get our things," Kyril said in an irritated tone, motioning Joelle to join him. "We are much later getting here than we had planned."

He turned and started walking, but before Joelle could follow, Kaldar put his hand on her arm.

"Stay with me for a moment," he beckoned, his voice going deeper than she had remembered.

Joelle's stomach fluttered in response to his words. His hand still rested on her arm. It felt warm but not uncomfortable.

"I'll be there in a few minutes, Kyril," she called out, her voice cracking a little. He had no right to order her around.

Kyril turned his head and frowned a bit. But Kaldar just smiled and waved his fingers at him, which didn't help the situation.

Kyril took a step back toward them, but Joelle shook her head and he stopped. With a quick turn he continued toward their rooms.

"Don't tease him so much," Joelle said, swatting Kaldar's hand down. "He's a good person. Really good."

"I'm sure he is," Kaldar said, "but quite young and boring if you ask me. Is it his magic that attracts you to him?"

"Attract? Me and Kyril?" Joelle gasped. "Oh, no, me and Kyril are not…oh no, no. We're just friends."

"Good to hear," Kaldar said with a broad grin. He turned slightly, leaned over, and put his crossed arms on the railing. "Such a beautiful place," he whispered almost to himself.

"It is."

"So much magic." Kaldar said. "Will you show me around the island, Joelle?"

Joelle shook her head. "I would love to, but…I'm not sure I'll…I mean I don't know if I'll have time. Kyril and I are…" She didn't want to tell him that they were here on an important mission, but it was hard not to.

Kaldar smiled as if he knew something, then nodded. "Ahh, I understand. It's just that I'm sure you know so much about the place, where the most important things happen, where the magic is."

"Magic?" Joelle smiled. "That's what you're interested in?"

"In a way," Kaldar said, his eyes seemed darker than they had the previous day. "There must be powerful magic here. Such powerful magic. Magic like your friend Kyril has."

Joelle jumped with a start. "What do you mean?"

"Come on now, Joelle," said Kaldar, "I saw what he did. He has a very unique medallion. Where did he get it?"

"That's not for me to say," Joelle said, trying to steer clear of the subject. She knew she had a tendency to babble and didn't want to accidentally say anything she shouldn't. "What's all this interest in Kyril all of a sudden?"

He turned toward her and cupped his hand under her chin. "Is this more to your liking?"

She stiffened at first, but then his eyes caught her attention and his face softened. His eyes bore into her. They were dark and drew her in, their depths filled with emotion and sentiment. And something else too, but she couldn't tell what it was for sure. They seemed somehow older than they should be.

"Your friend must be very important to be given such a medallion," Kaldar said in a soft whisper. "Don't you deserve that kind of power? Wouldn't you like to use it to help people?"

Joelle nodded. She did want to help people. She loved healing and the way it made her feel. Oh not the exhaustion part, but the part when she saw a patient's smile or the relief on the face of a loved one when she healed someone close to them.

"You could heal so many more people," Kaldar said as he moved his right hand up to her cheek. "You have the biggest heart of anyone I've met. I can tell how much you care and want to help."

Joelle could only nod once again. She couldn't find her voice. Deep down inside she wondered what was happening. He brought his lips close to hers and she felt her breath quicken.

"Too bad there is only one medallion," he whispered, his lips inches away. "I would do anything to give it to you."

"But there are more," Joelle whispered back, her voice cracking on the last word. "That's why we are here at the wizard school. To find information on the others."

She felt a quick jab of pain in her temple and noticed that one of Kaldar's fingers was now touching her there. She shook her head to clear a moment of fogginess and tried to remember what she had just said. Kaldar lowered his lips further and brushed them over her lips.

She closed her eyes and felt like she was a million miles away. Her power responded to him for some reason and swelled up inside her, enhancing the emotion behind the kiss. Thoughts of the medallion and their mission to find more information on the others scurried freely across her mind. She tried to push those thoughts away and concentrate on the kiss, but she didn't have much control.

Kaldar pulled away and lowered his hand back down to his side.

She glanced back toward shore and realized they had traveled much farther than she would have thought in the short time since Kyril left.

"Maybe I could free up a few minutes to show you around White Island, Kal," she said in response to his last words before their kiss. At least...that was what she *remembered* happening before the kiss...but it was all a bit blurry. Maybe that's what kisses did. She was a bit embarrassed to not have any previous experience in that area.

Kaldar smiled, but it appeared more forced now. "That won't be necessary, Joelle. I'm sure you have more important things to do. I'll be gone before you know it. Now you'd better hurry and catch up to Kyril. We don't want him to worry about you."

Joelle was a bit flustered. He seemed to be brushing her off now. She took a few steps away from the railing, then stopped and turning back around, caught a glimpse of Kaldar's face—a face that was not as beautiful anymore. A face that held a wolfish hunger for something. It surprised her for a moment and she let out a small gasp. But then he turned and smiled, and his handsome looks returned.

That kiss is definitely playing tricks with my mind.

CHAPTER FIFTEEN

Disembarking the ship and meeting Kyril a half an hour later, Joelle watched Sir Hughes and his son, Maddox arguing as they entered a nearby inn. Sir Hughes appeared confused about where he was and staggered a bit into the building.

The dark hair man she had seen a few times with Kaldar—including on the ship before Sir Hughes had showed up to find his son who had fallen overboard—stood now with a smirk on his face following Sir Hughes and his son with his dark eyes. But Kaldar was nowhere to be seen. Joelle was just about to comment on it to Kyril when they were directed to a cart that would take them up the hill to the wizard school. They left the bustle of the sailors, ships, inns, and stores near the docks.

A few other carts rode in front and behind them and so the going was a bit slower than she would have liked.

"I still think you brought too much," Kyril grumbled.

"Oh, lighten up, my friend," Joelle said, not allowing Kyril to spoil her lingering good mood. "Isn't it beautiful here?"

Kyril and Joelle took a moment to look around. Flowers and bushes lined the road leading up to the ornate gates of the wizard school itself. The Cremelino fields stood off toward her left, and the sea was to her right. A slight breeze blew by, bringing relief from the growing heat of the day. The sky was pale blue with only a wisp of stray clouds. Nothing could ruin her return to the wizard school.

As they approached the gates she turned and glanced behind them.

"Looking for Kaldar?" asked Kyril.

Joelle couldn't tell if he was teasing or irritated. What had gotten into him? She almost wished he was the shy, introvert that he used to be. Maybe the power was going to his head.

"No," Joelle answered politely, "I haven't seen him since I left him on the bow of the ship."

"I saw him stumble off the ship just before you got back," Kyril added. "What's gotten into you?"

Joelle slapped Kyril's arm. "Are you spying on him?"

"Are you going to see him again?"

"I don't know, Kyril," Joelle said, starting to get irritated. "If I want to, yes, but it's none of your business."

"It is if it detracts from the mission." Kyril's eyes grew hard. "Something wasn't right on that ship. Gamal, or his followers could be anywhere right now. We are no closer to finding him or the medallion than we were three days ago when we left Gildan. We need those medallions, Joelle. The safety of many kingdoms rely on us finding them, and you're batting your eyes at a man I don't trust."

Joelle felt a bit foolish. She had indeed been distracted. *That kiss.* Shaking her head, she tried to clear Kaldar from her thoughts. Kyril was right. What they were doing was more important than a schoolgirl crush on a handsome man she may never see again.

"I'm sorry," Joelle said, wiping a few stray tears from her eyes.

Kyril let out a puff of air. "Don't cry, Joelle. I didn't mean to be so harsh. I just feel so much pressure to find the other medallions and we don't know where they are."

"No, you're right, Kyril. I was distracted. We'll be at the school soon, and then we can meet with the headmaster and head librarian and gain access to their records. I'm sure we'll find something!"

"I hope so," Kyril said.

The cart moved from the dirt road onto the cobblestone driveway of the White Island wizard school. They soon came to the gates and had to wait their turn to enter behind dozens of other carts. White stone walls rose up in front of them, forming parapets and towers at the top of the school. A picturesque lawn, highlighted with water fountains and dotted with statues, came into view as they rolled slowly closer.

Soon they were dropped off in front of the school, and some younger students took their bags. One had hair like Kaldar…Joelle wondered where he was at the moment. She hoped she did have a few minutes to show him around before they left.

"He isn't a bad guy," she said, turning to Kyril.

"What?" Kyril said, obviously not following.

"Kaldar; he isn't that bad. He helped me with my things, stood with us when Sir Hughes didn't want us to heal his son, and has been nothing but polite to you."

Kyril shrugged as he followed her towards the front doors of the school. "Maybe. Maybe not. I didn't like the way he stared at my medallion."

Something in the back of Joelle's mind tickled a memory about Kaldar and the medallion, but she couldn't quite remember what it was. It didn't matter anyway now that they were at the school.

"Come on, Kyril!" Joelle grabbed a hold of his hand and led him up the steps toward the enormous door. She stopped for a moment and peeked upward at the school. "Can you feel it? Can you feel the power here?"

Kyril nodded. "It's different than Gildan."

"It's less formal. Magic is much newer in the Realm. There's still a freshness to it."

"Hey, Joelle," said someone off to their left. It was one of the younger students she knew from her classes, and she responded with a wave of her own. It was nice to be back.

After sticking his hand down in his shirt, Kyril pulled out the medallion. "Well, here it goes, Joelle. Remember this isn't just a social call."

Joelle sobered for a moment, remembering again what they were there for. Leading Kyril up the steps she squared her shoulders and tried to appear as important as she could.

"Kyril Siravan and Joelle El'San," she announced to the doorman. "We are on a mission from Emperor Mezar Alrishitar of Gildan and need to see Headmaster Penrose immediately."

CHAPTER SIXTEEN

A deafening, earsplitting blast knocked Kyril off his chair where he had been waiting to see the headmaster. Joelle appeared to fare a little better. Others in the room began screaming. One young wizard suddenly produced a ball of fire in his hand and circled around, looking for the source of the blast. Just as Kyril reached his hand out to help Joelle to her feet, an echo of the first blast shook the room once again. Bits of plaster fell from a growing crack in the ceiling, and a glass figurine, along with a dozen books, fell from shelves lining the room and crashed to the floor.

"What was that?" Joelle said, gaining her feet.

Kyril heard running steps coming down the nearby hallway, and shouts began to fill the school.

"We're under attack," said an older lady in the room.

"Who would attack the wizard school?" said a younger boy, hardly old enough to be in school.

"Gamal!" said Joelle and Kyril at the same time, but the others were paying them no attention. They had no idea who Gamal was or what he could do, but both Kyril and Joelle had seen the havoc he had wreaked upon the Wizard Academy in Gildan. The man would stop at nothing to find the medallions.

Kyril was the first to reach the door. Pulling it open he then stepped out into chaos. Flashes of wizard's fire splayed down the hallway, but didn't seem to be aimed at anyone in particular. Joelle headed deeper into the school pulling Kyril with her. As they rounded the corner, three hooded figures ran right toward them. One brushed by and kept on running. Kyril watched him for a moment when a second one knocked into him hard.

Grunting, Kyril fell hard onto his rear end and the back of his head smacked the cold hard marble floor. He yelled out in pain and grabbed both sides of his head, trying to keep from passing out. Sparkles filled his vision as he strained to stay alert.

He heard Joelle scream and turned his head in her direction to see her untangling herself from a woman—one of the hooded figures whose cowl had fallen back from her head. The one that had knocked into Kyril stood and looked over him for a moment, a slight frown forming on his young face. He was dressed like a student, but something tickled the back of Kyril's mind as he examined the stance of the man. He almost appeared recognizable but the ache in his head precluded him for figuring it out at the moment.

"Come on," said the female to the young man standing over Kyril. She pointed toward the third attacker who was now heading toward the door. She was dressed in student robes too, but upon closer study appeared to be at least ten years older than Kyril. "Our work is done here for now. We need to report back."

"Not yet!" With no warning, the man leaned down, grabbed at the chain holding the medallion around Kyril's neck, — and pulled harder than Kyril was prepared for.

"No!" Kyril cried out and tried to turn away—but the chain broke and the medallion skidded across the marble floor.

The other two were now running toward the front door at the end of the hallway. They beckoned back to their partner, but the young man was more intent on getting the medallion than escaping.

Kyril couldn't see how he could reach it before the man did, but even with ringing in his ears and his head still pounding, he brought up his palm, the mark of the medallion glowing brightly in quick response to his summons.

He reached toward the medallion on the ground just as the man leaned over it. The medallion lifted up in the air in response to Kyril's power and flew back toward his outstretched hand. The man tried to grab it in the air, but it sped by too fast, nicking the side of one of his thumbs.

The man roared in pain and spun around to fight Kyril, but Joelle stood up and blocked his path. She now had her staff out in front of her and began to spin it in a broad arc. Colors flew around her as she pushed the man back farther away. He stared at her for a moment and reached his hand out toward her.

"Joelle…" the man whispered.

Joelle hesitated as the man caught her eyes.

"The headmaster!" yelled a man down the hall in front of them. "The headmaster is hurt."

The news took Joelle out of her trance and with a smack of her staff she knocked the man to the side. Taking advantage of the distraction the man took off running past Kyril toward the front door. Kyril followed the man's gait for a moment, as if trying to remember something, but with an urgent yell from Joelle he spun around and followed her down the hallway.

Kyril entered the headmaster's office just steps behind Joelle to find utter chaos surrounding them. A half dozen people, including what appeared to be three students and three teachers, stood around a man on the floor. The windows at the end of the room were blown out, furniture was spewed throughout the room, and papers were still floating around from empty shelves that had been blasted.

Joelle pushed through to the headmaster.

"I'm sorry," said one of the female teachers without actually looking in her direction. "Who are you?"

"I'm a healer," Joelle said defiantly.

"Amanda, it's Joelle," said a man.

"Professor Warren, let me help," Joelle begged the man.

He nodded his head and the others stepped aside.

"She was always one of my best students," said Warren. "As a wizard of the heart she surpassed me long ago."

The others had their attention on the headmaster while Kyril walked around the room and surveyed the damage. He blocked out the noise of the school and tried to summon his powers as a wizard of the mind. As the chain was broken, he still held the medallion in his hand. It warmed to his touch but didn't burn him. Its power augmented his own and his mind started cataloging all he saw.

Although the room was a mess, not much besides the windows was actually broken. There was very little glass on the floor of the office, so he figured that the blast had taken place inside the room and had pushed the windows out. He walked to them and peered outside. Streams of people continued to pour out of the wizard school. He could see teachers and other adults trying to calm down the younger students. A barrier of wizards—primarily earth wizards, he presumed—took up position around the perimeter of the grounds. Whoever had done this would surely be caught.

"Who would attack the school?" said the other adult in the room, a man about ten years older than Kyril.

"Marcus, there are still those that distrust magic," said Amanda.

"I didn't think they were this organized," said Marcus. "To try and destroy the school…"

"It was a distraction," Kyril said softly.

Amanda and Marcus glanced over at him and opened their eyes wide at the color that still swirled around his hand from the medallion.

"And who are you?" Marcus asked, taking up a defensive posture. "We haven't seen you before. Maybe you are with them."

He and Amanda walked forward, hands outstretched. Marcus flicked his wrist and the last standing chair came flying behind Kyril and ran into his knees, forcing him to sit down.

"Warren, take the students out," Amanda commanded. "I think we caught one of them."

Warren left Joelle's side and crooked his finger at the three other students in the room.

"No," Joelle said in a whisper. Her eyes remained closed as her hands ran over the headmaster. "Leave Kyril alone."

Warren hesitated.

"I didn't do this," Kyril said and moved to stand up.

With another flick of his hand, Marcus sent a book from the desk toward Kyril's head. He barely dodged it, but then jumped up and pushed his hands out toward the attacking wizard.

Light shot out from the medallion and knocked the man backward. He stumbled but kept his footing. Now, with apparently more effort, Marcus motioned for a small footstool to lift from the ground and hurl itself toward Kyril. But filled with the power of the medallion, Kyril was now ready.

In the blink of an eye he transported and now stood behind Marcus, allowing the stool to crash against a bookshelf behind where Kyril had just moments earlier been standing.

"What?" Marcus said.

"Stop!" Amanda put her hands out between the two warring wizards. "Enough."

With a glare from Marcus, the man lowered his hands.

"Son, you too," Amanda said to Kyril. "I am in charge of security here."

From behind Kyril, Joelle began to cry softly. Everyone's attention turned toward her and the headmaster. She opened her eyes and tears dripped down her face.

"His injuries…" She shook her head. "They are too extensive. It was a quick-acting poison. I…I…tried to draw it out, but I couldn't."

Kyril raced to her side and knelt down next to her. "What about with the power of the medallion?"

Her eyes brightened for a moment, and he handed the medallion to Joelle. Her face lit up as she tried to access its powers. She bent over the headmaster once again and grabbed his head in her hands, the medallion touching him on one side. A dim light surrounded the headmaster, emanating from all over his body.

There was a gasp and the headmaster opened his eyes slowly. Joelle continued to hold onto his head. But now her face was turning pale and she began to sag to the ground next to the headmaster.

"Joelle, no!" Kyril called out. "It's too much power for you. You have to stop."

"I can do it," Joelle breathed. "He can't die."

"Imposter," croaked the headmaster.

Kyril leaned down closer.

"Look for the imposter," Headmaster Penrose repeated. "He's not who he seems."

They all looked at Joelle now, who still held the medallion in one of her hands. She barely kept her hands on the headmaster's head as she laid on the floor next to him. Kyril could see the veins showing through her skin and her hair losing its color.

"She's burning herself out," said Warren.

Kyril reached his hand over and took the medallion from her.

"No," Joelle said. "He'll die."

"Who was it, sir?" asked Amanda, now kneeling down next to the headmaster. "Who did this?"

The headmaster took a shallow breath and coughed before answering. "He said it was unfortunate that he had to kill a wizard of the mind, but that it was necessary for the greater good."

"Was his name Gamal?" Kyril asked, wondering if the evil wizard had indeed found a way there ahead of them.

The headmaster groaned and shook his head. "It was one of the students—but it wasn't at the same time. He acted and spoke differently. I think he may be a…" The headmaster coughed again without finishing his sentence and closed his eyes. His breathing shallowed and slowed.

"Be a *what*?" asked Marcus "What was he searching for?"

But there was no answer.

"He's dying," Joelle said. "Give me the medallion, Kyril."

The headmaster's eyes didn't open, but his mouth parted slightly.

"He was searching for information about a medallion," he said with his last breath.

Everyone in the room turned to Kyril, who was still holding the medallion in his palm.

How was Gamal always one step ahead of them?

"At least he didn't find it yet," said Joelle to Kyril, her coloring returning. "At least we still have a chance."

CHAPTER SEVENTEEN

Joelle felt like she was in a nightmare. In her time at the school nothing even close to this had ever happened. Now the school will forever be changed and she felt bad for all the students there who would now define their time at school by this one event.

When men came into the room to remove the body of the headmaster, Kyril led Joelle down the hallway and out the front doors where most of the students and teachers had gathered. A few people said hello to her, but she was barely able to nod her head in response. She didn't know what she would have done without Kyril next to her. He took control and brought her over to a spot away from the others on the grass against a small retaining wall.

She laid her head back, closed her eyes, and tried to breathe. She had healed many times before, but with the power of the medallion she had never had access to so much power. She was exhausted and could barely think.

"Oh Kyril." Joelle had thought she was stronger, but now tears flowed freely down her face. "How could they have done this? I've known the headmaster for years. He was kind and good and…" As a healer it was getting harder and harder for her to see someone die in front of her. Especially someone who had always had a caring word for her.

Kyril shook his head but didn't say anything for a few moments. When he finally spoke, his voice was low but firm.

"Gamal will answer for this, Joelle. I heard that aside from the headmaster, there were few deaths—but *any* are too many. It was all a diversion to get to the headmaster and to find information on the medallion. I'm not sure how he orchestrated it so fast, or if he had already been working on it, and we just happened to get here at the right time. With the attack on the wizard academy and now the wizard school, the world of wizards will not sit back and let him destroy magic."

Joelle listened to others crying and talking around the school grounds. She wiped her own eyes and took a little consolation from Kyril's words. "But what can we do?"

"We can bring balance back to the world of magic, Joelle," Kyril said. "That is our task. We need to push forward and start studying the books in the library."

"Surely not now?"

Kyril nodded his head a few times. "We can't wait too long, Joelle. If he attacked here, the Kingdom of Arc will surely be next."

"Sylvie?" Joelle asked.

"Yes, we need to get back to her soon," Kyril said. "If we don't find anything in a few days, we will have to leave."

"I can get us help, but…" Joelle began. "They need time to grieve. Headmaster Penrose has been the only head of the wizard school since it was founded over eighteen years ago. He is close friends with the king. It will be a difficult time for them here.

"We can't wait, Joelle," Kyril said softly. "We must keep searching until we find the next medallion."

Joelle closed her eyes and put her head back against the wall. "Just give me a few minutes to recover. I need something to eat."

"Oh, Joelle, I'm so sorry," Kyril said, stumbling on his words. "I'll go find some food for you."

She kept her eyes closed but she let a small grin appear on her face. She didn't mean to be so hard on him, but he didn't know these people like she did. This was where she had lived for the past five years.

"Thank you," Joelle said. "I know you are right. Just let me rest for a few minutes."

She heard Kyril walk away before sinking into a deep sleep.

***

It only seemed like a minute before Joelle was startled awake by a loud shout. Still dazed, she found herself on her feet and peering around, looking for the source of the commotion. A man stood on top of a garden wall and was pointing in the direction of the docks.

"Fire!" he yelled out.

Joelle followed his gaze and saw a dark plume of smoke billowing up into the blue—and previously clear—sky. After taking a few steps closer, she had to put a hand against a tree to steady herself. Closing her eyes for a moment, she took a few deep breaths.

"Are you all right?" asked Kyril from behind her.

She jumped in surprise, then pointed toward the smoke.

"There's a fire at the docks," she said. "What if Kaldar is still there?"

"Joelle…" Kyril began

"I know our mission, Kyril," Joelle snapped at him. He didn't have any right to lecture her right now. "But I can care what happens to others."

"I…" Kyril said, then pushed a chunk of bread and cheese at her. "I'm sorry. You're right. Here, this is the only food I could find. It's all chaos in there."

"We need to get to the docks," Joelle said then took a bite of bread. It felt good in her hollow stomach.

"You're not in a position to go anywhere," Kyril pointed out. "The other wizards will take care of it."

"But what if that's where the headmaster's killers went?" Joelle waved her hands around frantically in the air. "What if we can find them before they leave?"

Kyril seemed to think for a moment before he nodded his head. "You're right."

"You've been saying that a lot lately," Joelle teased with a small grin.

Kyril sighed, but then smiled. "I'm new at this, Joelle. I don't know what I'm doing."

"Neither do I," Joelle said, then pointing toward the stables beside the school, continued, "Maybe we can get a horse and get there quicker."

"Good idea," Kyril said, and the two of them began walking toward the stables. "I think I'm too tired to transport."

As they walked Kyril let out a small laugh.

"What's so funny?" Joelle asked. She couldn't see the humor in anything that had just happened.

"Oh, not really funny," Kyril said shaking his head. "But everyone is running around here worried about the school and the fire and all, but all of them are oblivious to what we are here for. None of them know about Gamal or the medallions or anything that we are doing. A much greater threat looms over all our kingdoms than one attack at one school."

Joelle agreed with his assessment of the situation. It was definitely a lonely quest they were on. More than once she had wondered why three teenagers were chasing around a powerful maniacal wizard and trying to find a trio of mythical medallions.

Coming to the stables they met a man trying to calm down a beautiful white horse. He turned to them as they entered. The thin, but fit, man appeared to be in his early thirties, had light brown hair that came down over his ears, and wore a welcoming and calm smile.

"Hello, Joelle," he said. "I haven't seen you in a while."

"I've been in Gildan at the wizard academy," Joelle said. "This is Kyril, a friend of mine." She turned to Kyril. "This is Jacob Widing, the master caretaker of the herd of Cremelinos and all the other horses at the school."

Jakob smiled at Kyril, but then with his hand still on the Cremelino he turned his head as if listening to something. He nodded before turning back to Joelle and Kyril.

"Seems you need to get somewhere fast," Jakob said.

Joelle gave him a surprised look.

"She told me," Jakob said, patting the horse.

"But…" Kyril said, then stopped to gather his thoughts. "But I thought they only speak to whomever they are bonded."

Jakob laughed and his eyes sparkled. "Oh, Cremelinos are a mysterious breed for sure." The horse next to him snorted in response. "They do bond to one rider and share thoughts with that rider, but they also avail themselves to any wizard in need. And you two…appear to be in need."

Kyril reached his hand toward the Cremelino, then hesitated. "She's beautiful."

Joelle felt pure power emanating from the tall and majestic creatures. It was different than anything that came from a wizard of the mind, heart, or earth. Known for their speed, grace, and ability the Cremelinos used the fourth power—the power of the spirit, the same power that dragons and other mythical creatures wrought. And they always seemed to come forward during times of great need.

"Hop on," Jakob said, motioning to Joelle and Kyril.

After a moment the two were settled on the horse and ready to leave.

"What's her name?" Joelle asked Jakob.

Before Jakob could answer, Kyril blurted out, "It's Solace. Her name is Solace."

"How do you know?"

Kyril twisted around from in front of Joelle, grinning from ear to ear. "She told me. I heard her speak."

Joelle frowned a bit, suddenly a bit jealous of her friend. She had lived on White Island and around the grand creatures for years without ever hearing anything.

"You've been given a rare honor," Jakob said.

Kyril nodded to Jakob his agreement. "We won't be long."

Kyril had grown up on riding horses in the meadowlands of Gildan and used his knees to turn the horse toward the door, and Solace took off with a jump. Joelle had to grab tightly onto Kyril to keep from falling off the back of the speeding horse.

"Can you tell her to slow down a bit?" Joelle grumbled in Kyril's ear.

But he only laughed with delight as they sped out of the school's gate and down the dirt road toward the harbor.

The entire southern sky was now filled with black smoke. As they headed down the curving road, Joelle caught glimpses of orange, yellow, and red flames and once again thought about Kaldar. She hoped he was all right.

CHAPTER EIGHTEEN

Kyril couldn't believe the speed with which they traversed the road. It was almost as if they floated, none of the rough spots or potholes impeding their ride. As they got closer to the docks, he could see ships burning in the harbor, flames now spreading onto the docks and toward the shops and homes in the area. His stomach fell, thinking of the senseless loss that once again he would hold Gamal responsible for.

You must stay calm, young medallion holder, came a soft voice in his mind.

"But this chaos is so foolish," he said out loud.

"Who are you talking to up there?" Joelle said.

"Solace. She wants me to stay calm," Kyril said. "But how can I stay calm? Gamal is wreaking havoc from Gildan to the Realm. He's going to make people afraid of magic."

They came to a hill on the road, ready to head down into the dock and small village there, when the Cremelino stopped.

"Why did you stop?" Joelle asked.

"I didn't. It's Solace." Kyril urged the horse forward, but it wouldn't budge. "She won't move."

"Look."

Kyril looked. A small boat had escaped the fire somehow and was leaving the harbor and heading toward the mainland. On its stern stood two people. Kyril couldn't discern their looks, but by their stance and size he thought it was the woman and one of the men that had attacked them in the wizard school. But where was the other man, the one that he had fought?

Without thinking he brought the medallion out of his pocket and accessed its power. He felt the sudden surge of energy and clarity of thought that always came with the power of the medallion.

"I'm going to stop them," Kyril said, readying himself to transport to the receding boat.

One is not enough, neither is two, but the three together will defeat chaos and restore balance. Solace spoke into his mind and sent a calming influence over him.

"Uh," Kyril grunted. "This horse speaks in riddles."

"What's going on?" Joelle urged. "We need to get down there and help. I can help."

"I was going to transport to the boat and stop those two from leaving, but the Cremelino told me not to and said something about…needing all three to restore balance."

"The three medallions," said Joelle.

"I know." Kyril let out a puff of air, taking one last glance at the boat now leaving the chaos behind. "Let's go," he urged Solace out loud and in his mind. "If you don't want me to stop them now, then at least get us down to the docks so we can help out."

With a burst of speed, the Cremelino took off, barely allowing Kyril and Joelle a chance to grab on for dear life. In a matter of moments they were as close to the fire as they dared get.

Joelle slid off the back of the horse and started running toward a group of people hovering over a man on the ground. He had wet brown hair and a black cloak.

"Kaldar?" she questioned as she pushed her way through. "I'm a healer! Let me through!"

The crowd parted and she kneeled down by the man, turning his body over with a tender touch.

"It's not him," Joelle said to no one in particular.

Kyril could see the disappointment on her face. But she ran her hands over the man's body and used her power of the heart to heal him enough to stand up and walk.

An explosion shook the air as part of the dock exploded next to them. Kyril stuck his hand out and immediately the power of the medallion formed a shield of blue between the people and incoming debris.

"Oil," said a man in the back. "There were drums of oil being unloaded from a ship."

Joelle led the people back toward a nearby inn, while men ran around with buckets of water, trying to put out the fire.

"Can you do something about this?" Joelle asked Kyril.

He didn't know. He wasn't a very strong wizard and didn't have the powers of an earth wizard to manipulate the wind or water. He wished that Sylvie was with them. Joelle scooted off to try and help others that were hurt and Kyril was left standing, wondering what to do.

Use the medallion.

He turned toward Solace and she urged him on with a bow of her head.

He knew the medallion augmented his own powers, but he was a wizard of the mind. Yes, he could move small objects and conjure fire if needed—which they definitely didn't need right now. His real power, however, was his mind and ability to figure things out in his head first.

The main ability that the medallion had given Kyril was the ability to transport. How could he use that to stop the fire from spreading and protect the people? He watched a man running past him with the bucket of water and suddenly had an idea.

It was a little crazy, but it was worth trying. He saw a large empty barrel rolling at the end of the walkway between the docks and the shops. He ran to it and rolled it to the water's edge. Now he would see how strong he truly was. He called on the power of the medallion and used it to lift the barrel off the ground, then submerge it under the water, filling it up as quickly as he could. Closing his eyes, he struggled to bring it back up from the water—it was horrendously heavy. But he finally did it.

As soon as it was above the water he grabbed the medallion in his hand and transported two hundred feet away—this time moving slower than he had done in the past. As he did so he brought the barrel of water with him, pouring it out in the air over the fire. He repeated the process again, pouring water from the barrel on his way back.

Steam rose up around him now and he stopped and took a breath. The fire still burned.

"I need to do more," Kyril mumbled.

He wondered how he could use his transporting abilities and the medallion to completely put out the fire. Suddenly he had an idea. He moved as close to the water as he could without getting burned by the fire. He coughed as smoke and ash filled the air around him. Bringing his hands up in front of him; the right holding the medallion, while his left carried his familiar scar. A golden glow erupted between his outstretched arms and he directed it toward the edge of the water.

He had learned how to transport himself and others, but could he transport something else entirely—an object? Within the golden glow he gathered water. After it slipped away a few times he finally got a grasp on it. Closing his eyes and putting all other distractions out of his mind he projected his thoughts toward the other side of the docks and he felt rather than saw with his eyes the water transport there.

Rather than dumping it directly onto the fire he began to create a barrier of water between the fire and the part of the docks and shops that hadn't burned yet. The explosion of oil earlier had spread the fire to a few nearby buildings, but Kyril stayed focused on the major part of the fire.

Soon there was a wall of water stretched out between him and the other side of the docks. It wavered in a few places but held fairly steady. The flames nearest to it began to fizzle out as the water did its job.

But soon his powers started waning.

Help is on the way, said Solace in his mind.

Kyril felt a renewed surge of energy, but didn't know if he could go on much longer. His mind was growing fuzzy and his head pounded with the amount of power he held.

Finally he heard someone shouting to him and he stopped for a moment and gazed at the wall of water he had created.

"My boy, however did you do that?" came the voice of a woman behind him.

Turning around, he saw half a dozen wizards—ranging in age from barely older than him to gray haired and stooped over—ogling at him.

A portion of the wall of water on the far side began imploding in on itself and blackness was starting to obscure his vision. Stars were sparkling in front of him and he knew he was going to pass out.

"I can't hold it any longer," Kyril declared.

But then, the others put their hands out in front of him and with a sizzle of light they poured their own earth powers into the wall of water and held it steady, as Kyril released the medallion into his pocket and fell to the ground. Putting his head down he breathed deeply, trying not to faint. He felt a hand on his back encouraging him to move farther away from the wall of water.

"I'm not sure how long we can hold it," said one of the wizards.

The wall was at least thirty feet high and three feet thick. A roadway, walkway, and buildings stood on one side, and the burning docks on the other. Kyril knew that if the water collapsed toward the buildings, all his efforts at keeping them safe from the fire would be washed away with water damage instead.

The water began to wave and slosh around.

"It's failing," called out one of the younger wizards.

"No!" Kyril muttered, barely able to talk. He brought the medallion out once again in front of him. He couldn't let the water fall the wrong way and add to the destruction.

Give me your power, he spoke in his mind to Solace. His demand was harsher than he intended, but he didn't know what else to do.

There was a moment of stubborn silence in his mind. What was wrong with the Cremelino? Why wouldn't she help him?

Solace, please! he thought. *These people don't deserve this. I need to help them. I have to help them.* "Give me your power!" he shouted aloud.

As you command, wizard, she said angrily.

Solace came up behind Kyril, and he placed one hand on the medallion and the other on the horse. Power instantly surged through Kyril like he had never felt before. This was not the power of mind, heart, or even earth—this was the power of the spirit. The power to bind all other powers. And with it he took control of all the powers of the wizards on the docks, and wove them together in a tapestry of colorful and mighty magic.

The wall of water held still for a few more seconds and then with once last ounce of effort and power, Kyril threw it back over the fire. As if it was a solid object, the water lifted up into the air and with one giant splash fell back across the docks and burning boats and then flowed out to sea.

With a loud hiss and sizzle permeating the air around them the water put out the fires. Kyril lowered his hand and once again fell to the ground, this time slumping against the Cremelino.

Don't ever command me again. The words jarred Kyril's mind with a stab of pain.

Sorry, was all he could think to say in his mind. He didn't mean to, he was just so desperate. The irritation subsided and calmness prevailed.

But you did do well, came the Cremelino's soft words. *The medallion chose well.*

Kyril afforded himself a small smile before the darkness closed in.

"Kyril!" came Joelle's high voice. "Kyril, where are you?"

But her words did nothing to stop him from fainting.

CHAPTER NINETEEN

Joelle ran through the crowds of dazed people—wizards and non-wizards alike. Broken and charred pieces of wood and stone littered the ground in front of her. She, like everyone else in the area, had seen the giant wall of water rise up between them and the burning docks. When it all came down she looked around frantically for Kyril—she could tell it had been his doing.

She spotted the brilliant white of the Cremelino horse and ran toward her.

She wiped sweat from her forehead and her hand came away covered with black soot. She pushed her wild hair back behind her ears and thought about how messy she must appear to others.

Stumbling twice Joelle pushed through the crowd and finally made it to the Cremelino, only to find Kyril slumped on the ground next to her. She fell down at his side and shook him a few times.

"Kyril, Kyril!"

Joelle didn't know what was wrong with him and if he needed healing, she didn't know if she had any energy left in her to do so. She had done more than she should have already. But it was *Kyril*—she had to try. She reached her hands over to him when a soft but firm voice spoke to her mind.

No!

She jumped and looked around. Then Solace brought her head down and nudged Kyril.

The horse had just spoken to her!

"That was you, wasn't it?" she said to the horse, then glanced around, feeling foolish for talking to a horse.

You've done enough, was the response.

"Oh, it *was* you. I was worried you didn't want to talk to me. I mean, I know that Kyril has the medallion and everything. But I've lived here for five years without ever hearing anything. I know most wizards don't—especially students. I understand that, but I always hoped. But now…"

"Joelle," croaked Kyril, barely opening his eyes.

"Yes?" Joelle said, relief washing over her.

"Please stop talking."

Words sputtered on the edge of her lips and she felt a brief moment of mirth surge through her mind from the Cremelino.

"Well, if that's how you feel about me," she said to the horse and Kyril. She wasn't going to sit here and be laughed at. She moved to stand up, but both her own weak legs and Kyril's hand stopped her.

"Please don't leave me alone," Kyril moaned, his hand touching her arm, his eyes still closed. "Just sit with me quietly for a few minutes. Then I'll be all right."

Joelle settled down next to him, feeling the Cremelino's legs behind them strong and sturdy. She closed her eyes and stayed quiet. She must have dozed for a moment, because she was startled awake by a voice next to her.

"Miss," said a woman. "You're a healer, aren't you? I saw you helping before…"

"Yes," said Joelle, opening her eyes at the question.

Kyril stirred next to her and sat up a bit straighter.

"My husband owns the inn there," she said, pointing with a weathered hand. "The one closest to the docks. He's trapped inside with others and I'm afraid he's hurt. The door collapsed, and…"

The woman's voice caught in her throat and she wiped her eyes. Joelle moved to stand up.

"Joelle, you're exhausted," Kyril said beside her. "Let others do it."

Joelle shook her head. "I need to try, Kyril. They need more help than I do."

"Then I'm coming with you," Kyril said.

She pulled Kyril up to his feet next to her. "Are you sure you can walk?"

"Yes, I just needed a little rest."

"Liar," Joelle said with a smile. "You can hardly move…not much different from me."

Turning to the woman she told her they would be along shortly. They walked carefully over the littered roads and walkways. Other wizards were helping injured people to more accommodating areas. Joelle didn't know how much more she could do at the moment, and looking at Kyril she thought he actually appeared worse than she herself felt.

They followed the woman to the front of what used to be an inn. A cracked sign lay on the ground in the shape of a bed with the words *A Good Night's Rest* written across it. Kyril stepped over it and toward the building, then climbed over a pile of rubble and into the front door. Joelle and the woman followed.

Half of the tables and chairs of the common room were out of place, many of them sprawled on the floor. A wooden beam from above had fallen to the middle of the room, which was where the woman led the two young wizards.

They heard the groaning before they arrived. Joelle picked up her pace and found an elderly man's legs pinned to the ground under the beam. She cringed thinking about how smashed his legs would be. Kyril looked at her with questioning eyes.

"We need to get him out from under the beam," Joelle said. "The medallion?"

Kyril sighed, but nodded. He grabbed a hold of it and closed his eyes. Soon, a bright light engulfed him. He stretched his hand forward toward the fallen beam and the light circled around it, and with renewed strength, Kyril began to direct the beam up into the air.

At first nothing happened.

Joelle heard the woman whimper in anticipation.

Slowly, the beam began to rise. It went up two inches and then stopped. Joelle glanced at Kyril. He wouldn't be able to do much more, but they needed another inch or so. So she brought up her own power, depleted as it was. This man's life hung in the balance and she couldn't let him die on her watch.

Supporting Kyril, Joelle lent strength to the light under the beam and it lifted another inch.

"Pull him out," Joelle directed the woman.

She leaned down and began to push his crushed legs out from the beam. The movement caused the man to bellow in agony. The woman paused.

"Hurry," Kyril groaned. "I can't hold it much longer.

With tears in her eyes the woman pushed her husband's legs out from under the beam, and within moments the beam crashed back to the ground, shaking the room around them. The man let out a scream and then fell unconscious. In the quiet moment that followed, a lone picture frame on a back wall fell off and shattered on the floor.

Joelle leaned over the man and swayed on her knees for a moment. Blackness threatened to overtake her. But Kyril was at her side and held her shoulders up.

"You need to rest, Joelle," Kyril said softly. "You'll be no help to anyone if you collapse."

"Just a minute," Joelle said as she brought her hands over the man. "I'll only stabilize him."

Running her hands over the man's leg, Joelle flinched at the damage. Bone, sinews, and muscles were crushed beyond her current abilities, and maybe even beyond what she could do at full strength. But she couldn't let him die. Drawing upon the strength of Kyril's presence next to her, she did what she could. After a moment she looked at his heart and head, making sure his breathing and mind were stabilized.

Falling back on her rear end she breathed out a deep sigh. "That's all I can do. Find the other wizards."

The woman nodded her head and leaned down next to her husband's lifeless body. She lovingly touched his forehead with her fingertips.

"Thanks for what you did," the woman said. "We've been talking about retiring. It may be time."

Kyril and Joelle smiled at the woman and Kyril helped Joelle to her feet. She leaned on him for support and the two of them struggled to the door. Exiting the inn, they stood for a moment and surveyed the damage.

"Why?" Joelle said. "It's all so pointless. And who were those three attackers in the school?"

Kyril shook his head. "I only saw two on the ship that escaped."

"Maybe the other one was hurt in the blasts before they left."

"Let's hope so," Kyril said, anger seething from his clenched teeth. "Gamal has much to answer for."

Eyeing the Cremelino still standing at the edge of the docks, they began toward her…but then they heard a quiet groan.

Joelle stopped and looked around. Kyril grabbed her right arm and pulled her away.

"No, Joelle," Kyril said. "No more."

Joelle sighed. She knew that Kyril was right. But her drive to help others was hard to dismiss.

"We'll get someone else to help," Kyril said.

The groan grew louder and Joelle turned her head. "Let's just see who it is."

"Then we'll get help," Kyril restated. "No more for you, Joelle. I need you well for our research. Do you remember why we are here?"

"Yes, I remember. It's hard to forget the evil we are up against at the moment."

She pulled away from Kyril. How dare he lecture her? Just because he had the medallion, it didn't mean he always knew better. This attack had done nothing but further her resolve to find the other medallions and bring Gamal to justice. This attack on the wizard school was personal to her. These were people she knew and had lived with.

"This was my home," she mumbled as she glared at Kyril.

He at least had the good graces to look ashamed for questioning her.

She climbed on top of a pile of rubble from which she thought she'd head the moans, and began tossing off scraps. First she saw a leg, she dug harder, then found an arm. Finally she moved up to where the face should be. She pulled off some rocks and gasped out loud, hand flying to her mouth.

"What is it, Joelle?" Kyril called, moving up behind her.

She pointed her finger at the man under the rubble. A man whose face was partially burned. Blood pooled on his forehead and dripped down his face, and bruises marred any unburned skin. His hair was singed and covered with ash and dust. But the things that grabbed her undivided attention were the eyes that blinked once and then closed.

"It's Kaldar."

CHAPTER TWENTY

Joelle fell to the ground and began frantically clearing away the rest of the rubble that covered Kaldar's body. He must not have left the docks before Gamal's accomplices had escaped and set fire to the docks.

Kyril knelt down beside her and had the good manners to say nothing. She knew he and Kaldar didn't like one another. He assisted Joelle in clearing the area around the injured man.

"Kaldar!" Joelle whispered, bringing her hand up to heal him.

"No, Joelle!" Kyril said.

Joelle ignored his pleading. She knew what his argument would be. But it was *Kaldar*. She had to try and help him.

"Kaldar." Joelle cupped a hand lightly beneath the unburned part of his face. "Kaldar, can you hear me?"

Kaldar's eyes flickered a few times and then held her own but he didn't appear to recognize her or understand her. But he was alive.

Kyril put a hand on Joelle's back. "Solace will carry him to the school."

Joelle turned her head, surprised that the Cremelino would carry a non-wizard.

"It took a bit of convincing," Kyril said with a bark of a laugh.

As if on cue, they heard the hoof beats behind them. Kyril called a nearby man over to help them. He watched the Cremelino with round eyes and hurried to do Kyril's bidding. Soon they had Kaldar slung across the back of the Cremelino.

"There won't be room for us," Kyril said.

Joelle nodded. She didn't care. She just wanted Kaldar to be all right. With thoughts of his kiss she ran a finger over her lips.

"We'll have to walk," Joelle said.

The Cremelino ran out in front of them with directions from Kyril to take Kaldar to the wizard school. Someone there would surely understand he needed help. All the other available horses and carts were being used for other seriously injured people, so Joelle and Kyril had to walk slowly up the broad dirt road.

Joelle looked over at Kyril. His face was scrunched up and he appeared to be thinking hard.

"What is it?" she asked.

"I'm not sure," Kyril said. "Just trying to make sense of it all, I guess."

"None of it makes sense," Joelle said. In her exhausted state she wondered if they would actually ever make it back to the school. "Gamal attacks the wizard academy and now the wizard school. To what end?"

"Chaos," said Kyril simply. "If the three medallions that Anikari handed out are to bring balance to the wizarding powers of our continent, then Gamal's black medallion—the one that was made from blood—brings chaos. It seems he has been planning this for a while and has been recruiting others to do his bidding. He is frantic in his search to find the medallions now, and doesn't care who or what gets hurt in the meantime."

"How can someone have such evil intents?" Joelle asked.

"I don't know," Kyril admitted. "But I'm trying to figure out how Kaldar fits into all this."

"Kaldar?" Joelle missed a step and tripped on a small rock. Only by a miracle did she stay standing. Her face heated up at her clumsiness. "What do you have against Kaldar, Kyril? He's been nothing but kind to you."

Kyril held his ground and lengthened his stride to pick up the pace. Joelle grunted but was determined to match him.

"I just don't think it's coincidence that he's here, that's all," Kyril began, but Joelle interrupted him.

"You think he did this?"

"I don't know!" Kyril threw up his hands in the air. "But he did notice my medallion, and now he's here where Gamal's people escaped…"

"Sir Hughes also seemed greedy for it, though," Joelle said. She couldn't believe that Kyril thought that Kaldar had anything to do with it.

Kyril shook his head in apparent frustration and grumbled. "I wonder where he is. Maybe they're all in it together."

Joelle took a deep breath and tried to calm herself before she lashed back at Kyril. "You're tired, Kyril, and both of us have used too much of our magic. Neither of us are thinking clearly. We'll just have to ask Kaldar what he knows when he wakes up. Then you'll see."

Kyril grunted again and matched her stride when she picked up the pace.

A tired hike later they entered the wizard school grounds once again. They had been gone a few hours at most, but the grounds were already in better shape and the wizards they saw were clean and organized. A few wizards were already working on repairing the outside of the building. Joelle was impressed, and admittedly proud of her alma mater.

Spotting Jakob with Solace heading toward the stables, Kyril rushed off in that direction.

"Kyril!" Joelle called.

"Hold on," he said.

But Joelle didn't have time to wait, and continued into the school without him. She didn't know what Kyril was doing, but she needed to find and tend to Kaldar. Upon entering the school she asked about him. A student pointed her toward the healers' rooms. She knew her way.

Walking down the long hallway she noticed that much of the rubble and many of the scorch marks had been repaired, but there were still obvious signs of the recent attack. She glanced up and saw a partial chandelier swinging above her with all of the candles burned out.

Joelle remembered the first time she had entered the wizard school. She had been eleven years old and had just come for a brief summer session to test her recently evident wizard powers.

She remembered stopping in this hallway and looking up at the very same chandelier. Of course, back then, it was fully lit then with over a hundred candles. It had impressed her and ignited a flame in her heart and a desire to pursue her magic wherever it would lead her.

The wizard school was the newest on the continent, established by newly-crowned King Darius DarSan Williams about ten years before she had first entered. Headmaster Penrose, previous governor of Mar, had been named as the school's first headmaster. And now he was gone.

She shook her head in frustration once again. Kyril might not think she cared as much as he did. But she did! She would get to the bottom of this before it was all done. There would be accountability for what Gamal and his followers had done to her school.

First, though, she needed to make sure that Kaldar would survive and recover from his wounds. Walking into the healers' rooms, she looked around for a moment to find him. The room was crowded with new and makeshift beds lining every wall. A few healers, most that she recognized, frantically raced from one bed to the other offering their healing services.

Coming up to Kaldar's bed she recognized Shyla, one of the few visiting wizards from Elvyn. She breathed a sigh of relief knowing that Shyla, although younger than her, was a very competent healer. She had studied under Kharlia Attah, a famous healer from one of the southern kingdoms and frequent companion to the Dragon King.

"How is he?"

Shyla turned to her and her slanted green eyes, although they held traces of exhaustion, lit up upon seeing Joelle. Her long, silky blonde hair was pushed back behind her pointy ears and swirled around her as her smile faded and she shook her head.

"Not good," Shyla said. "Do you know him?"

Joelle knew she blushed but pretended to not notice, and Shyla had the good graces to not say anything about it. How could she explain her relationship to Kaldar? She didn't understand it herself. She felt they shared something, and she had been drawn to him when they were on the bow of the ship to a degree that she knew didn't make sense.

"A new friend. We met on the ship to White Island." Joelle glanced out a window and noticed that the smoke from the earlier fire had almost totally dissipated, leaving the sky a hazy blue. "I found him at the docks."

Joelle studied Kaldar. His burns already looked better; he still had some swelling, but not as black and scarred. The blood had been cleaned up and his face washed. His eyes were closed and his chest rose slowly but steadily.

"Mind if I help?" Joelle offered.

Shyla lifted up one eyebrow to question her. "You are tired, Joelle. Why don't you rest first?"

"You don't seem much better," Joelle said back.

Shyla only blinked her eyes. But Joelle was a bit older so protocol held, and with a small nod of her head she acquiesced to Joelle's request.

Working in tandem, they stimulated new growth of his skin. After doing as much as they could for his face they moved to the rest of his body. Somehow, he had managed to avoid severe wounds, and they did what they could, leaving some wounds to heal on their own.

Joelle put her hand on his forehead. There was no fever.

"Kaldar?" she said quietly, then repeated louder, "Kaldar!"

The man's eyes fluttered open for a moment.

"How are you feeling?" Joelle asked.

Kaldar appeared in thought for a moment. "All right, but I've been better."

"I was so worried about you. When the explosion happened at the docks I wondered where you were. Kyril and I were up here at the school when it happened. But then we rode the Cremelino down…have you ever seen a Cremelino? Well, when you get better I'll take you to see them like I promised. They're beautiful. She was so fast; we made it to the docks so quickly. After Kyril and the other wizards put out the fire, we found you. Well, first I heard you moaning and then had to dig you out. Do you remember that?"

Kaldar laughed a bit, then groaned at a pain before looking up at Shyla. "Is she always so talkative?"

Joelle put her hands on her hips. *How dare he? I saved him.*

Shyla nodded her head and without a smile, spoke. "Yes, she is. But she is a talented healer. You are lucky she found you."

Kaldar looked at Joelle again and smiled. "You have beautiful hair. I've never seen anything like it before."

Joelle smoothed down what she knew were unruly locks of her red hair. "That's all you have to say to me, Kal? After that…" She was going to say "kiss," but with one quick look at Shyla she changed her mind. "After…saving you?"

"I'm sorry, miss." Kaldar's face fell a bit. "I am grateful for whatever you did to help me, but I don't know who you are, or who you think I am."

CHAPTER TWENTY-ONE

The crowds of Hasari, the capital and largest city of the kingdom of Cyrene, jostled Sylvie and Bale as they walked from the city gates in the east toward the harbor.

Bale complained under his breath the entire time, and Sylvie knew it was all he could do to not jump out in front of her and blaze a way forward with the point of his sword.

"There's no discipline here," Bale said under his breath. "What kind of kingdom does King Shafer run?"

Beside the road two wizards dueled with each other in the street. A sizable crowd had gathered around, cheering. Sylvie moved around Bale and tried to push through the crowd to get by—then somehow became separated from him.

Sylvie, hooded cloak over her head, stood up on tiptoes to peer around. A heavy breeze from the western blue sea blew across her face and pushed her hood off.

"Look, Papa, she's from Arc," said a younger boy, pointing at her blonde hair. "Is she a wizard?"

Sylvie tried to ignore the man and his son and continued searching for Bale. But the man stepped in front of her. He was a larger fellow and his dusty brown forehead held drops of perspiration. He ran large meaty fingers through his black hair and peered down at Sylvie.

"Are you here for the contest?"

"What contest?" Sylvie asked.

The man's eyes popped open wider. "The wizard fights, of course."

"I thought those underground matches were outlawed," Sylvie said.

"Oh no," the man said with a booming laugh. "Our young king enjoys the sport. It's all official now."

Sylvie tried to push her way around the man. "I'm only looking for a ship to get home."

She left the man and his son behind and let out a deep breath. Things indeed had changed here recently. Young King Shafer had inherited the throne two years earlier, when his father had gone in league with a woman trying to take over many of the southern kingdoms. They had been defeated by the Dragon King and his friend Roland, and Shafer had taken over the throne while his father spent the rest of his life in prison.

Shafer was young—only twelve when he had been named king—and so a regency had been formed with authority to help him run the kingdom until he was sixteen. Sylvie guessed it was the regency behind the newest upsurge with these wizard contests. One more sign of chaos among wizards—a situation she was sure that Gamal was supporting, or was possibly even behind.

The sun lowered in the western sky as she continued to search for Bale. She had all but given up hope and was going to the docks to secure passage when she heard a ruckus off to her right. Curious, she followed a growing crowd that was heading to the center of the city. Over the heads of the crowd she saw the spire-topped golden dome of the palace glowing in the sunlight.

She let the crowd sweep her forward, until it stopped. Climbing up on a small wall she peered over the crowd and groaned.

"Oh no," she said out loud.

In the middle of six local teens stood Bale Nabhani, cloak hanging off his back and sword in his hand. They were definitely trying to attack him, or at least bully and jostle him up a bit. He turned around in a circle trying to find an opening but each time he did so one of the teens flicked their hand toward him and engaged with a bit of magic.

A young man sent a small bolt of fire toward Bale, but he deftly swerved out of the way and blocked it with his sword. A smattering of applause and a few cheers rippled through the crowd. Then a young woman stepped forward.

"Do it, Tabbi," yelled a second, taller woman.

Tabbi then put both hands in the air in front of her and began spinning them around. Suddenly a dust storm formed around Bale, forcing him to lower his gaze and cover his mouth. As he did so, another young man pushed his hand out in front of him and Bale stumbled on the ground from a considerable blast of wind.

"Way to go, Oban!" said another young man, and they all laughed.

"Go back to where you came from," sneered Tabbi. "You're no match for magic."

"Can't he stay?" said the taller woman again. "I need a new pet."

Sylvie gasped and put her hand over her mouth. She couldn't believe what she was seeing. This was barbaric.

"Enough!" she yelled, without actually thinking what she was going to do.

Those in the back of the crowd turned to her.

"A wizard from Arc," shouted a woman close by.

Well, enough for not being noticed, Sylvie grumbled to herself. But if they knew she was a wizard, then she would use that to her advantage. With a wave of her hand, the ground underneath the six young taunters began to shake. They stopped teasing Bale and turned to their newest foe.

"Oh," said Oban. "Now here's a true opponent: one with magic."

He thrust his hand toward Sylvie and a flash of light sped toward her. Instinctively, she jumped into the air and performed a somersault over the blast before landing on the ground. With a wave of her hand she pushed people back from both sides and walked carefully toward the group.

Bale had backed up to one side and glanced back and forth between Sylvie and the group of six, a look of worry on his face.

"What is the meaning of this?" Sylvie said. "It takes six of you to take on this honorable foreigner who is here on request of the emperor of Gildan?"

A few of the young people seemed to hesitate. Emperor Alrishitar was very mighty and well-known among all the kingdoms of the western continent.

One of the others stepped forward, the youngest of the six. His black hair was cut short and he wore loose-fitting silks over his brown skin. A golden wristband encircled his left hand. The ornament reminded Sylvie of Zaidan, prince of Gildan—though that's where the similarities ended. While Zaidan was good-natured and respectful, this man was uncouth and clearly arrogant.

The crowd quieted as he approached Sylvie, a smug smile growing on his youthful face.

"I don't believe you," said the young man. "The mighty wizard of Gildan would not employ someone as weak and non-magical as this man. You're lying."

Sylvie couldn't believe what she was hearing. She took a deep breath and thought about what to do. She glanced around at the ground, the nearby trees, and even the moisture in the warm and humid air. It all held power for her.

She brought her hands up in the air and power gathered around her. She looked at Bale and she could have sworn she saw him holding back a smile. Three of the other young people stepped forward to join the one that had spoken. The other two hung back next to Bale.

She did not want to hurt these people, but they needed to learn not to pick on those that didn't have magic either. Doing so just emphasized Bale's previous bias against wizards. She had done a lot to try and teach him otherwise.

Power crackled in the air around them and the crowd took a few steps back. She closed her eyes for a brief moment and felt the power of the Blue Sea only a short distance away, and a thought came to her. Without hesitation she opened her eyes, smiled at those standing in front of them, and began twirling her hands in the air. She gathered in the moisture around her and then fed it with extra water from the sea. Sylvie let herself feel a moment of gratitude for all she had learned from her headmaster Danijela Anwar—especially her control of the elements.

Up overhead, a turbulent dark black cloud formed. The crowd in front of her looked up with wide eyes. With a quick nod to Bale, Sylvie brought her hands together. Thunder and lightning echoed from her hands and the clouds above. Water gushed forth from the sky as if pouring from a giant bucket.

People screamed and backed away. Three of the aggressors in front of her grabbed the fourth and tried to run away, but they were not fast enough. Just before the water hit, Sylvie threw up a barrier over both herself and Bale.

The water slammed into all six of the attackers, forcing them down hard onto the cobblestone street. Loud screams ensued as elbows, knees, and heads cracked together. Many of the crowd ran off, covering their own heads, while the few that stayed watching had horrified expressions on their faces.

Down the road, from the direction of the palace, ran a dozen guards, led by a man with flowing blue robes. He leapt down the street moving ten feet at a time and arrived ahead of the others.

His graying hair blew in the rising wind, but his face was as chiseled stone. His dark brown eyes flashed in anger at Sylvie and then toward Bale. Before the rest of the guards arrived he ran over to the young man that had called Sylvie a liar and lifted him to his feet. Blood trickled down the side of his head and he limped with a swollen knee.

"Your Highness," he said softly to the young man. "Are you all right?"

Your Highness? Sylvie groaned and caught a mirrored expression of worry in Bale's own eyes.

The others stood back up as Sylvie allowed the clouds to dissipate. The newcomer, with the young man in tow, marched toward Sylvie, and Bale moved to her side. He gave her a nod of respect and thanks but appeared prepared to continue the fight if needed.

"What is the meaning of attacking King Shafer?" said the man.

Sylvie knew her face turned red, and not from the exertion of the storm. To his credit, Bale stepped forward to spare Sylvie the questioning.

"May I introduce Sylvonna Hickory. She is a renowned wizard of the earth from Arc. She learned her craft under the tutelage of Danijela Anwar, High Wizard of the Wizard Conclave. She is here on a grave mission from the emperor and highly regarded wizard of them mind, Mezar Alrishitar of Gildan."

Bale ended with a flourishing bow toward Sylvie. She kept the smile hidden but knew that Bale had done exactly what was needed. Those in Cyrene and Turg prized power more than anything, and the people around her all bowed their heads low. All except the king and the man with him.

"I am Merikh Shaamon, wizard Counselor to His Highness King Shafer Hadad," Merikh said with a small nod of his head toward Sylvie, something she could tell rankled him to have to do. But after her titles, tutelage, and power had been professed he had no choice.

"Lock these two up, Merikh," King Shafer said, his voice still high due to his age. "They attacked me."

Merikh watched his king for a moment as if questioning what had actually happened, but then turned to the soldiers with him and nodded his head toward Sylvie and Bale.

"Escort them to the castle," he said. "We will take care of this business here, out of the sight of the commoners."

Bale stood his ground, not moving.

Sylvie put her hand on his arm and shook her head. "No more fighting, Bale. We'll be fine."

His body relaxed and he nodded. However, when the guards came to grab them, Sylvie spoke to Merikh.

"We will go voluntarily," she said. "There is no need for restraints."

The king appeared ready to argue.

"I do have the power to get away, you know," Sylvie said with a sweet smile toward both the king and Merikh.

The guards stood awaiting direction. Merikh agreed and motioned for all to follow.

The king ran his hand over his wet hair and then tried to wring water from a sleeve of his silk shirt.

"Here, let me help with that," Sylvie said.

With a quick flourish of her hand she gathered in the heat of the day and wrapped it around the young king. Within moments he was dry.

Shafer's eyes grew wide and his companions looked at Sylvie longingly. They also were drenched to the bone. But

Sylvie only smiled and continued walking with the group toward the palace. The others would get no special treatment from her.

CHAPTER TWENTY-TWO

After Joelle left Kyril and ran off into the school to find Kaldar, he continued toward the stables. Jakob was leading Solace back toward a small pasture behind the stable. He grabbed a brush on his way, and the stable master began to groom the Cremelino horse as Kyril joined them.

"They are quite amazing," Kyril said.

Jakob's eyes lit up. "Yes they are."

"How long have you cared for them?"

"My entire life," Jakob said. "My father was the caretaker before me. I've grown up around them."

"So, you've lived here on White Island your entire life?" Kyril asked, curious how a non-wizard could communicate with the Cremelino horses, but not wanting to ask outright. He wanted to know the extent of the Cremelinos' powers.

Jakob nodded his head, then hesitated. "Well, for a short time when I was a bit younger than you, I was with the king taking care of his Cremelinos. It was a grand adventure. We traveled across the desert and to Sur." He paused for a bit, lost in the memory. "It was all grand until the queen was kidnapped and the king had to find the path of peace to save her and our kingdom."

Kyril knew there must be a good story there, but there was no time to hear it. He needed to get back inside with Joelle. He still didn't trust Kaldar. And that's why he was here.

"Tell me about the Cremelinos' power," Kyril said. "What can they do?"

"It's more about what they know than what they do—though they can do plenty." Jakob finished brushing Solace.

The horse whinnied and went over to where water and hay was left out for her.

"The Cremelinos are ancient magical creatures," Jakob said.

"Like dragons?"

"Yes, like dragons, and the phoenix, and I'm sure some we don't know about yet. Have you seen a dragon?"

Kyril nodded his head. "Once from a distance—the Dragon King came to Gildan on his mighty blue one," Kyril said with a smile. "And I've seen the emperor's Cremelino."

"Ah, Star," Jakob said. "I haven't seen him since I was young."

Kyril watched as Solace ran out in the pasture and joined other Cremelinos.

"You asked about what they can do," Jakob continued. "I'm sure you were taught in school that all magical creatures have the power of spirit—the power to bind. This wasn't always known. My family has cared for them for hundreds of years and we carry a special bond as their caretakers—maybe something left over from their original wizards who took care of them. When I was a boy we knew they bonded with others, but didn't know about their powers or connection to wizards."

"Do they understand what goes on around them?" Kyril asked.

"What do you think?" Jakob said. He leaned over the fence and watched as three of them ran past. "Solace chose you for a reason."

"So they do know what's going on?"

"I'm afraid they probably know more than they tell us," Jakob said with a laugh. "They are quite secretive."

"Will they tell me something?"

Jakob glanced up in surprise and then with concern. "They are not to be used for trivial matters. They do not answer to your whims."

"Oh, no," Kyril said, putting his hands up in the air. "I would never do that. But I am on an important quest from Emperor Alrishitar and would appreciate any help I can get."

Jakob appeared in thought for a moment. Kyril wondered if the Cremelinos would help him or not. Solace had spoken to him and helped him to stop the fire. They had already intervened once. Would they do it again?

With a brief whistle, Jakob called Solace back over to them. He reached out and touched the horse and then nodded his head once and released her. He motioned for Kyril to do the same.

"She will speak to you," Jakob said. "But beware of the riddles."

Yes, Medallion Holder?

"What can you tell me about Gamal's plans and what happened here today?" asked Kyril, both out loud for Jakob's sake and in his mind.

The future is not ours to tell or know, but beware of the duplicity of a man who is not who he seems, she began. *The ruse is not what you think it may be. Trust the one you know, but beware of knowing the right one to trust.*

"What?" Kyril shook his head, repeating the words to Jakob. "That doesn't make any sense."

Jakob chuckled and shook his head. "It rarely does. Like I told you, they speak in riddles."

"But why can't they just tell us what they know?"

Because you do not know as much as we do.

"Kyril," Jakob said seriously, placing his hand on Kyril's shoulder. "I've worked with Cremelinos my entire life. Besides my own human family, they are my closest friends. And there are two things I can tell you. The first is that they are always cryptic in their answers; I think it's just the way they communicate to us lowly humans."

Kyril felt the mirth bubbling up from Solace through his hand still on the horse.

"The second thing," Jakob continued, "is that they are pure and untainted by man's lies and deceptions. They will never steer you wrong. You can trust what they say."

Kyril nodded. "I just wish I could understand what they said."

Open your mind, came the Cremelino's sudden command.

Kyril jerked a bit at the force of the words, but tried to clear his mind as he had been taught many times in class. As a wizard of the mind, he had been schooled on discipline. He pushed out all thoughts of the physical world around him and opened his mind to the Cremelino.

He found himself in an empty room. The walls were made out of gray blocks, the floor was worn wood, and the lone window was dirty.

Where am I?

Be still and watch, came the reply.

The door opened and two men came in wearing hoods that partially fell down over their faces. One turned toward the window. It's dull light caught the man's face and Kyril sucked in a breath of air.

Gamal!

Kyril looked around for a place to hide, but realized he was seeing a vision or there in spirit. The evil wizard didn't seem to see him so he stayed still and watched.

"We have received word that the girl is in the kingdom of Cyrene, in Hasari," said the other man. He stood taller and thinner than Gamal and was quite a bit older. His light brown hair with edges of gray and light skin marked him as being from the Realm or possibly the eastern side of Arc.

"Now what would she be doing there, Fenton?" Gamal asked, his fingers twitching around the black medallion that he wore around his neck.

"Our sources say she is traveling to Arc to find the third medallion, shadow master," said Fenton.

Shadow master? The words made Kyril shiver. What powers had Gamal accumulated?

Gamal's eyes glazed over in anger. "The third medallion? And what about the first two? Have your people found those yet? That boy should not have gotten away!"

The man shook his head. "They followed the two wizards to White Island, but I have not heard back yet."

Gamal held his medallion tightly and with a wave of his hand opened up a small portal in the air. It hovered in front of the two men like a hole in the room. Through it Kyril could see what appeared to be a small boat floating on water. He was trying to figure out if it was real or an illusion when suddenly a woman's face came into view. It was the woman that Kyril had fought in the wizard school, one of the three attackers. Though now she did not wear a school uniform, but instead wore a dark cloak over gray clothes.

"My Lord," the woman said, bowing low.

Gamal waved his hand at Fenton to do the talking.

"Myna, did you get the medallion?"

Myna shook her head, her eyes darting around the boat. It rocked for a moment and then settled down. "We questioned the headmaster but he told us nothing and so we poisoned him. The school is in chaos. We followed the two wizards and tried to get the medallion from the young boy, but we failed and he got away from us." Her face fell in shame. "I fear he may be more powerful than we thought."

A man that Kyril recognized came into view. He had been the one that attacked him and tried to take the medallion. "Only two of us made it back out to the ship, Fenton."

Fenton nodded but didn't appear pleased. "And where is your companion? Did you run when he stayed to finish the job?"

The man and Myna appeared nervous. And suddenly Kyril remembered seeing these two before on the ship. They had been in the dining room together.

"Are you sure the headmaster didn't know where the second medallion was?" blurted out Gamal.

The two on the boat in the portal turned their attention to Gamal. The edges faded in and out a bit making Kyril a bit dizzy as he watched.

"The headmaster mumbled something about Belor when we questioned him," said Myna, obviously trying to get back in Gamal's good graces, "but nothing concrete or coherent."

"And you just killed him before he gave you more information? You have failed to get the medallion from the boy and to find any concrete information," said Gamal. "You are useless to me. Useless!"

"Where are you now?" asked Fenton, trying to salvage a bad situation.

"On our way to Mar on a small boat and then south to Belor," said the man. "It's the only clue we have."

With no other words, Gamal waved his hand in the air, and the two disappeared.

"Utter fools you have sided with me, Fenton. I hope for your sake your last man can get the medallion from the boy."

"He does have special abilities, sire," said Fenton. "They will not discover him until it is too late. We will get the medallion, I assure you."

Gamal sighed with exasperation. "I cannot be everywhere at once. But I will have to try and do more myself it seems." A shimmering black light appeared around him as he began to transport away.

"Where are you going, sire?" asked Fenton with wide eyes.

"To Cyrene to check on the girl and then to the Kingdom of Arc," Gamal said. "I must ensure she does not succeed. Now get me the other medallions!"

Fenton bowed and mumbled his assurances before Gamal faded away from the room.

Kyril realized he had been holding his breath, and let out a long sigh.

We need to find that medallion before Gamal does, Kyril said to Solace in his mind. *Can you tell us where it is?*

The library holds the key.

Kyril sighed at another cryptic answer.

The room around him swirled and he was once again standing at the fence of the stable.

"Was I here the entire time?" he asked Jakob, who was leaning against the fence next to him.

"Yes," sighed Jakob. "I could tell the Cremelino had taken you somewhere. You've been standing there with your eyes closed for ten minutes or so."

"So I wasn't really there?" Kyril wondered aloud.

"I've been around wizards a lot here at the school, Kyril," Jakob said. "Nothing much surprises me anymore.

"Hmmm," Kyril mumbled.

The magic stream. Solace once again spouted out a cryptic sentence that Kyril could not understand.

"What?"

Jakob looked at him with questioning eyes.

"Solace," he tried to explain. "She said 'the magic stream.' But I've never heard of that."

"Me neither," Jakob said, "but there's a lot of things I don't know about magic."

Kyril tried to reason out what had actually happened. It had *felt* real. He knew that he had seen something that was actually taking place. And he recognized Gamal and the other two. What was it that the man had said? That the third attacker…was still here. His mind worked quickly and suddenly a thought came to him.

"Kaldar!" Kyril said out loud and turned toward the school. When they found him by the docks he may have been trying to escape with the others. And he had been in the dining room with them on the boat. He never had trusted the man.

"I need to find Joelle," Kyril said to Jakob as he began his way back to the school.

"And I need to get back to work," Jakob said. "Nice talking to you. Good luck in your quest."

Kyril began walking faster, then it turned into a trot, and finally into a full run. He had to get to Joelle before she spoke to Kaldar.

CHAPTER TWENTY-THREE

Shyla had cut Joelle's conversation with Kaldar short, insisting that he get some rest. Now Joelle found herself pacing the hallway of the wizard school. Her emotions jumped between worry and anger. How dare he pretend not to know her? Shyla had said it was common sometimes with extreme head injuries and concussions, but Joelle didn't buy it. The man was insufferable. He was playing a trick on her and she didn't like it one bit.

Twice she headed back toward the door to the healers' rooms to give him a piece of her mind, and twice she had walked back away. Now for the third time she had her hand on the handle…but this time she began turning it.

"Joelle!" called Kyril from down the hallway toward the entrance of the school. A few other wizards nearby turned and stared at the young man running—none of them knew who he was.

Joelle watched as Professor Halsey jumped into the middle of the hall and intercepted Kyril. He skidded to a stop, almost knocking the woman over. Two other students about Joelle's age were following Professor Halsey in the hallway. Power already sizzled around one of them.

"Who are you and where are you going?" asked the professor.

Kyril took a moment to catch his breath, looking at Joelle for help.

"He's with me," Joelle said, walking up to the three blocking Kyril's way.

Professor Halsey peered over her glasses at Joelle with pursed lips. Then she nodded her head. "I remember you from your second year. You are a wizard of the heart, if I remember.

Joelle smiled, hoping that the situation was being diffused. "Yes, I am Joelle El'San. This is Kyril Siravan from Gildan."

The professor appeared deep in thought, and then with a snap at her fingers at Kyril and Joelle, she spoke matter-of-factly. "You'll come with me. We can't have young wizards running around the school, especially in times like this. There must be order."

"But…" Joelle stuttered for something to say.

"At a loss for words?" said one of the other young wizards next to Professor Halsey.

Ruthorford was from the Realm and Joelle knew him for being quite a condescending wizard. He wore his light brown hair back in a ponytail and his robes marked him as being from nobility. His family owned hundreds of acres of cattle fields around Sur. Even though everyone was supposed to be treated equally at the school, the fact was, they weren't always. Joelle's father worked at the governor's offices in Belor, but they were not nobility. She'd never been treated horribly, but certainly not as well as the nobility.

"That's a first," laughed the second young wizard, Thane. He was of lesser nobility, but his bulky stature and proficiency with weapons as a wizard of the earth marked him as being one that would be an officer in King Darius's army someday. "Joelle, I was expecting more from you. More words, that is."

Ruthorford laughed.

"You two!" yelled the professor to the wizards on either side of her. "That's quite enough. Off you go now to your studies."

"Classes have been cancelled today," said Ruthorford with a smirk and a wink at his friend.

"Then off to the kitchens," said the professor. "Tell the cook that you have an hour of kitchen duty tonight."

"What about them?" asked Thane, pointing at Kyril and Joelle, his face red and angry.

"They are not your concern."

Joelle smiled at the treatment of the young apprentice wizards. After dealing with Kaldar she wasn't in the mood for more games. "Yes, off, you two apprentices. We wizards have more important work to do."

Before she knew it, Professor Halsey grabbed Joelle's arm, her fingernails almost breaking the skin. She reached out to grab Kyril's arm also, but he quickly turned and she missed. Together, they all began walking down the hallway.

"Everyone's tempers are riding high today," the professor said to Joelle. "You should not goad them such. You *are* a full wizard. Act like one."

Kyril's eyes went wide. Joelle lowered her eyes and gulped hard. The woman was right; she should have acted better.

"I'm sorry," she whispered.

Professor Halsey weakened her grip on Joelle, but didn't let go. She strode down the middle of the hallway, making others scatter to the side. The professor was known as a strict teacher and expected her students to be serious about their studies. She was a wizard of the earth and taught about weapons and defending the Realm.

At a stairwell, she led them down. The stairs were not big enough for her to keep a hold of Joelle, and so she and Kyril followed closely behind.

"Where are we going?" Kyril said softly.

Joelle glanced over her shoulder. "Both the library and the dungeons are in this direction."

The professor snorted in front of them. "Have you done something worthy of the dungeon, young wizards?"

"Of course not, ma'am," Joelle said. "We just got here this morning." *Have we not even been here for a whole day?* "We came in on a ship with a message for the headmaster, but then the attack happened and he died. But we saw the fire down by the docks and so then took a Cremelino down there…"

"You took one of the Cremelinos?" Professor Halsey asked.

"Jakob gave us one," Kyril said defensively.

Coming to the bottom of the first flight of stairs, the professor turned right and headed toward a set of double doors.

"Solace said it was all right," said Kyril.

The Professor stopped and twisted around, glaring at Kyril. "And who is this Solace to give you such permission?"

Kyril gulped hard and glanced at Joelle. She smiled at him, encouraging him to continue. She couldn't wait to see the professor's face at his answer.

"She's, well…" Kyril began. "She's one of the Cremelinos, ma'am."

Joelle was not disappointed. Professor Halsey put a hand on the doorframe and took a deep breath, her eyes bugging out of their sockets. Joelle knew she shouldn't be so vindictive, it was not her nature. Kaldar had gotten to her and she didn't like that.

The door swung open and another adult stopped upon seeing the three of them.

"Professor Halsey," he said, noticing her pale face. "Are you all right?"

"Yes. Yes," she said to assure all of them, as well as, most likely, herself. "These two have been stirring up trouble."

"I've heard," the man said darkly. "Come in."

Joelle and Kyril followed Professor Halsey into a library. At a table sat Professor Warren, Marcus, and Amanda. They were directed to empty chairs around the rectangular table.

"Why are they here?" Marcus asked.

"Because I think they know more about what is happening than they have said," said Warren with a small smile toward Joelle.

Joelle nodded her head back to them.

"What could they know?" said the man that had met them at the doorway. "From what I've heard from you, they only arrived today. In fact, they arrived just when the trouble started. Maybe they are part of the problem."

"Fielding," said Warren. "Let's reserve judgment. We've all been through a lot today. Hear them out."

Fielding grumbled but waved his hand at the two for them to speak. They all looked at Joelle, who was from the Realm, but it was Kyril who spoke first.

"In Gildan, there is a man named Gamal Turomi, a powerful wizard who pretended to be a scribe while stirring up trouble there. He kidnapped the headmaster of the Gildan Wizard Academy earlier this week. His goal is for wizards of the mind to be running everything—with him at the head."

Amanda frowned, but Fielding smirked a bit. Joelle knew Amanda was a wizard of the earth, but Fielding was a wizard of the mind, just like Gamal.

Joelle grew suspicious of Fielding. She didn't trust or like the man.

"And what does that have to do with you or what happened here today?" asked Warren.

"The Emperor of Gildan has sent us here to find information," Kyril said.

At mention of the powerful and well-known Emperor Wizard Alrishitar, everyone at the table sat up straighter and leaned toward Kyril.

"What kind of information?" asked Marcus with some suspicion. "The libraries in Gildan are extensive, you can probably find your information there."

"They are," Kyril said, "and we've combed through them for as long as we dared. But we don't have much time. As you can see, Gamal's followers were already here today. He has been planning this for quite some time."

"And he was looking for a medallion, from what we learned from the headmaster," said Amanda, concentrating deeply on what Kyril was saying. "But what does that have to do with you two?"

Kyril turned his head to the side and caught Joelle's eye. She nodded, and he reached inside his cloak pocket, brought out the medallion, and laid it on the table in front of him.

"This does," Kyril said. "He knows I have this one, and besides trying to get it, he has set his eyes on the other two. He thought that one may exist in the Realm. That's the information he was after."

"What is this medallion?" Professor Halsey asked.

"A medallion of immense power," Joelle said. "Years ago, three medallions were given by King Anikari to three wizards of Gildan, Arc, and the Realm. Their purpose, among many other things, is to restore balance to magic. They are the way to defeat Gamal. But if he gets his hands on them, he will turn them to dark and evil means. He has a black medallion that he uses to further his purposes."

The room was silent for a moment as everyone soaked in the information. A few whispered side conversations ensued, as if they had forgotten about Joelle and Kyril.

"Have you seen Kaldar?" asked Kyril, leaning in close to Joelle.

"Yes, I have," Joelle said, her anger rising again. "He says he doesn't know who I am."

"Really?" Kyril asked, looking both surprised and like he was trying to hold a laugh in.

"What?" Joelle asked. "You think this is funny?"

"No," Kyril said. "Quite the opposite. I think Kaldar was one of the three that attacked your headmaster. He must have been in disguise."

Suddenly the room went quiet, and Joelle realized they had all heard what Kyril said.

"That's not true," Joelle said, her face heating up. She was angry at the man, but didn't believe he should be condemned so easily. "That's impossible. We saw the attackers."

Kyril just shrugged. "Anything's possible with magic."

"Who is this Kaldar?" asked Warren, interrupting Joelle and Kyril's side conversation. "Is he the young man with the burns that you brought into the healers' rooms?"

"Yes," Joelle said.

"He travelled with us from Belor," Kyril said. "His two companions got away, but they said the third one in their party didn't make it to the ship in time."

"How do you know what they said?" Joelle rounded on Kyril. This wasn't fair for him to bring up here without telling her first.

Everyone's gaze was on Kyril. Sweat beaded up on his forehead and he fingered the medallion in his hand.

"Well?" Joelle asked. "This is news to me. Who told you?"

After another slight pause, he said softly, "The Cremelino."

Both Marcus and Fielding jumped from their seats and rushed toward Kyril.

"How dare you insult us with your lies!" Marcus said. "Cremelinos don't just share information with strangers from other lands."

"Give us that medallion," Fielding said, reaching his hand forward. "Leave it to the adults to figure out."

The others stood up also, and everyone started shouting. Kyril grabbed the medallion, pushed his chair back and reached over and grabbed Joelle's hand. With only a moment's notice, a glow erupted around Kyril and they transported from the library.

CHAPTER TWENTY-FOUR

It was early the next morning when Joelle was awakened by a soft noise. She sat up in bed and took a moment to reorient herself to where she was and what had happened recently. After Kyril had transported them from the room full of wizards back outside, the two had argued for a while—mostly about Kaldar.

Taking a deep breath to keep from getting frustrated again, Joelle tried to clear her head. She stood up and then walked across the cold stone floor to a window and pushed it open. The early colors of pre-dawn were just beginning to show out to the east over the Blue Sea, while a few stars still twinkled off toward the west. It would be a clear day and most likely very warm—but bearable with the constant sea breeze that wrapped around the school.

The room she had been given was much more pleasant than those she had lived in while a student here at the wizard school. She had slept well despite her argument with Kyril, and now felt almost fully recovered from all the healing she had done the day before. Changing out of her nightclothes, she pulled on a new green dress that she had purchased in Belor while buying supplies. It fit a little snugly but would do for now. Lacing up her boots she thought about home in Belor. She had been hoping to visit her family when they had transported there. *Maybe on the way back.*

Grabbing her staff she exited her room, looking up and down the hallway as she did. No one else was up yet, it seemed. Turning left would take her down to the back steps and out of the school, while turning right would take her to the main stairs and down to the ground floor where the healers' rooms were. She chose the right.

Walking softly down the stately and curved stairs from the third floor to the ground level, Joelle saw a few early morning servants scurrying around the school. Yesterday had been chaotic, but she surmised that today things would begin to get back to normal—that was the way with wizards. The morning meal would be prepared as usual and Joelle wouldn't be surprised if at least some classes didn't resume. On the way to her destination a few servants bobbed their head at her and she returned the greeting with a smile but continued on without stopping. Coming to the door of the healers' rooms, she put her hand on the knob but then hesitated.

What if Kyril was right about Kaldar? Were her feelings for him clouding her judgement? The thought made her pause and rethink whether she should see him or not. Oh, she hated the indecision and ground her teeth in frustration. Finally she pushed the door open, harder than she had intended. An elderly man jumped up from his chair, his eyes going wild for a moment until settling on Joelle.

"What in the blazes are you doing?" he whispered loudly to Joelle, taking a few steps closer to her.

"I'm truly sorry, Grantham," Joelle said with a warm smile. "I just wanted to check on Kaldar, your patient there." She pointed to him. "How is he doing? Did he sleep well? He wasn't too cold in here was he? What about all the other patients?"

"Joelle," Grantham sighed with a small chuckle. His face was wrinkled and wispy gray hairs were scattered around the top of his head, but his blue eyes were bright. It was rumored the man was the oldest healer—and maybe even wizard—in the Realm. It was said he had lived and practiced his arts in secret in the city of Sur for years before wizardry was accepted again in the Realm. His ways were unconventional at times, as he'd had no school to teach him, but his methods were effective. "You always did move around faster than I can keep track of."

Joelle took a deep breath and tried to slow down. Grantham gave her a warm smile and put his fingers to his lips. Joelle took the hint and followed him over to Kaldar's bed. Peering down at his resting shape she resisted the urge to run her hands over his untidy hair.

"A friend of yours?" Grantham asked.

Joelle felt her cheeks begin to burn, but the old man didn't seem to notice—or was too polite to show he did. "We only met on the way here a few days ago."

Grantham nodded. "He woke last night mumbling incoherently and thrashing about in the bed. I had to give him a powerful sleeping draught to get him back to sleep. He'll be out most of the day, I suspect."

She let out a long sigh before realizing what she had done. Was she relieved to not have to talk to him? He had frustrated her the night before, pretending to not know who she was. Why would he do that?

Grantham motioned her away from Kaldar and the rest of the still-sleeping patients. Looking around the room, she was glad that more hadn't been more injured.

"His mind is not well," Grantham said.

"What do you mean? Why do you say that?"

"I'm not sure," Grantham said. "It just doesn't feel right to me. Something's wrong."

"He pretended not to know me last night," Joelle admitted.

"He may not be pretending, my dear."

Joelle stood quiet for a moment and thought. She glanced over at his sleeping form and thought of his lips on hers the other day. Not wanting to get caught up in that memory again, she whisked back around to the elderly healer.

"Maybe I can help him," Joelle said.

Grantham shook his head. "Not now. He needs to rest. As healers we can do a lot for people—and from what I've heard you've grown in your powers this past year—but we cannot do much for the mind yet. We need to study it more. We could hurt him more than help him if we don't know what we are doing."

Joelle knew that Grantham was right, but she didn't like knowing that there was something she couldn't heal. She glanced around at the other sleeping shapes and her lips parted into a small smile.

"But I will come back and help you with the others," she said.

"That would be wonderful," Grantham said. "I'm sure we can get them all back on their feet in no time. But let's let them sleep longer. It's still quite early." He lowered himself back into a worn but comfortable chair and laid his head back. "I could use a bit more rest myself if you don't mind."

Joelle chuckled softly. She had interrupted his sleep and he was an old man. She gave the elderly healer a short bow and then turned and headed out the door—this time opening and closing it much more quietly.

She headed toward the stairs that would take her back down to the library. One thing that Kyril had been right about the previous day: she *had* let Kaldar distract her from their mission. They were here to learn where the other medallions might be, and the library would be the best place for that. She would show Kyril she could get the job done!

From around a corner, she heard laughs before she could see who was there. Luckily she slowed down, because bursting around the corner came Ruthorford and Thane. Ruthorford was holding something tightly in his hand, and Thane was urging him forward.

Joelle pulled herself back against the wall, barely missing colliding with the two students.

"Watch where you're going!" shouted Thane, the larger of the two.

"What are you two doing down here at this time of morning?" Joelle shouted at the two as they sped past her.

Ruthorford came to a quick stop, turned around, and glared at her. "We don't answer to you." His eyes were harder and darker than she remembered…and for some reason it reminded her of Kaldar the other day.

"Actually," Joelle said, putting her hands on her hips, while pushing thoughts of Kaldar out of her head, "you do answer to me, because I'm a full wizard and you two are only apprentices. Now, what do you have there?"

Rutherford stuck his hands behind his back and Thane jumped out in front of him.

"What are you doing down here?" mocked Thane in a high-pitched voice. "It's a bit early, isn't it?"

Joelle rolled her eyes at the miscreants. She didn't have time for their antics.

"Be on your way." Joelle waved her hand at them dismissively.

"Like I said, we don't answer to you," said Thane.

Joelle smiled. He obviously wasn't that bright. "All right then, stay here."

Thane appeared confused, but Rutherford nudged him. "Come on, let's go. I got what I came for."

Joelle stepped forward. She was curious as to what they had been after so early in the morning. But before she could say anything, she heard a crash in the library, and turned back to her original destination. Pushing the door open she glanced back one more time down the hall in time to see Ruthorford and Thane turn a corner.

A sick feeling filled her gut as she rushed into the library. Lying on the floor next to a small broken shelf was Kyril; a jagged cut on his forehead oozed blood. Books were strewn around him on the floor.

Joelle rushed to his side, dropping her staff on the floor.

"Kyril!" she said with a soft touch to his forehead. "Kyril!"

A small groan escaped his lips and his eyes fluttered open for a moment before they closed again.

"Kyril, what happened?" Joelle asked.

"I'm not sure," Kyril whispered, eyes still closed. "I came down here to research the medallions. I was back a few shelves when I heard the door squeak open. I asked if someone was there, but there wasn't any answer. When I went to investigate, something hit me on the back of my head. I never saw who it was."

Joelle ran her hand softly over Kyril's forehead and with hardly any thought brought down the swelling and closed up the small gash.

"A few minutes ago I heard voices outside of the room and tried to stand up, but when I did I got all dizzy and fell back again." Kyril opened up his eyes. "Hence the mess," he said, smiling weakly. "I must have knocked over the bookshelf.

Joelle brought her hand carefully under Kyril's head and began to help him up, but he yelped at the pressure.

"Can you heal that bump too?" Kyril asked, pointing to the back of his head.

Kyril, still sitting on the ground, leaned over and Joelle placed a hand over the back of his head. She closed her eyes and delved inside his skull. She felt the swelling pushing against his skin. She carefully examined the blood flow and brain matter itself. She had to be careful around the brain.

Kyril let out a breath of air. "That feels better already."

"What's this?" Joelle said, opening back up her eyes and focusing on a strange abrasion across the back of his neck.

Kyril put his hand back and ran it over his neck. "I don't…"

He stopped and his back went rigid. He reached his other hand down beneath his blue cloak and came up empty.

"My medallion!" he moaned. "Someone took the medallion."

CHAPTER TWENTY-FIVE

Kyril still felt a bit groggy from falling over, but the reality of the medallion having been taken was bringing clarity to his mind. He couldn't believe he had been so careless.

"It was Ruthorford and Thane," Joelle said. "That's who I was arguing with outside in the hallway. They had something, but I couldn't tell what it was."

"They took the medallion?" Kyril cried out. "We have to get it back." He headed toward the door.

"We can talk to the head wizards," Joelle suggested. "They'll get it back for us. Those two are up to something."

Kyril shook his head. "We don't know who we can trust at this point. Someone else must have known what they were doing! They're only apprentices; they had to be working for or with someone else."

They arrived at the library door and went to push it open when the door swung in their direction instead. With a yelp, Joelle jumped back and they both barely moved out of the way before being trampled by Fielding, the wizard of the mind they had met the night before. Three guards followed behind him. He took a moment to gaze over the mess of books and shelves on the floor.

"Guards,"—he motioned with his head—"apprehend these two!"

"But..." Joelle blurted out. "We didn't do anything."

Kyril suddenly felt helpless without the medallion and he realized with sudden clarity how much he had learned to rely on its powers in the short time he had possessed it. He never had been a very great or strong wizard and knew that he was no match for Fielding and his guards. He glanced over at Joelle who was trying to wriggle out of the grasp of one of the guards.

To the guard's surprise, Joelle twisted her staff in her hands and whacked the guard in the shins. He yelped and loosened his grip. Joelle took the moment to swing the staff around in a wide arc around her. A bright light erupted and kept the guards at bay.

Fielding brought both hands up in the air and the sleeves of his loose blue robe fell down, exposing his thin pale arms. He took a deep breath and clapped them together. What resulted was a deafening explosion that rocked Kyril backwards. He and the guard still holding him tipped sideways. Kyril struggled to get away, but the man was much stronger than he was.

Joelle's staff left her hands and flew through the air, arriving in the now outstretched right hand of Fielding.

"How dare you!" Joelle yelled, her wild red hair whipping around her face in the residual breeze of the clash of magic. "You have no right to hold us."

Fielding flicked his hand toward her and the guards grabbed back onto her—one on each of her arms, and they held her firmly this time. Kyril tried to catch Joelle's eyes, but the guard stood in the way. He didn't know how things worked in the Realm, but he surmised that Fielding was overstepping his bounds.

"Actually..." Fielding flicked his tongue across his lips before continuing. "In light of yesterday's attack and the absence of a headmaster, I have been given the responsibility of securing the school. By order of Marcus, one of the senior councilors I have all the authority I need to apprehend you two."

"Isn't that usually the job of an earth wizard? What about Halsey or Amanda or one of the other earth wizards?" Joelle asked.

Annoyance flitted across Fielding's face. "Amanda is not feeling well, and I don't know where Halsey is. She seems to have gone into hiding."

"But we have done nothing," said Kyril softly. It seemed his confidence was also lacking since losing the medallion.

"Ahh, there you are incorrect, my young foreign wizard," Fielding said. "Now, Joelle may have some rights here and will be afforded that as her station as a wizard of the Realm, but you...no one knows who you are, and quite honestly there are many good students and wizards who worry that you might be behind this attack."

"What?" Joelle said. "Kyril wouldn't hurt anyone."

Fielding's eyebrows lifted up in a surprised look. "We shall see. There are some faithful students that say otherwise who saw him fighting two students yesterday during the attack."

Kyril shook his head. He must have been hit harder than he thought or Joelle hadn't healed him as well as she usually did, because he surely wasn't following Fielding's line of reasoning. "I never touched any students."

"Do you admit to fighting two people in the hallway yesterday during the attack on the school?"

"Well," Kyril said, "yes, but they…"

"Do you admit to using the medallion—a foreign object of power—in the halls of this school?"

"But I was…"

"Do you admit to riding a Cremelino that you were not authorized to ride?"

"Solace gave me permission," Kyril said in exasperation. Fielding wasn't allowing him to explain himself.

"The Cremelino herself gave you, a young untrained wizard from Gildan (if that's really where you are from) permission to carry you on her back?" Fielding said, almost spitting out the accusation. "You must see how this looks! You have no authority here, young wizard, and as such I am placing you under arrest."

"You can't do that!" Joelle said, trying once again to break free of the two guards. "The two he fought in the hallway had just *killed the headmaster!* We already told you they work for a man in Gildan who is trying to find the medallions and make himself leader. They were in league with him and I'm not even sure they were students. We are here to help you."

"Maybe," Fielding said, "maybe not. It will take some time to figure out."

"Talk to Kaldar," Kyril pleaded.

Joelle shook her head at him, but he continued anyway.

"He was part of it," Kyril continued. "Make him tell you what they were doing here."

"Kaldar?" Fielding furrowed his eyes. "Oh, yes, the man that *you* two brought to the healers' rooms. I'm afraid he doesn't seem to remember who he is."

Kyril watched as Joelle's face turned white and she slumped in the arms of the two guards. He was at a loss. He tried to think but couldn't see any way out of their current predicament. He felt his palm grow warm and a spark of hope blossomed in his heart.

"Take me then, but Joelle doesn't belong in prison. She is a wizard of the Realm and attended school here. That should count for something."

Fielding nodded his head. "I see at least you have some respect for your fellow wizards. She will be confined to her rooms for now while we work through this mess."

Joelle's face lifted and Kyril could see she was about to protest, but he gave a quick shake of his head toward her. She narrowed her eyes in confusion, but then a quick glance of her eyes toward his right hand showed her his intention. He had experienced the powers of the medallion even before he possessed it. He would once again have to rely on those as they searched for the medallion. He could transport out of the cell as soon as they left him.

With a jerk, the two guards dragged him out of the room and toward the dungeons. Out of the corner of his eye he watched the others take Joelle up the stairs and back toward the main part of the school. He wondered with no one else around that knew him how he was going to get out of this mess.

CHAPTER TWENTY-SIX

After alternating between sitting and pacing in her room for the past three hours, Joelle hadn't come up with any way to help the situation. There were others at the school that she was sure would help her, but Kyril's mention of not knowing who to trust made her second guess everyone she knew. She hated it.

If the wizard school here on White Island had been infiltrated like the wizard academy in Gildan, and if Gamal was behind both of them, she surmised that he would have targeted wizards of the mind to help him. Fielding and Marcus were both wizards of the mind and so that immediately cast suspicion on them. That left Warren, Amanda, or Halsey on the wizard council that she might be able to trust.

Halsey was the most strict wizard on the council, but Joelle knew she would be fair. First, however, she had to get out of her room.

Almost as if her wishes had been magically granted, there was a knock on the door and then it opened. One of the guards peered inside, then stepped back and allowed someone else to enter.

"My dear," said Grantham, the elderly healer, "you had promised to come and help me heal the others today. What are you still doing in your room?"

He said the last as if he hadn't noticed the two guards stationed outside.

"I…" Joelle glanced at the guard at the door who seemed bored by his current duties. "I would love to come and help you, Master Healer, but I am not allowed to leave my room."

"Not allowed to leave your room?" he said with a glance back toward the guard. "That's preposterous. After yesterday's attack we need your healing expertise."

"There seems to have been a misunderstanding," Joelle said, "and Wizard Fielding under orders from Marcus has sequestered me in my room."

There was a brief flash of annoyance across Grantham's face, but he quickly put his dull smile back on his face and walked back toward the guards.

"We need the young woman in the healers' rooms," he said to them.

"Wizard Marcus has ordered her to stay here," said one of the guards. "He has assumed temporary command after the headmaster's death."

"Oh, he has, has he?" Joelle said. *Maybe he and Fielding were behind the attacks in the first place.*

"Surely they would understand," pushed Grantham. "Her skills are desperately needed."

One guard seemed to hesitate, while the other stood his ground. "His orders are that she remains in this room." One hand sat on the pommel of his sword as if expecting trouble.

"Oh dear," Grantham said, shaking his head. "This will not do at all. There are people that need healing." He tottered over to a wall and put his hand to it as if to steady himself.

The hesitant guard came to his aid and kept him standing. As he did so, Grantham touched his hand to his shoulder and whispered a few words that Joelle couldn't decipher. The man instantly slumped to the floor.

The other guard went to draw his sword but Grantham's hand snaked out quicker than Joelle would have thought possible, and did the same thing to his shoulder. It only took a moment for the second guard to join the first on the stone floor.

Glancing up and down the hallway he motioned to Joelle. "Hurry, get them inside your room before anyone notices."

Joelle stood in shock at what she had just seen, speechless for once.

"Come on, girl," Grantham said. "Jump to it."

The words drew Joelle out of her stupor and they dragged both guards into her room. Shutting the door, Grantham put a hand on the handle and after it glowed for a moment, he stepped back with a mischievous grin.

"They won't be leaving for a while."

Joelle snorted a laugh, then covered her mouth and glanced around. A few servants were walking farther down the long hallway but no one appeared to have noticed the scene at her room.

Grantham took hold of her arm and instead of heading toward the main stairs that lead down to the healers' quarters, turned and headed in the opposite direction.

"Where are we going?" Joelle asked.

"Hush," said the healer. "Not now."

Joelle opened her mouth to protest, but with a quick glance at Grantham thought better of it, and despite a slew of questions, kept her mouth closed for now. They came to the end of the hallway and pushed open a door that led down the back stairs, normally used by servants. Stopping at a landing halfway down to the next floor, Grantham put his hand to the wall and suddenly the outline of a doorway appeared.

Joelle gasped, but once again was shut down by a stern look. So with only a huff she followed him through a new opening. Once on the other side, the door slid shut with a soft click and she found herself standing in darkness.

Soon a glow filled the small area about ten feet in front of them and Grantham stepped forward, beckoning Joelle to follow. She had always suspected these types of passageways existed, and had read about them in books about ancient castles, but as she was generally not one for much adventure, she had never found one herself.

A dozen steps later Grantham put a hand up and rapped softly on what appeared to be a wooden door. He knocked in a strange pattern and stood as if awaiting an answer. After only a few short moments, the wooden door opened slowly. Grantham pushed her forward in front of him with urgency.

The person that greeted them on the other side startled Joelle. She had medium length blond hair, wide green eyes, was about four inches taller than Joelle and at least ten years her senior. Her leather clothes appeared more akin to battle garments than appropriate for the atmosphere of the school. At least three weapons hung from a brown belt. Joelle realized now she was the Realm's battlemaster--a wizard of the earth. Her name was Kittoran.

A moment later she noticed a man behind the woman. He stood hunched over a bit with a dark cloak wrapped around him and a cowl covering up most of his face. All she could see were a few strands of brown hair and grim mouth void of emotion

The newcomer walked up next to Kittoran, but before she said anything she put a finger to her mouth. His eyes grew wide but he stayed quiet. After a moment of listening at another door in the room, Kittoran opened it and motioned them to follow.

The air grew stale and the walls damper as they descended steep stone steps. Joelle used her staff to help steady her way, and she wondered where they were going. Grantham seemed surprisingly spry for his age as he preceded her down the stairs.

Soon they came to a landing and a sturdy iron door stood in front of them. With a touch to a lock by Kittoran, a soft glow emanated around the door and it swung open without a sound. The four of them stepped through and into muted daylight. Joelle glanced around, and the strong scent of horses filled her nostrils. They were in what appeared to be in a small storage room in the back of the stables.

Three others stood in front of them—two young wizards of the heart apprentices that she recognized, and Halsey. Her mouth was held firm and accusations filled her eyes when she looked at Joelle.

All three bowed their heads low toward the mysterious man that had come with them. She looked back and forth not knowing what to expect.

Grantham looked confused. "Kit, who is this man you have brought to us? Can he be trusted? I sense he is a wizard of the mind and may be in league with the others. What have you done?"

Kit? How does Grantham call the Realm's battlemaster by a nickname?

"Grandfather," said Kit, "you have no need to worry." She pointed toward the man and he pushed the cowl from his face.

Joelle instantly knew who he was.

"The prince!" Joelle couldn't help the gasp leaving her mouth. It was Liam Dar San Williams, prince of the Realm and son of the king. He was a year her senior and she had seen him quite often at the wizard school until he had become one of the famed Dragon Riders a few years before.

A tug of a smile barely reached the corners of Liam's mouth. He stood a few inches taller than Joelle. He had brown hair down to his shoulders, had broadened out since she'd seen him last, and was looking much like his father, the king.

"Joelle El'San, I presume," Liam said. "My father has sent me to help you."

CHAPTER TWENTY-SEVEN

Joelle couldn't believe that Prince Liam was speaking to her. She glanced around for a moment to regain her composure.

"My dragon is out back," Liam said with raised eyebrows as if mocking her. "If that's what you're searching for."

"My Prince, be nice," said Kit.

"Yes, Battlemaster," he said again with a mocking voice.

"Please ignore the prince," said Kit with a sigh and a wave of her hand. "He forgets himself sometimes."

"It is my father's battlemaster who forgets herself sometimes," Liam said, his eyes flashing darker once again. "I am not beholden to your commands."

"My apologies," said Kit with a low bow. "What is the Dragon Rider's wish in this regard? Do you have a plan to find who is behind this attack and to establish stability once again at the school?"

Liam glared at the woman for a brief moment and then leaned back against a wall, favoring his right foot a bit. Everyone in the kingdom knew the prince had been born with a club foot, and the birth defect had marred both his fighting abilities and his personality until he had been selected as one of the few dragon riders in the western continent. The time with his dragon had both healed his limp considerably and had loosened his tongue.

The others in the room glanced back and forth between the two of them, obviously uncomfortable with the casualness with which the prince was being treated.

"You have my permission to continue, Battle Master," said Liam with raised eyebrows and a grin toward Joelle. "I surmise our famous healer has a few questions of her own."

Joelle smoothed down her hair a bit, an action to hide her presumably blushing face. But she did indeed have a few questions and after a brief breath, began asking them.

"Where is Kyril? Is he all right? Why are we meeting out here?" The floodgates opened and she couldn't stop. "Do you know who is behind the attack? It's Gamal, a wizard from Gildan. He's using wizards of the mind to take control…"

The Prince coughed and Joelle remembered that he himself was a wizard of the mind.

"Well, I meant no offense to you, Prince Liam," Joelle stuttered. "I'm sure we can trust you." She looked around the group for confirmation. Kyril had told her to trust no one, but surely he didn't mean the prince of the Realm and the battlemaster, Kittoran.

Grantham put a hand on Joelle's arm and she flinched a bit. He was trying to hide a small smile, but wasn't doing very well.

"Of course we can trust him," Grantham said.

"But can we trust her?" The prince posed his own question with a shake of his head toward Joelle. "Seems to me she was the one that brought the stranger here."

"The stranger? You mean Kyril?" Joelle grew angry and she let it show. "He is here on an errand from Emperor

Alrishitar of Gildan who trusts Kyril explicably. Kyril saved his life and the life of his son. The power that he holds in that medallion—well, the medallion that was stolen from him—is a third of the power that is needed to defeat Gamal and his followers and restore the balance of magic to our kingdoms!"

The two younger wizard's mouths flew open in surprise at Joelle's ramblings. They obviously hadn't heard all that was going on and perhaps she had said too much. But Liam threw back his head and laughed loudly. When he finally got control again he turned to Joelle.

"Oh my, you are a feisty one from Belor, aren't you?"

"The stranger the prince was referring to was the man in the healers' rooms with no recollection of who he is," said Kit with a small grin of her own.

"Oh," Joelle moaned. She berated herself for flying off the handle. How was she supposed to know what they meant? She had been escorted from her room, down stairs, through hidden passageways, and now stood in the Cremelino stables with, among others, the prince of the Realm. She still wasn't used to all this adventure.

"Why didn't you say so?" Joelle said in response to Kittoran's comment.

Halsey now took a step forward. "This is getting us nowhere, Your Highness," she said to Liam, but then addressed the rest of the group. "We've heard this story about Gamal before…"

"It is not a story," Joelle said.

Halsey held her hand up in the air. "All right, we have heard what you and Kyril have said. And yes, you may need to find Gamal and the other medallions, but first we need to reestablish control of the school. Marcus has gone too far in presuming leadership of the council and in imprisoning your friend. This is not the way things should be handled."

"I am here at the king's request to ensure the council's smooth transition," said Kit.

Joelle wondered how the king had heard of everything so quickly. But she didn't need to wait long for an answer.

"The Cremelinos told the king the seriousness of the situation. That is why we summoned one of the dragon riders to assist us," Kit explained. "Liam happened to be close by."

"I'm sure we could have handled things ourselves, Your Highness," said Halsey, trying to save a bit of face in the current chaos of the school.

"Wizard Halsey," said the Prince, "while we appreciate your support here, the headmaster of the school is appointed by the king and he has taken a personal interest in this situation."

"But in the interim?" Halsey asked, eyes growing a bit hard. "We do have a school to run."

"How bad is it?" Grantham asked.

"It's hard to know," Halsey said, and let out a sigh. "It does seem like many are in support of Marcus, but it's hard to be sure where his loyalties lie. That is why we have gathered each of you here. We will need to quietly determine the extent of this growing insurrection. Emory and Lisbeth here have agreed to help. They are both on the student leadership council and can find out about the other students. Warren can stay in the school and I on the council, so we can ascertain loyalties there. It appears that Amanda has gotten sick and has shut herself in her rooms."

"What about me?" asked Joelle. "And what are we going to do to get Kyril out of the dungeon and get the medallion back?"

"You will work with Healer Grantham here to bring the memories of this Kaldar back," Halsey said. "I'm afraid he might be the key to understanding the attack. We need to know what he remembers and if he is in league with anyone that he can name."

"He was not involved," Joelle said in a firm tone. "He couldn't be."

"Then why was he here at the same time as the attack?" the prince asked. "Everyone is a suspect."

Joelle opened her mouth but then thought better and closed it again. Liam gave her a small grin as if mocking her control over her tongue.

"Bring me word of Kaldar's progress if there is any," Halsey said. "Only directly to me and I will only share it with the council if I feel it is safe. It's indeed hard to know who to trust at this moment."

"The council meets tomorrow to try and determine who will lead the school until a new headmaster is named," Kit said. "The prince and I will leave now and return publicly tomorrow morning to oversee the council's actions. That gives us only 24 hours to figure out who is behind the plot and who we can trust on the council."

"And to get back the medallion," Joelle said. "Someone had Ruthorford and Thane steal the medallion."

Kit raised her eyebrows at her. "That will have to wait."

Joelle fumed inside. She wasn't going to let Kyril stay in the dungeon and surely wasn't going to wait to find the medallion until the school had settled down. By then, the medallion may have made its way toward Gamal. And that was not something she could allow.

"Joelle El'San," Halsey said directly to her. "You must not trifle in matters of the council. You do understand the seriousness of this."

Joelle let out a stifled laugh and with a shake of her head she eyed each one in turn: Grantham, the prince, the battlemaster, the two other young wizards, and then Halsey. "I understand far more than you might know, Wizard Halsey."

The battlemaster assumed a fighting stance. Halsey shook her head at Kittoran before turning back to Joelle. "That sounds like an underlying threat, my young wizard. I hope for your sake you stick with our plan."

"I will do what you ask in trying to regain Kal's memories," she said out loud, truly meaning what she said. But what she didn't promise was not to try and find Kyril. "But you have to do something about my own imprisonment. Council member Fielding with authority from Marcus has put guards on my room and ordered me to stay there."

"I will take care of that," Halsey said, "as long as you and Grantham stay in the healers' rooms."

"I'm sure Joelle will do what she must," said Grantham. His words seemed to pacify the others, but Joelle felt he was also giving her permission to move forward with her own plans.

"Good," said Halsey with a broad smile. "Classes will resume this afternoon, and as far as other students are concerned, normalcy will begin to be restored here at the school. The students must get back to their schedule."

The meeting broke up when Halsey and the two student wizards headed back toward the school. Kittoran gave a hug to her grandfather Grantham, and then she and the prince snuck out of the stable, leaving Joelle and Grantham to make their way back through the hidden passageways and to her room.

Upon arriving, they dragged the two still-unconscious guards back out into the hallway, and Grantham left Joelle back in her room to finish getting properly ready for the day.

A half an hour later she heard a ruckus outside of her room.

"I heard there was trouble here," said Marcus, his angry voice unmistakable. "Where were you two?"

Joelle heard a mumble of words from one of the guards but couldn't make it out.

"Open the door," Marcus ordered.

Keys jangled and the door began to open.

"She's escaped, sir," said one of the guards before fully seeing the room. "She and an old man knocked us out and…" His words trailed off as Marcus pushed the door wide.

"Wizard Marcus," said Joelle with a sweet voice. She held a brush in her hand and began untangling her unruly curls. "Is there a problem? Coming to let me go so soon?"

Marcus ground his teeth and looked back and forth between the two guards.

"The guards said an old man helped you to escape."

"An old man?" Joelle smiled broadly. "You mean, little me and an old man escaped under the eyes of these two strong guards? I'm confused."

"And so must they be," said Marcus. He turned to the guards. "Report to your captain and tell him you are on waste duty for the rest of the day."

The two guards groaned and then almost tripped over themselves backing toward the doorway.

"It seems your skill has been requested by the healers to help them with the injured from yesterday's attack," said Marcus. "And it is said you are to try and help the stranger there to regain his memories and see what he knows."

"Oh?" Joelle said. "Are you interested in what he knows, Wizard Marcus?"

"Of course I am," Marcus said. "This school suffered an unfortunate attack yesterday."

"An attack that puts you in a viable position as possible next headmaster of the school," Joelle ventured.

Marcus's face grew flushed. "Are you insinuating that I had something to do with the attack? As far as I know your shifty friend from Gildan and your memory-missing friend were in this together. I don't envy the position you are in. I'm giving you this courtesy of leaving your room because you attended school here, are a talented healer, and other members of the council have requested it. Don't give me reason to put you back in here again."

Joelle took a step back at his vehemence. He was a dangerous man and she had pushed him too far. She needed to be more careful. There might be more enemies than friends around right now.

"Can I see Kyril?" she asked.

Marcus shook his head. "Not right now."

"And the medallion? Where is that?" Joelle asked, not really expecting an answer.

"How am I to know?" Marcus said, throwing up his hands. "If that boy can't keep it safe, maybe he doesn't deserve to have it. Maybe someone more experienced could get better use out of it."

"Like you?" Joelle said, knowing she shouldn't push again.

Marcus clenched his teeth. "You go too far again, Healer Joelle. You have no right to question me, a council member of the school. I don't have to convince you of my loyalty to the school. I will do what I must to keep the peace here."

Joelle held her tongue. She needed to find the medallion and stop him from assuming permanent control of the school.

"I will be visiting the healers' rooms later today and expect to find you working there. And you will report directly to me if Kaldar regains his memories—nobody else. He may have information behind the attack."

Joelle opened her mouth to respond, but Wizard Marcus only pivoted and headed out the door, leaving it wide open and not saying another word.

Joelle sat on the bed and tried to calm her racing heart. She definitely was not made for this intrigue.

CHAPTER TWENTY-EIGHT

Kyril paced the small dungeon room for at least the hundredth time since waking. It was not a typical dungeon with bars, but instead was an actual room with four walls, no window, and an iron door. Within the door was a smaller locked door toward the bottom—Kyril hoped it was for food. Upon being thrust into the room the night before he noticed immediately that all of his wizard powers disappeared. It was unnerving and would make escape extremely difficult.

He must have slept soundly, because there was a plate of food and a cup of water left for him just inside the door. He berated himself for not waking up and taking advantage of the situation. But what could he really do? He wasn't large enough to fight the guards and he wasn't a strong enough wizard without the medallion. Besides, his powers were gone. Well…not gone per se. He could feel them lingering as he usually did, but they didn't respond when he tried to bring them forth. The room definitely blocked magic.

He finally stopped pacing and sat down on the rickety bed. Besides one thin blanket on the bed, the only other item in the room was a chamber pot. Two dim candles flickered on the wall, sending dancing shadows about the room. It wasn't the size of the room that bothered him—he had never grown up in much luxury. But not having any windows made him disoriented. He didn't know what time of day it was.

Opening his right palm in front of him, he ran the fingers of his other hand over his scars. He still remembered that fateful night two years earlier when his mother, father, and sister had died in the fire. For a long time he felt guilty for not being there. Finding his mother's medallion—the one that had burned his hand after the fire—had finally given him purpose in life. And now it was gone. And so was his power.

Some of his magic had manifested itself through the mark in his hand even before he had retrieved the medallion, but try as he might, nothing was happening now. He realized, a bit surprisingly, that he wasn't overly afraid—something that would have been the case before finding the medallion. Before then he had been unsure of himself and unpopular. He knew part of it had been his own fault. He had been negative, timid, and not very friendly to others, but once Targon and his group of followers had befriended him, he had awoken to the possibility that others might like him. He now realized it had most likely all been a ploy to manipulate his powers, but he had grown fond of his mentor and still missed his attention sometimes.

Glancing around the blank room Kyril knew that somehow Joelle would find him, or one of the other council members would override Marcus's decision. Gamal had used wizards of the mind in Gildan, so it didn't surprise him to learn he had also used one at the wizard school on White Island. From what he had learned from Joelle, Marcus was a longtime professor and council member and had always thought he should be headmaster. However, the previous headmaster, Wizard Penrose, had been appointed by King Darius when the school first opened about fifteen years earlier and had stayed on ever since. Often at odds with the headmaster, Marcus never hid his desire to run the school in the way that he deemed better. Marcus thought Penrose was too soft and coddling of young wizards and that the wizard school on white island could do more to establish itself as the premier wizard school on the western continent.

Gamal must have offered Marcus that chance.

Kyril wondered if Marcus would try to use the medallion or just get it to Gamal. He feared what the old scribe would do with it and hoped that he hadn't found either of the other ones yet.

Kyril should have been more attentive. He couldn't believe he had let those two students knock him out and take the golden medallion. He sighed in frustration and lay back down.

He must have drifted off to sleep because the next thing he knew he heard the small door opening at the bottom of the bigger door. Two large meaty hands grabbed his old dishes and pushed through another plate of food. The door closed—but not before Kyril noticed something.

In that brief moment when the small door was open, he had felt his palm grow warm. It still tingled, but the power had already receded.

"That's it," Kyril said out loud to himself.

That small opening to the exterior of the room had also opened up whatever was shielding his power. Now he had something to look forward to. The next meal.

But before that came he had many hours to wait. So he grabbed his meal—a thin soup with an inadequate amount of potatoes and carrots swirling around one small chunk of meat. A hardened, crusted bread sat next to it. Hungrily he gobbled up both and then began pacing again.

Kyril needed a plan. When that small door opened again he wanted to test out his theory one more time. Then the next time, he could try and escape. It was a thin plan—but the only one he currently had.

***

"Sylvie, this is unacceptable," Bale said. "We should be honored guests, not held in this dirty cell like common criminals." He wrinkled his nose up at the stench.

Sylvie agreed about the stench, but she didn't have Bale's sense of entitlement. "We did fight with their king."

Bale threw his hands up in the air. "They attacked me—us, I mean—first! Come on, I know you can break out of here."

Sylvie glanced around. She could indeed break out with little use of power. The cell bars were no match for her powers and the three guards stationed only a short distance away would not be a problem for her.

As she and Bale had gotten closer to the Blue Sea she felt her powers grow stronger. The water seemed to hold vast power for her…even more than the earth did. That would be something interesting to speak with her High Wizard about. Most earth wizards had more strength when on land than the sea. With barely a thought she could blow the doors off, but she decided to let things play out –hopefully to the degree that no one else was hurt.

"Be patient, Bale," she said. "It won't be long."

Bale only sighed, then fell quiet.

"I'm not much of a spy, am I?" he said a few minutes later. "Couldn't last a day without being caught."

"You're doing fine," she said in effort to comfort him. "It's just that you need to learn to not take things so personally. You need to fade more into the background."

"I wasn't raised for that," Bale grumbled.

Sylvie laughed. "No, I guess you weren't. You were raised to take over your father's barony and be a ruler, right? So what made you turn to the spymaster's office then?"

Bale stopped his pacing and came up to the bars that separated their individual cells. His black brows creased, knitting together, and his lips pouted.

"Fine, I'll tell you," he said as if coming to a conclusion. "Our Barony has been losing money for years. My being brought into the spymaster's office was a way to try and curry favor with the emperor and hopefully to find a wife from a richer barony that could help us back to financial security."

He turned away from her as if in shame.

"Politics," Sylvie said, "are a nasty business sometimes."

Bale stayed quiet and resumed his pacing around the cell. A few minutes later, the sound of footsteps echoed down a nearby hallway. Within a matter of moments Wizard Merikh appeared in front of them. Both Sylvie and Bale moved to the front of their respective cells.

"How dare you hold us here!" Bale said, voice raised.

Sylvie shot him a look to be quiet, but he missed it. Merikh didn't even acknowledge Bale's words but kept his gaze focused on Sylvie. He offered her a short bow.

"My lady, your power and control were quite impressive," Merikh said. "And you have kept your honor by not escaping, when I surmise you could."

Sylvie smiled and nodded her head to him in acknowledgement. "As mentioned before, we are on a mission of incredible importance. I have no desire to cause any problems. The altercation earlier was indeed unfortunate."

Merikh raised his eyebrows and pushed back his long gray hair behind his shoulders. "I agree. Our young king can be brash, and if I might add, a bit foolish at times."

Bale grunted his agreement and Sylvie shot him a dark glare. Bale rolled his eyes but held his tongue.

"But we have a problem," Merikh said with a shrug of his shoulders. "You embarrassed the king in public. Even though you are very strong magically, we cannot let his subjects see him as weak."

Sylvie thought for a moment. She knew from her studies that the people of Cyrene and Turg put a lot of credence in the power of magic. Their entire social system was based on levels of powers. This was indeed a delicate situation. She had already bested King Shafer and his friends in public so everyone knew she was more powerful. If she bowed to him in apology, it would come off as false. However…

She turned and looked at Bale, and an idea began forming in her mind. And she was sure that Bale wasn't going to like it.

"I have an idea," Sylvie finally said.

The older wizard lifted his brows in curiosity.

"My companion, Bale Nabhani, will bow to your king and issue a public apology," Sylvie said, trying not to watch Bale's reaction. "He is from a noble house of Gildan. This will put Gildan in Cyrene's debt and the king will save face with his people.

"I will not," Bale spat. "I did nothing wrong."

"A wonderful idea, young wizard," Merikh said, still not acknowledging Bale. "Those without magic do have their uses sometimes.

"Is no one listening to me?" Bale said more loudly.

Sylvie waved a hand at Bale as if dismissing him. She hated doing it, but it was for their own good. It was the only way they would get out of the cell—well, at least without causing more problems. She needed to get back on her trip to the Wizard Conclave and try to find information on the medallions.

"I will set up a time with King Shafer and will return when he is ready," Merikh said with a clap of his hands. "This is wonderful. The King of Arc is indeed lucky to have such a powerful wizard from his kingdom. Your people must be proud of you."

"I'm sure they are." Sylvie bowed with a smile, still playing the part of the arrogant wizard. "But I must ask one favor from you, mighty counselor."

"Of course," Merikh said with a nod of his head.

"I would like to freshen up before the public apology," Sylvie said, pointing to the dirty cell. "You must agree this is no place for such a wizard as I."

A smile grew on Merikh's face. "Yes, yes, I understand. Guards!" he called. "Please let Wizard Sylvonna out of her cell and escort her to a guest room."

"What about me?" Bale growled from his cell.

Sylvie waved her hand in his direction. "In good time, Nobleman Nabhani." When Merikh turned to leave, she quickly winked at Bale.

His eyes went wide and he stumbled on his words.

"I will not apologize," Bale said, his face growing a dark shade of red. "The emperor will hear about this."

Before she could catch up to Merikh's long strides, she turned toward Bale and glared back at him. "Play the part, spy," she whispered to him.

The words jolted him and he stiffened straight. She continued to glare at him until he gave a small but perceptible nod of his head. She hoped she had gotten through his haughty shell. As she had told him, if he wanted to be successful in the employ of the king's spymaster office, he needed to learn to blend in and play the part. Only then would he get the information he needed. It would be a hard lesson for Bale Nabhani to learn, but learn he must.

CHAPTER TWENTY-NINE

Kyril heard a jangle of keys outside his door. He was ready this time. Once the small door opened he would extend his mind outward and see how strong he felt. He wanted to test the mark on his hand. He needed to know what he could do in the span of only a moment with the power.

However, rather than the smaller door opening, the bigger iron door opened instead. To his surprise, Wizard Halsey stepped inside. Instantly he felt connection to his power once again. With a deep breath he tried to push his mind outward past the edges of the cell. He found it difficult at first; he had already become used to the medallion augmenting his powers and he felt weak.

With a warmth growing on the palm of his hand, he stuck it quickly inside the folds of his dirty cloak. He didn't want the wizard to see.

A smile spread across Halsey's face. "Kyril Siravan, are you well?"

Kyril nodded. "Better if I was out of here."

"Ah, I understand," she said. "I'm sorry I'm not at liberty to release you. Though, I promised Healer Joelle that I would look in on you."

"Is she all right?"

"Oh, yes," Halsey said. "She is helping Healer Grantham in the healers' rooms. The attack yesterday left a few of our wizards and students injured."

"And the man Kaldar?" asked Kyril. While talking, he continued to use his powers to discover what was around him. Without the actual medallion he needed to take a few more minutes to understand if he could really transport out or not. "I've asked her to try and heal him and see what he remembers. I hear you do not trust him."

Kyril shook his head. "No ma'am, I do not. I think he had something to do with the attack yesterday."

"Really?" Halsey said as if in surprise. "Joelle doesn't think so."

"Figures," Kyril mumbled.

"What was that?"

"Nothing," Kyril said.

"Now what can you tell me about the medallion that was stolen? I told her I would check into that for her."

"Two wizards—students, I believe—took it from me," Kyril said. "I need to get it back. It's dangerous in the wrong hands."

"Dangerous?"

Kyril opened his mouth to explain, but then thought better than it. Hadn't he told Joelle to trust no one? This wizard seemed very intent and focused on finding out about the medallion. In fact, her eyes had seemed to grow dark and penetrating as she spoke about it. It appeared hard for her to take her eyes off of it.

"Come on, Kyril," Halsey pleaded. "I'm doing a favor for Joelle. The council is trying to put this all behind us and get on with things. The students need to know they have a safe environment here at the school. But I am interested in studying this medallion you had."

"It's mine," was all Kyril said. "I need to get it back. If you can help, then I…and the emperor of Gildan would be very pleased."

"The emperor?" Halsey said. "I've heard he is a very powerful wizard and a friend to the King of the Realm. Of course I will help."

Kyril let out a slow breath in relief, though he still didn't trust her. "Thank you."

"I will personally talk to the two that knocked you out, as you say," Halsey said. "Though I have heard Ruthorford is sick and says he doesn't remember a medallion." Halsey laughed, but the laugh didn't seem pleasant to Kyril. "Those two are scoundrels from noble houses. I'm sure you can understand that they like to play games sometimes."

Kyril nodded his head. "I understand more than you know." He'd been picked on by Bale and his friends over the past few years and knew quite well how nobles could be to others. Would he never get away from it? "I can help find it, if you will let me leave. Ruthorford is lying if he says he doesn't remember."

Halsey smiled. "I will do what I can, Kyril, but I am only one lowly voice on the Council. I'm afraid Marcus and Fielding have quite a bit more sway than I do. These things take order and time, as you can appreciate."

Kyril frowned. This woman was as smooth a talker as most politicians he had met.

"I can't jeopardize my place on the council by letting you go," Halsey added. "I hope you understand. I am not a wizard of the mind like Marcus and Fielding. I must be careful."

Kyril almost felt the fullness of the power of the medallion in his palm now. Suddenly he felt a pull up and to the right. He jumped in response.

"Are you all right?" asked Halsey.

Kyril had somehow *felt* where the medallion was. Marcus's rooms must be in that direction.

"I think Wizard Marcus has it," Kyril said. "The medallion, that is."

"That's a strong accusation," Halsey said, pursing her lips. "You must tell no one else your thoughts. If he gets wind of that, I may not be able to get you out of here."

Kyril nodded his head. "So you will help me?"

"Of course," Halsey said. "But I fear it may be another day or so. The council is meeting tomorrow on it."

Kyril groaned to hide his displeasure. But he wasn't planning on still being in this cell at that point. The next time a meal came, he would be gone.

Halsey walked out with a smile on her lips and a promise that she would return soon if she had any more information.

By the time the door closed Kyril was confident in his ability to be able to transport next time he had the opportunity. He would find Joelle, and then together, they would find the medallion.

***

Joelle stood over the bed of a young wizard a few years younger than she was. The girl blinked her eyes a few times and then a low groan escaped her lips.

"How are you feeling?" Joelle asked.

After a brief moment of silence the girl nodded her head. "Better."

The young girl had been standing under a chandelier during the attack, which had shattered and rained sharp crystals onto her. She had taken multiple deep cuts all over her body. She had been unconscious while they worked on her. It had taken various rounds by no less than three healers over the past day and Joelle had been the last.

Grantham walked over and ran his hand over the girl's head where the worst of the gashes had been, then moved his eyes to her arms where new skin covered all but a slight discoloration of her skin.

"Amazing," he said, "You have a finesse in healing that I have rarely seen. Are your parents wizards?"

"No." Joelle shook her head. "My father works in the Belorian government building and my mother is a seamstress. I'm not aware of their parents having any powers either."

"I've never seen…" His voice trailed off. "Well, you are quite talented, Joelle."

"Thank you," said the injured girl. "Thank you all."

"A few more hours' rest here, and you'll be free to go back to your room," said Grantham. "You should be able to return to classes tomorrow."

Grantham and Joelle walked away but soon another voice called out to them.

"What about me?" called Kaldar.

"What about him?" Grantham shook his head toward the man.

Joelle walked over to Kaldar with what she was sure was a scowl on her face. "What about you?"

He was propped up with his head on some pillows. A slight grin covered his handsome face. In the day he had been in the healers' rooms his whiskers had grown thicker.

Joelle yawned and covered her mouth. "I must be tired," she said.

"When do I get out of here?" Kaldar said. "I feel fine."

"But you still don't know what you are doing here?" said Joelle with hands on her hips.

"No, I don't, princess," Kaldar said with a laugh. "Maybe I followed you here."

Joelle felt her face heat up but she tried to ignore it. He had hit too close to home.

"No memories?" asked Grantham with a worried look on his face. "I've seen this before after a traumatic experience, but they should come back in time."

"And in the meantime?" He began to sit up more fully.

"And in the meantime, you stay here," Joelle said with a push of her hand against his chest.

He grabbed her hand, held it, and peered intently into her eyes. She glared back, but quickly became lost in his eyes. This time they didn't seem as dark and deep as they had on the ship. Using her healing powers she delved deep inside of his mind to try and find the block. His mind was different than anyone she had encountered before. She couldn't make sense of it and it frustrated her.

"Tell me who I am," she heard Kaldar say to her, his voice pleading.

While still concentrating on trying to heal him, she spoke. "Your name is Kaldar. We met you in Belor."

"We?"

"Kyril and I," said Joelle. "But he doesn't trust you."

"Why is that?"

"He…he…" What could she say? Was Kyril just jealous or was there something else? "I don't know."

She reached further into his mind to try and find the block. The hardest thing was that she didn't have much information to work with. She realized she didn't actually know much about him. Remembering the lingering kiss on the ship, she withdrew her hand from his and dropped the eye contact.

"Now, that was quite intimate," Kaldar said with a wink and a look at Grantham. "Seems this young healer and I enjoyed a little kiss."

Joelle's hand flew to her mouth as she covered a gasp. "How did you know?"

Grantham tried not to smile. "Sometimes if you go too deep into someone's mind they receive residual thoughts from yours also. Maybe next time I should try."

Kaldar chuckled. "Well, at least I have good taste. I've never seen such beautiful locks of gorgeous red hair. Where I'm from we don't have many redheads."

Joelle backed away. She needed to get away from him. She couldn't think straight around him. But Grantham reached his hand out and stopped her, then turned back to Kaldar.

"You remembered something?" Grantham said. "About redheads?"

Kaldar thought for a moment and then smiled devilishly. "I guess I did. Maybe you did some good in my mind. Want to try again?"

"No. No," Joelle muttered. "Maybe later. I…" She turned around and almost ran straight into Wizard Marcus. Standing next to him was Wizard Fielding. She let out a small groan. These were not the two people she wanted to see right now.

"Sounds like you are making progress with our young friend here," Marcus said, looking from Joelle to Kaldar. "Soon we will have a confession from him."

"Confession?" Kaldar asked, concern on his face. "Did I do something?"

As flustered as Joelle was she walked over and put her hand on his sheet-covered leg. "Of course you did not do anything wrong. Wizard Marcus is fishing for something he knows is not here."

Fielding stepped forward and glared at Kaldar. "He knows something. I can tell. Let me try and get to his memories."

Joelle stood up straight and was still a few inches shorter than Fielding. "You are not a healer."

"No, but I am a wizard of the mind and might be able to reach his mind."

"To destroy it?" Joelle said in defense of Kaldar. "Is that what you two are trying to do? Erase what he knows? Maybe he saw or knows something that you don't want him to say."

Fielding pushed his way closer, but Marcus put his hand out. "Enough," he ordered, and called back Fielding with a crook of his finger. "This bickering will not get us the truth." He nodded toward Joelle and said, "Continue your methods. I will return later to check on your progress. I assume you will be here."

Joelle watched Marcus suspiciously. She didn't trust the man at all. He was hiding something, she was sure. "Where else would I be?"

"Where else indeed?" Marcus said with a smile. Then, turning to Fielding, he motioned him out ahead of him. "Now let's go see what that boy knows. I intend to have control in the school once more."

CHAPTER THIRTY

As soon as Marcus and Fielding left the healers' rooms, Joelle turned to Grantham with a questioning look in her eyes.

"Go!" he said with a nod of his head toward the door.

She moved to take a step forward, but not before Kaldar snaked his hand out and grabbed her arm. She tried to pull away but he held it tight.

"Let me go!"

"I'm going with you," Kaldar said as he moved to sit up. He threw off his blanket, then took a moment to get his balance.

"You are not well enough yet," Joelle said. She pulled her arm away from him finally and stood in front of him, daring him to take another step.

"Feisty one, isn't she?" Kaldar said with a sly wink at Grantham.

The older healer only grunted, but there was a hint of a smile at the corners of his lips.

"You are a prisoner here," Joelle said. "They won't let you just walk out and leave."

Kaldar raised his eyebrows at her and Joelle got the feeling this was all just a big joke to him. Maybe he did remember their kiss. With that thought his smile grew even broader and she felt the heat in her cheeks.

"Is something wrong, Joelle?" Kaldar asked as he reached his hand tenderly toward her face.

"Stop it." Joelle slapped his hand down, a bit harder than she had intended.

Kaldar shook it out for a second or two and then cocked his head to the side. "Seems to me like you aren't supposed to leave this room either. You are as much a prisoner here as I am."

"You have no idea what you are talking about." Joelle shook her head and her long locks of hair flew around her face. "Now, I need to go before I lose them. I need to find out where they are holding Kyril."

"Kyril?" Kaldar mused. "That's your wizard friend who thinks I'm behind the attacks that supposedly happened yesterday?"

Joelle had turned to go, but now swung her head back to Kaldar with suspicion. "How do you know about that? I thought you couldn't remember anything."

"I do have ears," Kaldar said. "That's all anyone around here is talking about. I need answers as much as you do, so I'm going with you."

Joelle looked at Grantham and he shrugged his shoulders. "Do what you must, Joelle, but you need to hurry. I can cover for you for a bit, but between Halsey and Marcus checking up on you you'd better be careful."

"Like a said, a prisoner," Kaldar said.

Joelle ground her teeth in anger, but time was slipping away. "Fine. Just don't expect me to save you if you get caught." As she turned toward the door she heard a soft chuckle along with light footsteps following behind her.

Why did she keep feeling that Kaldar knew more than he was letting on? She walked with purposeful strides down the stone hallway, her heels clicking softly on the marble flooring. She didn't believe, like Kyril, that he had actually been involved with the attack, but why was he really there on White Island? She ground her teeth in frustration. She was finding suspicion where there didn't need any to be.

"Where are you from, Kaldar?" she finally said.

Kaldar had caught up to her—which wasn't hard with his longer legs—and jerked his head in her direction. She tried not to look over at him, but she could feel his eyes burning into the side of her head.

"You know I don't remember."

"That's what you keep saying," Joelle mumbled.

"Look," Kaldar said, more softly than before. "As frustrating as it is to you, think of how it is for me. Am I the monster some think I am? Or am I innocent, caught up in some elaborate scheme by powerful wizards? I know my name is Kaldar. I know how to think and understand things around me, but I truthfully don't know who I am or where I come from. You and your friends are wizards; why don't you tell me what you know!"

Joelle let out a deep breath as his voice picked up near the end. A few others passing by glanced curiously at the two of them.

"Keep quiet," was all she could find to say. "You're drawing too much attention to yourself."

She knew he deserved more of an answer than that and she knew she wasn't being entirely fair. This adventure was getting to her. She was a healer and not made for this. She wished Sylvie was there with her. She'd know what to do. She was always more decisive than Joelle and her background as a wizard of the earth would be more practical for sneaking around and possibly fighting with others.

Grasping her staff harder, she motioned for Kaldar to follow her down another hallway. As they did so, she glimpsed Marcus and Fielding up ahead, opening a door. She pulled herself and Kaldar back behind a pillar and waited for the door to finish closing.

Standing there, she realized how close she was to Kaldar. The warmth of his body radiated over her, and she opened herself up to her healing powers momentarily and tried to delve inside him once more.

Next to her Kaldar stiffened and gasped. "What are you doing to me?" he whispered. "If you wanted me alone…"

"Don't go there," Joelle snapped at him. "I'm trying to heal you."

"That didn't feel like a healing," Kaldar said, his eyes dark and angry. Then he softened a bit and gave a toothy smile. "Though I do feel stronger and more energized, now that you mention it."

Joelle sighed.

"What else were you doing?"

Joelle put a finger over her lips as the door at the end of the hallway opened once again. Council member Halsey walked out of it and down the hall toward them. She appeared deep in thought and passed by their spot without noticing them. She appeared almost as if she were in a trance.

What was she doing down there?

"Who was that?" Kaldar said once she had passed by them. "She's been in the healers' rooms before, trying to get information from me. She seemed to know I came here on a ship with you."

"Wizard Halsey, one of the council," Joelle said. "She's on our side."

"Really?" Kadar's eyebrows arched up. "When she talked to me, it didn't seem that way." He paused for a moment, and before Joelle could say anything he smiled. "Hey, you said 'our side'—does that mean you trust me?"

"Trust you?" Joelle said with a glance toward where Halsey had gone. "I'm beginning to not trust anyone at this point."

They began walking back down the hallway toward the door.

"And where does this lead?" Kaldar asked.

"To the dungeon cells where they hold prisoners."

"Ah, your friend Kyril," said Kaldar. "And you're wondering why all the council members seem to be interested in him. He must be a mighty wizard. Maybe he orchestrated the attack."

Reaching her hand to the doorknob, Joelle turned to face Kaldar and he took a step back and put his hands up in defense.

"Kyril. Did. Not. Attack. Anyone," Joelle said angrily. "And no, he's not a really mighty wizard at all. At least not yet."

"Then why are they so interested in him?"

Joelle slowly opened the door and they walked onto a landing, letting the door close behind them before they continued. Torches at various intervals on the walls gave light to the stone steps leading down.

"The medallion," Joelle said with hardly more than a whisper.

Kaldar stumbled on a step next to her and she put a hand on his arm to keep him steady.

"Thanks," he said.

"What happened?" Joelle stood in the middle of the steps. "You look like you've remembered something."

"The medallion," Kaldar whispered. "It…it sounds familiar to me. A golden medallion…" His voice faded away. "What do you see when you delve into my mind, Joelle?"

"I…I…I don't know," she said. "I've never seen such a mind before. It's as if…" She trailed off. What she was thinking didn't make any sense. There were holes there that shouldn't exist.

They reached the bottom of the steps and with a finger to her lips, Joelle peered around a corner. In front of her was a short hallway with another door at the end. She guessed the prison cells were behind that door. But what else was there? How close would guards or Marcus and Fielding be?

Her heart pounded as they approached the door. She could hear Kaldar's breathing next to her and knew he had questions. But so did she. She risked a quick glance at him and caught him looking at her. His face was hard to read—it looked confused and full of questions. His lips parted as if he was going to question her again but she shook her head as they reached the door.

Putting her hand on the handle, she pushed it open as quietly as she could.

CHAPTER THIRTY-ONE

Kyril sat on the dirty bed thinking about his conversation with Wizard Halsey. Joelle had mentioned she was very strict and straight-laced. She seemed to want to help Kyril, and that was good. He needed an ally on the local wizard school council. Obviously Wizard Marcus had it out for him, and was possibly even working with Gamal on some level. But something about Halsey bothered him also. She asked a little too much about the medallion for his liking.

He was starting to mistrust everyone and he didn't like the paranoid way it made him feel. Kyril ran his hand over his scar once again. They had come to White Island to find information in their search for the other medallion, the one supposedly given to a wizard of the Realm many years before. But now he had lost the one that had been given to him.

Well, he hadn't lost it. It had been taken from him. He ground his teeth in frustration. His quest was moving backwards. How could he report back to Emperor Alrishitar without even the first medallion in his possession? No, he couldn't do that. He would have to retrieve it before they left the wizard school, and then they could resume their search for the other medallions elsewhere.

So far Gamal had infiltrated two of the three wizard schools in the northern part of the western continent. And if both of the attacks were any indication, he had been planning things for quite a while. The wizard community was moving toward chaos and only the three medallions could be used to bring balance once again.

A sound out in the hallway had him standing up again. Was it meal time already? He braced himself for the small door to open, and reached for his magic and the power of the medallion. He had to escape.

Instead of the small door opening, however, the full door swung open, catching Kyril by surprise once again. In the doorway stood a guard alongside Wizards Marcus and Fielding.

What do they want? Kyril groaned out loud.

All three entered through the doorway and Marcus took a step out farther than the other two. Kyril tried to feel for his powers, but the two wizards were doing something to hold him there. He couldn't move his arms or legs. Only his head was able to swivel from side to side.

"I see council member Halsey has been to see you," said Marcus. "I ran into her on my way in. She besought your release. What did you say to her?"

"The truth," Kyril said through clenched teeth, then looking down at his immobile body added, "Is this necessary?"

"I'm not sure what is necessary when it comes to you, Kyril Siravan," Marcus said. "I am trying to keep order here. This school is based on discipline and order and ever since you arrived on White Island, chaos has ensued."

"Me?" Kyril couldn't believe what he was hearing. "I've told you I came with the blessing of Emperor Alrishitar to search for information leading to the capture of Gamal Turomi and to find the other medallions. And now the one I did have has been stolen from me."

"Ah, yes, I remember that now," Marcus said condescendingly. "Maybe you are not responsible enough for this task."

"And you have no leads on who attacked the school either," said Fielding, his first words since entering. His face sneered with disbelief at Kyril's words. "These are very weak arguments for a wizard of the mind."

Kyril couldn't believe the conversation. They were obviously hiding something.

Through the mark in his hand, Kyril could feel where the medallion was now that the door was open. It was above him somewhere, but in a different spot than before. Marcus or Fielding must have gotten it from Ruthorford and Thane and hidden it. But Kyril didn't let on that he knew anything about it. He was about to say more, when he noticed Joelle and Kaldar sneaking up behind the three men.

"Nothing more to say?" Fielding said as he stepped forward toward Kyril. He brought his hand up to slap him, but Marcus spoke up first.

"No, Fielding," Marcus said. "That will solve nothing. It seems Wizard Kyril here doesn't want to speak anything of sense to us. Perhaps Halsey has her own reasons for letting him go. We need to speak with her more. I'm starting to wonder who to trust around here."

Kyril hid his response to Marcus's words with a cough of disbelief and tried not to watch Joelle and Kaldar creeping closer. But he didn't like the way that Kaldar appeared so close to Joelle. And what was he doing, free from the healers' rooms? He and Marcus were surely in league with each other.

Kyril's hand began to warm, but he still couldn't move it. Along with the warming came the familiar growing of power within him. It wasn't as intense as it was when he was in possession of the medallion, but it was familiar to him and reminded him of when he had first learned to transport—only now he was much more disciplined. But could he do it with his body frozen? The glow brightened and caught the attention of Marcus and Fielding.

"What is this trickery?" Fielding said, taking a step back. "Marcus, we need to get out of here. He's going to unleash his evil magic on us."

Kyril caught Joelle's eyes and nodded, hoping they understood what he intended to do.

Kaldar jumped ahead of Joelle and rushed through the doorway, knocking down the guard and Fielding on the way in. As he did so, the spell on Kyril was lifted. Marcus turned to leave, but Joelle brought her staff out in front of her and stepped into the room. With a whirl a bright flame of green and yellow formed a shield between her and Marcus.

Wizard Marcus brought his hands up in front of him and prepared a spell, but Joelle smacked her staff down on his right wrist. He yelped in pain and his spell dissipated.

"How dare you!" Marcus roared, his face red with anger.

At this point, Fielding and the guard had tried to stand up, but Kaldar did a roundabout with his legs and kicked Fielding in the gut, while punching the guard in the side of the face. Both grunted hard, Fielding falling to the ground. But the guard stayed standing and rushed back at Kaldar, trying to grab him around the middle.

Joelle cried out and Kyril turned his attention back to her. The guard, Fielding, and Marcus now stood back up between Joelle and Kaldar, and himself. Joelle was breathing hard and trying to move her staff around, but the space was small and it was difficult for her. A ball of lightning formed around Marcus's hand.

"Traitor," Marcus spat. "We taught you all you know and now you betray us."

"You're the traitor, Marcus," called out Kyril. "You'll not have the medallion or help Gamal anymore."

Marcus turned toward him and away from Joelle. As he did so, Kyril gathered his powers and transported out of the room.

"Shut the door," Kyril screamed at Joelle as soon as he landed in the hallway outside the door. Joelle jumped back out of the room, but Kaldar struggled to get away from the guard and fell to the ground in the doorway.

"Kyril, help him!" Joelle called out.

Marcus turned toward them and threw a ball of fire. Joelle spun her staff and deflected most of it, but a portion hit her in the shoulder and she screamed and went down.

Kyril took her place in front of the door and glared at Kaldar. He was going to ruin this for them. He began pulling the door closed on all four of them. Kaldar was surely in league with Marcus anyway.

"Please, Kyril," came Joelle's quiet voice from behind him. "Save Kaldar for me."

With a flash from the mark in the palm of his hand Kyril transported two steps in, grabbed hold of a surprised Kaldar, and pulled him back out of the room before the other three could understand what was happening.

"Close it now," Kyril ordered Kaldar. He didn't know if he had the strength to do it himself.

A blast of air from inside the room pushed Kaldar back into the hallway before he could reach the door again. Marcus was about to get away.

"Duck!" came Joelle's voice from behind Kyril.

Without thought, Kyril dropped to the ground and a stream of fire flew over his head from Joelle's staff, singeing the back of his hair. The force pushed the three men back inside the room. With his last ounce of energy, Kyril thought hard and used his mind to suck the air out of the hallway, bringing the door closed with a loud bang.

Falling onto the floor he felt blackness gathering around him. He glanced at Joelle, who lay gasping for air next to him.

"What did you do?" Kaldar croaked. He too was feeling the effects of the momentary lack of oxygen.

"What I had to do," Kyril whispered. "Can you open that other door and let the air in?" He pointed down the hallway.

Kaldar staggered to his feet and with a hand on the wall, shuffled toward the door. Before collapsing to the ground he pushed it open. Kyril now laying on his back and tried not to let the blackness overtake him.

As he felt himself faded further away he heard angry voices on the other side of the cell door. Kyril smiled at the thought that they would not be able to use their powers for some time.

And then he blacked out.

CHAPTER THIRTY-TWO

Before Joelle opened her eyes she heard faint voices as if from a distance. She assumed it was Marcus, Fielding and their guard. The last thing she remembered was Kyril directing his power toward the cell door and her suddenly not being able to breathe.

With a groan she blinked her eyes and sat up.

"Kyril!" she called out to her friend, still lying still only a few feet away from her.

He stirred and turned his head toward her.

"Are you all right?" Joelle asked.

Kyril nodded and sat up. He rubbed his hand over the back of his head and then frowned. "You're hurt," Kyril said, scooting over to her.

"I'll be all right," Joelle said with only a small grimace. Then she glanced at the door to the cell room. "Why aren't they blasting out of there and after us?"

Now Kyril smiled more broadly. "Magic doesn't work in there."

"But you transported out of there."

"Only after the door was open. The room has some sort of shield that blocks magic when all closed up."

Joelle nodded her head in understanding and then jumped up. She let a moment of dizziness pass before turning around.

"Kaldar!" Joelle called out, and took a few quick steps toward the door to the hallway where he was lying across the threshold.

Kyril joined her as she leaned down and softly touched Kaldar. With a trickle of healing magic into him, he stirred. Joelle put her arm under him and pulled him up to a sitting position. He rubbed his hands over his face for a moment.

"Why are you out here?" Kyril asked.

Joelle scowled at him. They didn't have time for this. They needed to get out of there before someone found them.

"Not now," Joelle said.

Kyril had the grace to agree, and with a nod of his head he reached over and grabbed a hold of Kadar's other arm and with Joelle, lifted him to his feet. He was still breathing a bit hard, but all in all didn't appear too worse for what they had been through.

"Kyril," Kaldar said with a nod. "I finally meet the wizard that has created quite a stir around here. Something about a medallion."

Kyril shot Joelle a pointed look, but she ignored him. "He still can't remember anything. We need to get out of here. Someone will be down here soon."

"And looking for you too, I would bet," Kaldar said to Joelle.

"Looking for you?" Kyril said. "What's going on?"

"Can you transport us out of here, Kyril?" Joelle asked.

Kyril's eyebrows furrowed in thought for a moment. "Without the medallion, I'm not sure. Maybe not all three of us, but…"

"Transport?" Kaldar asked, glancing back and forth between the two. Then his eyes brightened. "Ah, like you did in there? That's how you got out. Quite a neat trick."

"Where to?"

"Take Joelle first," Kaldar said, "then come back for me."

"Oh, no," Kyril said with a shake of his head. "You're not getting away that easy. For all I know you'll be freeing those wizards from that room in there."

"Kyril," Joelle began. "When are you going to learn to trust him? He had nothing to do with the attack. With my help I can take you someplace safe, then you can come back for him."

Suddenly, they heard the door up the stairs open and close, and then footsteps descending the stone steps.

"Fine," Kyril said as he grabbed a hold of Joelle's hand with his marked one. "Think of a safe place, Joelle. And don't let your mind wander."

Joelle growled. Would he never let her forget that? She could concentrate. She thought of a spot overlooking the sea. After a slight moment of dizziness they were there.

Kyril let go of her hand and leaned over and took a few deep breaths.

"Are you sick again?" Joelle asked.

Kyril nodded his head. "It's worse without the medallion, it seems. But I'm all right."

A slight sea breeze ruffled Joelle's hair and she turned and looked out at the Blue Sea. Taking in a deep breath of air, she let her beating heart relax. They stood a few hundred yards from the school between a thick line of trees and the bluff. The waves crashed about fifty feet below them.

"Are you ready?" she asked Kyril.

Kyril stood up. His face was pale and a sheen of sweat lined his forehead. He nodded, but Joelle wasn't so sure.

"You don't seem well," Joelle said.

"I have to get him," Kyril said. "I have no choice."

Joelle agreed, but didn't like it. She reached over and placed both hands on either side of his neck, transferring some of her healing power to him. He straightened with a twitch and he regained some color back into his cheeks.

"Thank you," Kyril said and took a step away. "Be back in a moment."

Suddenly he wasn't there. Joelle shook her head in amazement. The power of transportation she knew was very rare in the wizarding realm. She stood in the quiet for a few moments relishing the sounds of the waves below and the strong scent of salty air in her nose. Growing up in Belor along the coast, she had spent many youthful days collecting shells and chasing the birds. Sometimes she missed those carefree days before her powers had emerged.

Growing up with her mother, father, and younger brother, she would have never thought she would become a wizard someday. None of them had any hint of power. She had always wondered about that. Once she had begun exhibiting her wizard abilities she had felt a gulf rise between the rest of her family and her. She missed being a normal child sometimes. She had caught her parents looking at her at times with worried expressions on their faces.

Oh, she loved healing, and wouldn't ever dream of abandoning helping others, but every once in a while it was nice to get away from it all. There was always pressure on her to perform, to help someone, to heal something she'd never seen before. Like in Kaldar's case. She couldn't figure out what was wrong with him and it bothered her. Something in his mind was blocking his memories. When she delved into his body with her healing powers it was not… normal, not organized like others were. It was…

"Kaldar!" she said, twisting back around and facing the tree line. The top of the wizard school peered over the tallest tips. "Kyril!"

They should have been back by then. It was a relatively short distance and it didn't take him long to transport. She paced for a few more moments, and then she hiked up her skirt and began racing back through the trees, over the small garden fence, and toward the wizard school itself. Something must have happened.

CHAPTER THIRTY-THREE

Joelle jogged up the school steps and crashed through the doors and down the hallway. She turned a corner and ran into someone, knocking them to the ground. She winced at the pain that ran through her shoulder, but spared the stranger no notice and continued on her way until a voice called her back.

"Wizard Joelle," said Wizard Halsey.

The voice stopped Joelle in her tracks and she let out a groan.

"Where are you going in such a hurry?"

She turned around and took a deep breath, her chest heaving hard. She used her fingers to smooth down her hair and tried to give the council member her best smile.

"Just out for a breath of fresh air," she said hurriedly. She needed to get away from Halsey and find Kyril and Kaldar. Maybe Kyril was right. Maybe Kaldar did cross them.

"Surely you're not back from your errand to town yet?"

"My errand?" Joelle was confused.

"Healer Grantham informed me just now that he had sent you to town for some herbs, but surely you didn't go to the town and back again." Halsey's eyes looked puzzled.

"Oh yes, the town," Joelle said. "Well you see, I left, as you said, to run an errand for Healer Grantham. I know you said not to go anywhere, but Healer Grantham asked me to, and well, he is my elder, and so I couldn't disobey him. But I didn't want to disobey you, so after I got to the…umm, gate. Yes, after I got to the gate I turned around and came back here and find you."

"To find me?" Halsey appeared surprised.

Joelle didn't like how the lies came so easily to her lips. She wished she could better understand Halsey's intentions and what she was fishing for. Then she realized something and with a gasp, her hand flew to her mouth.

"Something wrong, Healer Joelle?" Halsey took a step closer.

If Halsey had just been to the healers' rooms, she would have known that Kaldar wasn't there either. She was trying to trick her into lying.

"N…no, Ma'am," Joelle lied again.

"You look nervous." Halsey took a step closer, her cloak swirling around her. "Can I help with something?"

Joelle took a deep breath. Why *was* she so nervous? Halsey was on their side. She shouldn't be afraid of her. And what if she had left the healers' room? They couldn't hold her as a prisoner here. She was a full wizard. She pulled herself up as straight as she could.

'I'm fine, thank you," Joelle said with a feigned smile. "Just need to get back to my healing."

Halsey cocked her head to one side. "What about your errand?"

"Oh yes, my errand," Joelle said with a gulp. "I'll send someone else. I should be looking after the patients. I would feel bad if something happened to them."

Halsey nodded and smiled. "Fine attitude. And so you know, I am doing what I can to help your friend Kyril out of his prison room."

"Oh thank you, wizard Halsey," Joelle said. "I appreciate that."

"Of course, of course. We're all in this together, Joelle. I hope you understand I am trying to help you, but the council is not as easy to work with as you might imagine."

Joelle allowed herself a small grin and turned to leave but Halsey took another step forward and lowered her voice so others around couldn't hear her. "You'll be sure to tell me as soon as you find out anything about Kaldar or the medallion won't you?"

"Of course, ma'am," Joelle said, her head buzzing with fear. If she had been to the healers' rooms recently as she had hinted at, wouldn't she know that Kaldar wasn't there?

"I'm on your side here, Joelle," she said. "I believe in you when you say Kaldar wasn't involved, but you know," she shrugged her shoulders, "others on the council want to be sure."

"Of course," she said.

"I talked to Kyril about the medallion. Shame he has lost it."

"You mean it got stolen," Joelle said. She was trying to get away from Halsey, but she continued to ask questions.

Halsey waved a dismissive hand in the air. "Lost or stolen, it doesn't really matter. He doesn't have it, that's all that counts, right? And you know how he uses it, don't you?"

Joelle was getting more uncomfortable with this line of questioning and moved once again to get back to the healers' rooms. "I need to get back and help Healer Grantham."

Halsey grabbed her arm. "Be careful, Joelle. I wouldn't want you or the other wizards to get hurt. You're involved with powerful magic that you don't know a lot about."

The wizard's dark eyes began pulling Joelle in closer. A door banging in the background brought her back to her senses and she pulled out of Halsey's grasp.

"I will," Joelle said, but didn't trust herself to say anything else. She turned and headed back toward the healers' rooms with a quick walk before Halsey could say anything else. She breathed a sigh of relief for finally being away from the woman. She must have known she was lying, but what did she gain by playing games?

She pushed open the door to the healers' room and glanced around for Grantham. What greeted her instead caught her by surprise.

"Joelle!" called out Kaldar from his bed. "Back from your errand so soon?"

"What are you doing here?" she said in a whisper, coming up to his bed. She glanced around the room. There were four other patients. One was with Healer Grantham. He glanced in her direction and raised his bushy gray eyebrows but said nothing, only turning back to his patient.

"Where is Kyril?" Joelle said to Kaldar.

He only shrugged and his mouth twitched as if he found the entire thing amusing.

"This isn't funny," Joelle said. "Was Wizard Halsey just here?"

"Yes, she was," Kaldar said, his mirth souring. "Like I said before, she's not a very nice wizard and didn't seem quite right to me. She was confused and focused on asking about the medallion. What is it about that thing?"

"Why, what did she say?" Joelle asked. Halsey made her nervous too, but she said she had believed Joelle so she had no reason not to trust her if Kaldar had been here when she had come in.

Kaldar crooked his finger at her beckoning her closer. "She said I'd better be careful or I might find myself on the next ship off of White Island."

"What did she mean by that?" Joelle asked. "Did she know where we had been?"

"I don't believe so," Kaldar said, "but she wanted to see if I had recovered any memories. She even asked about the medallion—like I'm supposed to know about some golden magical medallion!" Kaldar slammed his fist down on the bed. "I wish I had my memories. What kind of man am I to not know who I am or what I've done? Maybe they're all right. Maybe I *am* somebody to get rid of. Maybe I was a part of the attacks. But if I was, I didn't do it alone. So someone else here knows what happened and who I am."

Joelle put a calming hand on his shoulder. "We'll find out the truth Kal. Kyril and…wait, where is Kyril? He went back to pick you up. What happened?"

"Two guards came down the stairs to the dungeons and when Kyril didn't come right back I had to hide in a dark recess. When they passed I raced back up to the stairs and came here," Kaldar explained. "I don't know where Kyril is. Don't you?"

"No I don't," Joelle said. "Looks like I have to go and find him again."

"Then I'm with you again."

"Not this time; you stay here," Joelle said. "It's too dangerous out there for you."

Kaldar shook his head and stood up. "It's too dangerous for me anywhere. A man without a memory is dangerous to everyone."

"Even me?" Joelle said before she realized it. She blushed and tried to turn her face away.

Kaldar reached over and tenderly turned her face back to him. "No, not to you Joelle. You are the only one to believe in me."

She stared into his eyes for a moment, remembering the kiss. There was something about him that was dangerous, but also something that drew her to him. He leaned forward and she felt herself take a quick intake of breath.

"Leaving again?" came a voice from behind them, breaking the spell.

Joelle jumped away from Kaldar, who remained where he was, eyes intently following her. She tore her gaze from him and toward Grantham.

"Kyril is missing," Joelle said in a rush. "We need to go and find him again. Can you cover for me?"

Grantham looked from Joelle to Kaldar with a small grin. "He is going with you too?"

"Yes," they both said at the same time.

"Fine," Grantham chuckled. "I don't expect anyone else to check on you for a while. Just be careful."

"Thank you, Grantham," Joelle said.

He just waved his hand at that. "There's been more excitement since you showed up than I've had in years. I'm actually quite enjoying myself."

With a quick goodbye, Joelle and Kaldar raced out of the room once again.

"This is becoming quite a habit," Kaldar laughed. "Is your friend always this much trouble?"

CHAPTER THIRTY-FOUR

Kyril had transported to the first place that came to his mind—the Cremelino stables outside of the wizard school. When he had gone back to find Kaldar, the man was not where he'd left him. Before he could look around he heard voices coming down the stairs and knew that he couldn't stay there. So he left.

He paced around an empty area of the stables and fumed about Kaldar—the man that Joelle was blinded to. He didn't trust Kaldar, and was sure he had some role in the attacks, but he just couldn't figure it out. And the convenient way that Kaldar had lost his memory irked Kyril also. Why couldn't Joelle see past his deception? From the very beginning Kyril hadn't trusted the man—although he admitted reluctantly to himself that it may have been because he was giving so much attention to Joelle.

Even though Joelle was a much more powerful wizard than he was—at least without the medallion—he felt some form of obligation to protect her. She was too kind and friendly, and was not always aware of what went on around her. And although he was a bit younger than her and she had been a full wizard longer than him, he had grown up being bullied and pushed around by others. He knew his look at the world was a bit cynical, but he made a point of not trusting many people around him. Joelle, however, wanted to be friends with everyone.

They had been at the wizard school almost three days now and hadn't found anything new in their search for the other medallions. On top of that, he had now lost the one he had.

When he was outside the dungeons, he had briefly thought about transporting to where he felt the medallion might be—but he knew that would be rash without knowing if he could really do it or not—he had never been there before. He didn't have the strength to find out at the moment. Without having the medallion with him, along with the encounter in the dungeons with Marcus and Fielding, followed by the multiple transports, he was magically and physically drained.

He knew that Marcus and Fielding would soon be let out of the dungeon room he had put them in. And then, they would come directly back for him once again—and with better cause this time. Worried, he walked out of the stables and along the fence that bordered the pasture where in the distance a few Cremelinos grazed.

"What's bothering you, Kyril?" asked a voice, startling him out of his thoughts.

"Jakob!"

"Sorry to bother you," Jakob said. "But you do seem troubled."

Kyril glanced toward the school, knowing it was only a matter of time before Marcus and the wizard school council found him. Before answering, he let out a long sigh.

"Sometimes, it's just too much." Kyril peered down at his shoes as he kicked softly against a fence pole.

"Yes, I'm sure it can feel that way," Jakob said kindly. "I remember traveling with our young king years ago. He was a few years older than you and trying to prove himself as a new king—he was the first wizard king in the Realm in many years. Then, his wife was kidnapped. It devastated him and almost overwhelmed him. But with the help of his friends and the Cremelinos he pushed through and saved her. It wasn't always easy for him either. He was untrained in his powers and people were still wary of him."

Kyril jerked his head up. "What did you say?"

Jakob laughed. "I said a lot of things. What do you mean?"

"About who helped him?"

"His friends and the…"

"Yes, yes," Kyril said with excitement. "The Cremelinos."

Jakob's mouth opened into a wide grin and he gazed out over the small herd. One of the horses broke rank and trotted toward them. "The Cremelinos do know a lot, but as I've said before, it's just trying to understand *what* they know and if they'll help—that's the trick. That's just the way they are. They are mighty beings with the power of the spirit and are passionate protectors and companions of wizards. But they are secretive and cryptic at times."

"But they did help me before," said Kyril, watching as one of the Cremelinos came up to them. Kyril recognized Solace right away. "To get to the docks to help with the fire, and in giving me a vision of what Gamal was doing."

"Perhaps Solace will help you once again," said Jakob. "She does seem to have an affinity for you."

Kyril turned to the horse and put his hand out. She nuzzled up to him, her nose touching his hand. *What do you seek, medallion holder?*

"I've lost the medallion," Kyril said both in his mind and out loud.

But you still control its power, young wizard. The medallions were created to balance magic, not to be used to manipulate it. You must not allow another of evil intent to use it.

Don't you think I know that? Kyril snapped in his mind, a bit more aggressively than he intended.

Solace neighed loudly and pulled away.

"What did you say?" asked Jakob. "The Cremelinos are sensitive creatures."

"I'm sorry," Kyril said with a small wail, and reached his hand back out toward the horse. "I just don't know what to do."

The Cremelino and the two men stood in silence for a few moments as Kyril tried to put his thoughts together. As a wizard of the mind, he had been taught to think through things. He had let his frustration disrupt that process. He needed to think through it logically.

He surmised he had three problems at the moment. One, overarching everything was the need to find the other two medallions—one of which he was fairly certain was somewhere in the Realm but hadn't found out where yet. Second, he needed to get back his own medallion. And third, he needed to find out what Kaldar knew about the attack and who in the wizard school was behind it. He suspected Marcus, but as he told Sylvie, he didn't trust anyone at this point.

"That's it!" Kyril said out loud, but to no one in particular. "I need to take them in steps." Then, turning to Solace he asked, "Would you take me down to the harbor? I need to find out who might have seen Kaldar and with whom he had been speaking." If he could find out who was behind the attacks then hopefully that would lead him back to his own medallion and eventually the other two.

I will do as you ask, young wizard.

"Jakob, can you open up the gate?"

"She must really care for you, Kyril," he said.

Kyril shrugged. "Can't say about that, but I do feel they want to help me find the medallions and stop Gamal. Solace told me before to beware of the duplicity of a man and to be careful who I trust. I need to hurry, though. The wizard council will be after me soon."

Jakob opened the gate and then lifted his eyebrows toward Kyril. "Wizard Council? Kyril, What did you do?"

"I escaped from the dungeons and imprisoned councilors Marcus and Fielding in my place."

Jakob's barked out a laugh. "Councilor Marcus will not be happy."

"No, he will not." Kyril shook his head in agreement. "I think he is behind the attack."

Jakob looked startled. "I'm not sure I would believe that, Kyril. He has been here almost since the beginning. He is a hard man and harder still on the students, but I can't believe he would be behind this treachery. He loves the school and all that magic represents."

Kyril climbed up on Solace and he turned back to Jakob. "That's what I'm going to find out."

With a light swat on the Cremelino's flank, Jakob waved his goodbye. "Take care of each other."

"Quickly, Solace," Kyril said. "I'm afraid we don't have much time before someone uses the medallion for evil."

Hold on.

Kyril grinned for a moment, but then as Solace picked up speed his joy turned to fear for his life. He grabbed onto the horse's neck with all his might and tried not to fall off.

They raced through the wizard school gates, almost knocking over two guards. Then they headed down the hilly road. The ground rippled and trees blurred by beside him.

You're going to kill me.

The Cremelino neighed loudly as if laughing and picked up speed.

Kyril took a deep breath and tried to relax. In doing so he actually began to enjoy the ride. He had never thought to travel so fast in his life—well, besides transporting, but that was different. Around turns, past other riders and wagons, and over small stones, the Cremelino seemed to float in the air as she picked up speed. Kyril's mind cleared and he directed the horse toward the inn that he had seen across from the docks.

In a matter of a few minutes they were there. They came to an abrupt stop and Kyril rose up out of his seat on the horse and almost tumbled over her neck, but by sheer will he stayed upright.

You did say "quickly."

Kyril laughed at the duplicity of the horse's nature. She was secretive and mysterious on one hand, but she did have a wicked sense of humor and seemed intent on tormenting him.

Walking to the front of the inn, Kyril noticed a dozen men, some of them students from the wizard school, helping to put the finishing touches on rebuilding since the fire.

"Amazing," he said.

A woman looked over at him and smiled. She was the one they had helped earlier in saving her husband from being trapped in the inn.

"The wizards have been remarkable. I would have thought our inn was destroyed, but look." She waved her arm toward the door. "Good as new. We'll have patrons in it tonight."

"Still thinking about retiring?" Kyril asked.

The woman nodded her head. "Yes, my son will take over once we are all put together again."

"May I ask you a question about someone who might have been here two days ago?" Kyril asked.

She nodded.

"He is taller than me, brown hair, a few years older." Kyril knew that it was too generic, but didn't know what else to say. "Oh, and a gold ring on his right hand," he remembered.

"Ah, a good-looking fellow?"

Kyril didn't want to admit it, but grunted his agreement.

"Yes, he came in all dazed as if he didn't know where he was. Another man, a merchant named Sir Hughes from the ship joined him; he didn't seem real well either. They sat in the back but didn't talk too much.

"Did anyone else speak with them?"

The woman thought for a moment, then called out, "Gretchen!"

A woman in her twenties came over. She had medium brown hair down her back and clutched at her obviously pregnant stomach. A mark of dirt was smudged across one cheek.

"This is my daughter-in-law," said the woman, smiling broadly. Then she turned back to her. "This young wizard is asking if we saw anyone speak to the two men that sat at the back the other night. You know, the ones that were very quiet." Turning her attention back to Kyril she added, "Most of those we get here are parents of students and a few tradesmen. But these men were neither."

Kyril nodded his head and awaited an answer from Gretchen.

"Yes," she said. "There was someone else that joined them." She scrunched her eyes up trying to remember something. "Ah, it was a member of the wizard council."

Even though Kyril had expected it, he was still a bit surprised to actually hear it spoken out loud. "Marcus. Was it Councilor Marcus?"

Gretchen shook her head. "No, it wasn't him. It was…" She thought for a moment again, and then smiled broadly. "She is a strict one. I think it starts with an H. Oh yes, Halsey. I think it was council member Halsey. She came in as if looking for someone; she wasn't real happy."

Now, that news did shock Kyril. "Are you sure Marcus wasn't around?"

"I am sure, young wizard. The council members rarely come to town, and Wizard Halsey less so than the others. Not sure what brought her here…maybe to meet a new student. I don't know. But it was definitely her. Then they were joined by another man—dark hair in his twenties I would guess."

"Did you overhear any of their conversation?"

The older woman put her hands on her hips and gave Kyril a small glare. "Young man, it is not our place to gossip about what we overhear at our inn."

Kyril felt his face heat up a bit. "I'm sorry. But it's really important…my friend *did* heal your husband. Please, just this last favor?"

The woman's face softened. "Yes she did. And I am thankful." She turned to Gretchen. "Did you hear anything, dear?"

"I didn't hear anything, but…"

"Yes?" Kyril prodded her. "But what?"

"It sounds crazy, but…" Gretchen paused for a moment. "But when I was bringing over a refill one time I could have sworn that there was a brief shimmer of light, but I was tired. And it's probably all silly anyway. Soon after, Wizard Halsey left with the other man holding on to her arm as if to steady her. The other two stayed behind. Sounds crazy right?

"Must be the pregnancy," her mother-in-law said with a smile and a pat to Gretchen's belly.

"What did Kaldar and Sir Hughes do after that?" Kyril asked.

Gretchen shook her head. " That's when the fire started and everyone began panicking. "

Kyril thought about it a moment and realized he didn't have any other questions. He needed to get back and find Wizard Halsey now. Along with Kaldar, somehow she seemed to be in on the attack also.

"Thank you, thank you," Kyril said, his mind racing with possibilities. "And good luck with your inn."

Back outside he turned to call Solace when his mouth dropped open in surprise. Coming down from the sky was a brilliant, fierce red dragon. Two riders sat on top of him, one a young man a few years older than himself, and one a woman a bit older, wearing armor and with a bright sword at her side.

"Kyril Siravan, I presume," called out the man as they landed.

Kyril nodded his head, still in shock at seeing the dragon close up. "I am Liam DarSan Williams, Dragon Rider, and this is Kittoran, Battlemaster of the Realm. Your emperor has sent a message to my father, the king. Seems like we could use each other's help sorting out this mess."

CHAPTER THIRTY-FIVE

Sylvonna Hickory peered at herself in the ornate, gold-edged, full-length mirror and turned around with a short twirl. She smiled and let out a short chortle as the dress spun out from her slender frame. She ran her hands down over her sides, and the soft silky fabric barely scratched her fingers. It was the softest dress she had ever worn or felt and it somehow fit her perfectly.

She furrowed her brows for a brief moment trying to figure out how it had been made. The cloth had to have been sewn with spells by a powerful weaver. It would have been hard for even the most talented seamstress to make such a perfect fit. It fit her snugly in all the right places and then dropped with multiple folds of fabric down from her waist.

She smiled again as she noticed a split in the folds for her legs to move more easily—a perfect addition for a wizard of the earth who ended up fighting at times. A few hidden pockets could hold a myriad of other weapons.

Scrutinizing herself in the mirror once again, she noticed how the taupe material and deep blue layers made her own blue eyes pop out as a dazzling sparkle. She put a blue comb in the side of her chin-length blonde hair.

Walking over to a window, she looked north over the city of Hasari and toward her home of the Kingdom of Arc. It had been a bit over a year since she had been home. Her parents and older and younger sisters all lived in a small farming village where the meadows and desert met, an hour or so horse ride south of the capital city of Arc. Her mother had some minor wizarding abilities, enough to allow them to do better than others farming the land. However, ever since she had been young, her potential as a strong wizard was manifest.

Besides power, she had been blessed with a desire to learn, a friendly personality, and an ability to get along with most people. This had treated her well at the Wizard Conclave during her time at the school there. Sylvie almost felt guilty about wanting to be there again—over visiting her family. She loved them terribly, but the life of a farmer was not for her and she always felt a bit uncomfortable around them. She was most excited to speak with her mentor and High Wizard of the Conclave, Danijela Anwar. The recent help Sylvie had received from Zaidan, Prince of Gildan, in reaching more of her powers and becoming one with things, had strengthened her in many ways. She was excited to share the process with the High Wizard.

A knock on the door pulled her from her musings and she dropped a brush she had not realized she'd still been holding and moved toward the door. On the other side stood Wizard Merikh Shaaman along with two guards. All three looked resplendent in colorful and pressed clothes.

"Wizard Sylvonna." Merikh bowed his head to her as he spoke her name.

"Wizard Merikh," Sylvie said, "is everything ready?"

"Yes it is," Merikh said. "The king has a few minutes before the arrival of an important guest. His advisors and other nobles have gathered with him in the throne room to receive you and your companion."

As they began walking out into the hallway Sylvie turned her head around. "Where is Bale?"

"Oh, he'll be brought in once we are there," Merikh said. "We can't have him entering before you, now can we?"

Sylvie almost laughed out loud—but maintained her decorum thinking about what Bale's response would be to that. "Oh, no, we can't have that."

The closer they got to the throne room the more people on the side of the hallway bowed in deference to her. Beginning to feel a bit uncomfortable at all the attention, she turned instead to speak with Merikh.

"Have you had any other disruptions in Cyrene lately?" she asked. "Has anyone been stirring up trouble?"

"Not any more than usual," Merikh said. "Now that Wizard Roland Tyre has dismantled his golden empire and kept himself to Alaris, most of the relations we have with other kingdoms have grown more stable." The old wizard leaned in a bit closer and lowered his voice. "Though I am a bit concerned over the King Shafer's recent friendship, if truth be told."

Sylvie was about to ask more clarifying questions, but a sudden noise drew their attention. Coming from another door was Bale Nabhani, escorted by four guards. His head was down and his wrists were shackled in front of him. He had not even been granted a change of clean clothes.

He brought his eyes up, ran them over Sylvie's new outfit, and eventually they reached her face. She noticed a slight squint to the corners of his eyes and from the way he tightly clenched his jaw she surmised he may shatter some teeth before this was all done. But to his credit he didn't say anything or miss a step. Maybe he was learning.

"Ah, our friend, your companion," said Merikh with a flourish of his hand. "He will follow behind us."

"Why so many guards?" Sylvie asked, cognizant of her two to Bale's four, when she was definitely the more powerful of the two.

"The king shows great respect to you to allow only two guards," Merikh explained. "It's a sign of his trust in your keeping to your word. However, your companion is not to be trusted so more guards are needed to protect him from the king."

"He will not attack," Sylvie said.

Merikh raised his eyes as if questioning her statement. "We shall see."

Two trumpeters stood to either side of fifteen-foot-high double doors and drew their instruments to their lips. With three short bursts followed by a long blow, Merikh led Sylvie into the throne room. Despite having been in both the court of Arc and Gildan a few times, she almost tripped over herself at the display of gaudy wealth surrounding the room and those in it.

Men and women who were obviously wizards stood on either side of the room and with hands outstretched formed a colored rainbow over the entrance, leading all the way to the throne. King Shafer sat on a raised throne that appeared to be pure gold. Two gilded phoenix statues stood to either side of the throne. The young king himself had on layers of light colored silks and a crown that circled his head—both highlighting his brown dusty skin and dark hair and eyes. A seemingly warm but feigned smile covered his face as he crooked two fingers toward Merikh and beckoned them to him.

"My favored wizard and counselor Merikh, what have you brought to us today?" he said as if he didn't know.

Sylvie realized this was all a grand show for the benefit of his subjects. He didn't care about Sylvie or Bale. What the king lacked in respect he obviously tried to gain through showing his power over others. It was pathetic. Anger at the way he treated people began to rise from her heart, but she pushed it back down, knowing this was not the time for the king to get one of her lectures on serving the people.

But she couldn't let his arrogance go totally unchecked. As Merikh stepped aside and bowed, Sylvie instead raised her hands up in the air. The silks of her sleeves slid down to her elbows as power instantly came to her fingertips. Drawing from the ground beneath her feet, the stone pillars, and even the gold of the obnoxious throne, she clapped her hands in the air above her.

She felt more than saw Merikh stiffen next to her.

"What are you doing?" growled Bale behind her.

Two guards forced Bale to the ground as many in the room fell to their knees in awe of the power gathering around Sylvie. From outside she drew water into the air and formed the shape of a dragon high up in the room, where the rainbow colors of the other wizards were beginning to shimmer with a disruption of power.

Sylvie laughed with glee at the amount of power she held. She and the earth around her became one as she drew upon Prince Zaidan's teachings. In her mind she felt the power of the water dragon overhead and began to pour cold into it, forming a layer of ice.

Soon the entire dragon was a rotating ice sculpture in front of the crowd. Lowering her hands she directed it down on the floor, and then pulled the rainbow of the other wizards to the sculpture. She heard gasps from the wizards, surprised at her finesse and ability.

Sylvie was sure that she was no match for all of them together—not even close. But her delicate grace and subtle elegance had them in momentary shock. The colors of the rainbow splashed into the dragon ice sculpture to the delight of the crowd.

The look on King Shafer's previously arrogant face was priceless, but slowly was growing a bit dark and worried. She knew he had not expected her to show so much power. She knew it was dangerous and she had to balance out by also showing him deference. And so she did.

Going down on one knee she bowed her head low—he was a king of a sovereign land, and even though she was powerful, she was still only a wizard, and from another kingdom to boot. After hanging her head low for a substantial amount of time she raised it and caught a surprised expression on the king's face. She resisted the urge to laugh.

"King Shafer, I present to you this dragon ice sculpture. Its beauty is only rivaled by your grand palace, and the power the dragon represents is equal to the power and majesty of your people."

The king stood up slowly and clapped his hands together once. Then again, and again, and again, until he was applauding Sylvie. He stopped and with a raise of his hand directed her to stand. The rest of the crowd joined in the applause.

"And that's how you play a part," she whispered out of the corner of her mouth to Bale.

She heard him cough, but otherwise he stayed quiet.

The king resumed his seat and the crowd quieted down. Bale was then brought up next to Sylvie. When he didn't speak she elbowed him and he responded with a whispered murmur, keeping his face held forward. After a long and flourished bow to the king he spoke.

"My Lord King Shafer of Cyrene, my companion, the great wizard Sylvonna Hickory has just honored you beyond measure. Obviously she is a powerful wizard of eminent renown." Bale paused for a moment. "I am but a humble man, a mere mortal from a minor noble house in Gildan, and cannot think to even hold a candle to her power, but I beg your forgiveness."

The king nodded and glanced around at the gathering. They were looking at Bale with what appeared as agreement on their faces, but disdain at his appearance and lower status.

"More," Sylvie whispered and she felt Bale stiffen. She glanced at him through the corner of her eye and wondered how he was actually holding it together. They both knew that he had done nothing wrong and this apologizing would be hard for Bale's ego to take. But Sylvie figured this would be the quickest way to leave without causing more of a scene that they already had.

With a deep breath Bale continued. "My actions yesterday toward you and your friends were rash. As a representative of Gildan I pledge our emperor's good will to you, oh great King, and to your great and impressive kingdom."

"Wonderful, wonderful," King Shafer said with a prideful glance around the room. His people nodded their heads and appeared to bask in the glory of their young and powerful king. "I accept both the gift of a powerful wizard and the apology at her uncouth companion."

Sylvie elbowed Bale again.

"Will you stop that!" he said out of the corner of his mouth. "I didn't do anything."

"I'm just making sure," Sylvie said as she grinned and nodded at the king.

"Very well done," said Merikh to her side. "You do play the game well."

Sylvie chuckled. This was no game to her. She was here on a critical mission and she was only doing what she had to do to get on her way.

"Your Highness," Sylvie called out, and the room quieted down again. "Your hospitality has been gracious, but my companion and I are on a bit of a timely mission and would like to excuse ourselves to be on our way."

The king waved his hand in front of them. "Nonsense. I have another honored guest I would like you to meet."

A steward moved Sylvie and Bale to the side and shortly the horns at the door sounded again. A small crowd began to come through the door but Sylvie and Bale's view was blocked by guards with tall hats.

The king stood up in front of his throne and a broad smile covered his face. With a short nod of his head he spoke loudly.

"Wizards and honored guests, may I introduce you to my newest friend, the mighty, eloquent, and revered wizard, Gamal Turomi."

CHAPTER THIRTY-SIX

Joelle tried to walk calmly next to Kaldar but jumped every time someone glanced in their direction. She knew it would be only a short time before someone let Wizards Marcus and Fielding out of the dungeon room—and then they would come looking for her and Kyril.

"I'm sure he's fine," said Kaldar.

"I wish I had your optimism," Joelle said. "If you knew Kyril, he's…well…"

"A very powerful wizard?" Kaldar said with an arch of his brow.

His words caused Joelle to pause for a moment. Is that how people saw Kyril now? She covered her mouth with a chuckle.

"What's so funny?"

"Well," Joelle said, "I was going to say that Kyril is a bit timid, but I guess he has changed in the time I've known him."

"He didn't seem so timid down in the dungeons," Kaldar said as they turned a corner. "He took on two council members."

"That he did," Joelle said with a smile.

Running footsteps sounded down a hallway just in front of them. Joelle's stomach fell and she peered around anxiously. Her hand tightened around her staff as she prepared for a fight.

But Kaldar grabbed her arm and pulled her through a door, right before the intersection.

Joelle heard shouts and loud steps racing down the hallway outside of the door. All of a sudden she realized they were in the dark. Turning around, she bumped into Kaldar, who grunted in response.

With only a thought she brought up a small ball of light in the palm of her hand.

"Convenient," Kaldar said with a smirk.

The two turned to face the room, the pounding footsteps receding into the distance. Joelle knew they didn't have much time. Soon everyone would be on the lookout for them.

"It's an office," Kaldar said as he approached a large desk.

"Don't touch anything," Joelle called out.

She studied the room. It was not one she had been to before. The sturdy desk sat in front of what she thought would be a window that faced the gardens outside, but currently was covered by a heavy blue drape.

Books filled shelves on one wall, and another small table with three chairs sat in another corner. The office was clean and neat—almost as if it hadn't been used recently. Except for three pieces of paper on the desk.

Walking up next to Kaldar, Joelle glanced down at the papers. With a light finger she pushed them aside so she could see all three. As she began to read them a sick feeling began to fill her.

"It's him," Joelle murmured.

"Him who?" Kaldar asked.

"The traitor," Joelle added. "This is their room. These papers…one is a summary about the medallions; almost as if it was a small report written for them from someone. This one"—she pointed to another—"is a list of wizards and apprentices…many of whom I know. And the ones I know are all wizards of the mind."

"And the third one?" Kaldar asked, reaching for it.

Joelle batted his hand back and grabbed it herself.

"I thought you said not to touch anything," Kaldar growled.

Joelle ignored his taunt and picked up the paper in her hand. It was blank on the top. She flipped it over and stared at the list of names hastily written there. There shouldn't be any connection between them, but all were familiar to her…and one was standing only a foot away.

She took a step back from Kaldar and studied him for a moment. Could Kyril have been right?

"What is it, Joelle?" Kaldar asked. "What did you find?" He tried to step closer, but Joelle backed up farther.

"Tell me the truth!" she demanded, anger filling her. Perhaps she had been too trusting.

"What are you talking about?"

She shoved the paper into Kaldar's face. "How did your name get on this paper? Sir Hughes from the ship, yours, a student, and Wizard Halsey. Why is your name here, Kaldar? What is your connection to these three?"

Joelle's voice rose and she positioned her staff in front of her. Kaldar's eyes flicked around the room as if searching for a way out. Finally she had caught him in his lie.

"I…I…" Kaldar stuttered. Then he took a step backward and fell into a chair. His right hand rubbed a spot on the side of his head. "I don't know what to say. I…I…" His fist slammed down hard on the armrest. "I can't remember, Joelle!" he shouted. "I told you I can't remember who I am!"

Joelle glanced back toward the door and hoped no one had heard his roar. A loud sigh from Kaldar turned her back to him. His head hung low, his shoulders slumped, and eyes downcast to the ground.

"Help me," he said, this time in a pitiful whisper.

His anguish caused a lump to rise in Joelle's throat and she relaxed her stance. With cautious steps she moved closer to him and knelt down by his side. She reached a hand forward and laid it lightly on his knee.

Kaldar's hand snaked out and grabbed hers and held it tight. She resisted at first and tried to pull away—at the same time summoning her powers to be used if needed. Kaldar's head lifted and there was a new fire in his eyes. A hunger for something.

"Tell me," he whispered hoarsely, still holding tightly onto her hand. "Tell me how we met. Tell me about myself."

Joelle's heart skipped a beat. She took a deep breath and let it out slowly to steady herself.

"You seriously cannot remember?" she asked.

"No, not much," Kaldar said. "It's fuzzy, but…I do remember a ship—and you, sometimes."

"Do you remember kissing me?" Joelle said without thinking, and then felt her face heat up with the question.

"That is something I would like to remember, but no, I'm sorry I do not."

"Well, that's fine then." Joelle regained control over her emotions and tried to cover it up a bit with anger. "I'm sure it didn't mean anything to you anyway. Do you always kiss stray girls you find on ships? Is that your little game? Well, let me tell you about myself. I am a fool for falling for those deep dark eyes and roguish good looks of yours. You're too old for me anyway. I don't even know why I believe you. Maybe Kyril is right. How else did your name get on this paper in this office? Someone here knows you."

Kaldar's head had dropped during her tirade and now with his hand still covering hers she felt his body shaking a bit. Maybe she really was a fool for letting her tongue rattle on so much. She had hurt his feelings now.

"Kaldar?" she said, trying to get his attention. "I'm sorry. I'm not used to these types of situations. Don't be sad."

Kaldar brought his head up slowly but instead of being sad or mad, he was smiling and trying not to laugh.

"Oh my, Joelle, you are quite a woman, aren't you?" he said.

Joelle flashed her eyes at him in anger.

"Oh, don't be mad," he said. "I meant that as a compliment of the highest standard. I would be lucky to get a kiss from you."

Joelle let the anger subside and she felt the corners of her own mouth tugging up a bit. "I guess I do get carried away sometimes. But truly, you do not remember?"

He shook his head and at the same time, Joelle used their physical connection to delve once again into his mind. She still felt a struggling there, but nothing to imply that he was telling anything other than the truth.

"About the paper?" Kaldar finally spoke as he stood up, releasing Joelle's hand.

She was surprised at the momentary loss as he removed his hand from hers.

"Why is my name there with those other two?" Kaldar asked. "That's the question we need to ask ourselves."

Before Joelle could answer, they heard voices outside of the door. Frantically, Joelle peered around the room, wishing for Kyril's transporting ability. There was no other door. But…

"There's always a hidden door," she mumbled.

Kaldar waited for her to say more, confusion written across his face.

She ran toward a bookcase and began running her fingers back and forth on multiple shelves. Finally she heard a *click* and the shelf moved slightly, opening up a small space behind it. At the same time the doorknob to the room began to turn slowly, the voices of two people growing louder. With hardly a moment left, Joelle pulled Kaldar after her behind the shelf and closed it behind them just in time.

One of the voices was distinctly that of Wizard Marcus. Joelle realized they must have been in his office. He must be the traitor.

With heart pounding, she turned around and found they were in a short, rough-hewn hallway.

"We have to get out of here," Joelle said into Kaldar's ear. They couldn't take the chance that Marcus and his companions would open the shelf and find them there.

There was a narrow passage leading to their right, and a small narrow door in front of them. Moving quickly so their presence wouldn't be noticed, Kaldar tried to open the door but it was locked. Joelle pushed him aside and with barely a trickle of power into the door lock she used her wizard magic to unlock it. They entered a room barely big enough to hold a bed. And on that bed lay someone wrapped in a blanket.

Making the light brighter in her hand while moving closer, Joelle peered down.

"Turn them over," Joelle told Kaldar.

Kaldar nodded, leaned over, and gently pulled the person onto their back.

It was a woman. She shuddered a breath and opened up her eyes.

Joelle gasped out loud.

"Wizard Halsey, what are you doing here?"

Halsey shook her head back and forth a few times, while her eyes darted between Joelle and Kaldar.

"I do not know," she said with a quiet rasp. "And who are you again?"

CHAPTER THIRTY-SEVEN

Joelle glanced at Kaldar and then back at Halsey with concern. She had *just* talked to her in the entranceway of the wizard school. She didn't seem like the kind of woman to joke around with her. Joelle shook her head with the thought that something definitely wasn't right—first Kaldar and then Halsey.

"Why is everyone losing their memory?" Joelle said.

Halsey's eyes went wide as she glanced back and forth between them. Slowly she sat up and moved her feet toward the floor. Her cloak got tangled up around her and Joelle reached over and helped her.

"Who are you two?" Halsey asked as she stood up. "And where am I?"

A sound down the hallway alerted Joelle to possible danger. "I don't have time to explain right now, but we need to get out of here."

Joelle reached her hand toward Halsey to bring her along but she pulled her hand back. "I'm not going anywhere until I know what's going on."

"I don't remember much of anything either, but I trust her," Kaldar added. "Let's go." He grabbed hold of Halsey who was quite a bit shorter and more slender than he was, and pulled her by the arm.

Halsey resisted for a moment, but eventually she relented and went along. Walking back into the narrow hallway, Joelle directed them away from the office where Marcus and the other wizard were. Halsey stumbled once and Kaldar kept her from falling.

After turning down a short hallway, Joelle stopped and turned back toward Halsey. "I can help." She brought her hands up to the wizard's head. "I'm a healer."

Halsey flinched a bit, but let Joelle touch her. Her skin was hot with fever but Joelle quickly dove into the council woman's body and felt along the lines of her muscles and veins. Joelle heard a gasp as she energized her and put her body on the road to healing. She wanted to visit her mind also, but there wasn't time at the moment.

Pulling away, she once more directed them down a hallway only to pause at another crossroad.

"This way leads outside," Halsey said pointing in one direction.

"How do you remember that?" Joelle asked, a bit suspicious. Was the woman deceiving her and leading them somewhere dangerous? She had been asking a lot of questions of Joelle just a short time before.

"I just do," Halsey said seemingly perturbed by the entire situation. "But it's all so fuzzy."

Kaldar gave Joelle a questioning look. But they would follow her lead. They did need to get out of the secret passageways. If she was going to be caught, she would rather it be a public place where she could plead her case. With a nod of her head, Joelle followed the others down another short hallway so narrow that they had to turn sideways at one point to get through.

A small maintenance door about three feet tall was at the end. Kaldar reached it and pushed hard. At first it didn't budge but eventually there was a loud *squeak* and the door swung out far enough for them to crouch down and squirm their way out.

Blinking for a moment in the bright light, Joelle glanced around. Kaldar sneezed and she gave him a warning look. They were at an outside corner of the wizard school and for the moment shielded by a small grouping of bushes, two of which had fragrant white flowers covering them—most likely the culprit of the sneeze.

Both Kaldar and Halsey appeared to be waiting for further instruction from her. Their deference made her uncomfortable. Both were older than her, and council member Halsey was obviously a more experienced wizard. What should she do?

"We can't go back inside," she said in a whisper, mostly to herself. She wished she had the disciplined mind of a wizard of the mind like Kyril, but she didn't. And talking helped her to figure things out. "Marcus and the others may find us. We need to find Kyril, or the medallion, or something to help us. Maybe I could go back to healer Grantham or to council member Amanda. They would believe me." She looked at Halsey. "At least they would believe you, I think." She threw her hands up in the air. "Oh, I don't know!"

Kaldar put a hand on her arm and she jumped out of her reverie. She wasn't getting anywhere with this line of reasoning.

"What about us?" Kaldar asked her.

Joelle nodded her head. He was right. What about him and Halsey? What did they have in common? Both had a hard time remembering things. That was a connection. Both were on the list on the desk in the office.

"Sir Hughes, the merchant!" she said with excitement. "He was one of the other names on the list with you two."

Halsey appeared utterly lost, but Kaldar nodded his head, following her logic.

"If we can find him, maybe we can figure out what's going on," Kaldar said.

"Yes, we must get back to the town," Joelle said. "With the destruction yesterday to the docks, no other ships have come or gone so he's most likely still here."

Stepping out from behind the bushes, Joelle directed the three of them across the lawn, over the few walkways, past fountains spewing water high into the air, and toward the gate of the wizard school. Two guards moved out in front of them and Joelle groaned inside.

"We have orders that no one leaves the grounds," said one of the guards, a large burly fellow who appeared to take his job seriously.

"Why?" Joelle asked, standing in front of her two companions. "Has there been another attack?"

The guard shook his head. "An escape from the dungeons. A dangerous wizard from Gildan."

Joelle would have giggled at the thought of Kyril being described as dangerous if she wasn't so nervous.

"Who did this order come from?" she asked, already knowing what the answer would be.

"From Council member Fielding on orders from acting headmaster wizard Marcus," said the second guard, this one was trying to peer around Joelle and see who the others were. Kaldar was taller and stood out, and Halsey stayed behind him. "He has taken charge while a new headmaster is chosen."

"Of course he has," Joelle mumbled to herself.

"Excuse me, miss," said the first guard, "but you will need to go back to the school now. Classes are still in session today."

Joelle's face turned red and her ire rose. They thought of her as a *student* still! She clenched her fists and considered blasting them out of the way, but she didn't want to attract more attention.

"I'm sure his directions did not include a member of the council," Joelle said, allowing some of her anger to come forth. "Wizard Halsey has important business to attend to." She pulled Halsey up in the front with her.

The two guards looked back and forth at each other, clearly at a loss of what to do. Finally one of the guards bowed his head toward the wizard with respect.

"I will tell Marcus that you two were vigilant guards," Halsey said. Joelle noticed that her voice was a bit unsure, but she pushed on nonetheless. "I'm sure you will be rewarded well, but as this young woman has said, I…*we*…have important business to attend to."

Joelle was a bit surprised at how deftly Halsey picked up on her lead.

"Please," Halsey said politely, but the fire that grew in her eyes was one of frustration that came out more as anger.

The two guards surely didn't want to deal with the wrath of a council member. They parted to the side and with a wave of the larger one's hand, directed the three of them out of the gates and on to the road that led to the small dockside town.

After a few minutes of silence and now out of earshot of the guards, Joelle let out a long breath. "That was close. Thank you," she said to Halsey.

She grinned a bit but shook her head. "I'm not sure what is going on around here, but I figured if I am really a council member of the school, I had some power to exert over those two. I want to know what happened to me as much as you both do. Now, can you fill me in on who you are and what we are doing?"

A small trail a bit off the main road wound its way down the hill and toward the small harbor. Joelle led them this way rather than toward the more crowded road. Heeding Kyril's earlier warning she didn't know who to trust, and so tried to stay away from as many people as she could.

As they walked she filled Halsey in on what had happened recently that she didn't seem to remember. As the three of them spoke, some memories began to return to both Kaldar and Halsey, and they could start piecing together a short timeline of events. Joelle figured that finding the merchant would fill in the rest of the blanks.

After an hour they approached the town. All of a sudden, a loud screech filled the air and the three of them dropped to the ground behind an old dilapidated stone building. Turning their heads up above them, all three gasped.

"A dragon," Kaldar said, echoing all their thoughts.

"It's Dragon Rider Liam and the Battlemaster," Joelle said. "They said they would return."

"Who is with them?" Kaldar asked.

Joelle squinted against the glare of the day and then clapped her hands with glee. "It's Kyril! Looks like they are heading back to the school."

"The wizard who lost the medallion?" Halsey asked. "The one you came with?"

"Yes," Joelle said. She felt better about things than she had earlier. If Kyril was safe and with the Dragon Rider she didn't have to worry about him. But she *was* worried about Kaldar and Halsey—and their memories.

They moved quickly the rest of the way to the docks. She was surprised at how much had been repaired already. Things would soon return to normal. That's what happened when wizards were involved. The school made sure to care for the town around them.

Heading toward the *Good Night's Rest*, where she had helped the innkeeper earlier, Joelle noticed quite a few people standing together and staring up in the sky—apparently having just watched the flight of the dragon. Prince Liam, the Dragon Rider, had been seen often at the wizard school when Joelle attended.

"Excuse me," she said walking up to the only one she recognized—the innkeeper's wife. "I'm looking for Sir Hughes, a merchant. Would you happen to know where he might be?"

The woman's eyes squinted in a bit of suspicion.

"Please," Joelle said, confused at her reaction. "You do remember me, don't you?"

The woman nodded her head and gave a brief bob of it to wizard Halsey.

"I'm trying to find a merchant from Khazer," Joelle tried to explain, thinking that maybe she hadn't understood before. "Hughes is his name. He has his son with him."

"All of a sudden everyone is asking about Sir Hughes and these two?" the woman waved her hands to include Kaldar and wizard Halsey.

"Everyone?" Joelle asked. She was concerned if someone else had figured out the connection.

"Yes, the young wizard from Gildan just left," the woman said.

Joelle relaxed a bit. "That's my friend, Kyril. What did you tell him? Please, it's important."

"That's what he said," the woman said. "Sir Hughes met with this man,"—she pointed toward Kaldar—"right before Wizard Halsey came in and joined them with another man."

Joelle turned toward her companions. "You two have met before?"

Kaldar and Halsey only shrugged.

"You can trust them," Joelle said. "They're with me, but they've lost some memories."

The woman's eyes went wide with surprise before she finally gave Joelle some information. "They are not the only ones." She beckoned the three of them with the crook of her finger. "Come with me and I'll take you to Sir Hughes."

With a nod of her head, Joelle told Kaldar and Halsey to follow, and the three of them hurried to keep up with the woman. She passed by her own inn, a general store, and then stopped in front of a smaller inn. She paused for a moment, then walked up the single step and into the building.

The room was dark with only a few candles burning. It was obviously still being repaired and only a few people sat at the tables in the room. The woman pointed toward the back where two people sat in the shadows. One was the young merchant's son who had been so rude to her on the ship, the other was…

"Sir Hughes," said the woman, interrupting Joelle's observations. "He seems to have lost most of his memories also. His son hasn't left his side."

CHAPTER THIRTY-EIGHT

Joelle walked up to the table where Sir Hughes and his son, Maddox sat. She stood there for a moment not quite knowing what to say before Maddox turned his head and noticed her there. A brief flash of annoyance moved across his face but then his head dropped in apparent exhaustion.

"Healer, is there anything you can do for him?" Maddox said. The arrogance of his earlier outbursts on the ship was all but left behind at the sight of his poor father.

"I'm not sure," Joelle said as she stepped forward.

Placing both hands on either side of his head she once again—for the third time—tried to heal someone with recent memory loss. The man jerked under the use of her power, but she continued on. There had to be something she could learn from all of this. His mind was similar to Kaldar's—all jumbled up with what only as she could describe were holes. Both were slightly different than Halsey's. She figured that Halsey's was distinctive because she was a wizard and had additional training to protect herself from such harm.

She tried to realign strands and neurons in Sir Hughes's mind but it was difficult and taxing and she didn't know if she was doing anything helpful or not. It had already been a long day and she had used her powers multiple times. After she'd done what she could, she staggered for a moment until Maddox brought over a chair for her.

"Where am I?" Hughes mumbled after a minute. He glanced around at the group in obvious confusion.

The rest joined them at the table but no one said anything for a few minutes until Maddox started explaining to his father where they were. All listened intently, but Joelle tried hard to see the connection between her three companions with memory loss. They were all from different kingdoms with varied backgrounds, occupations, and ages.

"All right," Joelle said. "What is the connection between the three of you?"

"We both were on the ship," said Kaldar pointing from himself to Hughes.

"But I was not," Halsey said.

"Supposedly we were together for a brief time in the inn next door," Kaldar said to Halsey.

"And what do you all remember?" Joelle asked.

Her question was met with silence as everyone sat in thought.

"I remember coming into Belor with my son," began Hughes, "but not much after that."

"But Father," said Maddox, "don't you remember the trip here, me almost drowning, and um…" He glanced sideways at Joelle with a bit of embarrassment. "…the wizard here saving my life?"

Hughes shook his head, clearly confused. His head dropped down.

"The medallion," he whispered.

"What did you say?" Joelle asked.

"I…I don't know. I think I remember a medallion on the ship. A golden medallion with immense power."

"Yes, Kyril's medallion helped to save your son," Joelle said.

"The medallion," repeated Kaldar.

Joelle turned now to him. "What do you know about the medallion?"

"I don't know," Kaldar said slowly. "I'm starting to remember my ride into Belor. I had met a man on the way there. He talked about a medallion. Then I helped you to the ship. I spent some time withi the other man and his friends but they pushed me away from their small group." The more he spoke the more he seemed to remember. "You and Kyril saved Maddox there, and I remember Sir Hughes wanting the medallion and then…then…"

Kaldar slammed his fist to the table. "This is infuriating. It doesn't make sense. Why can't I remember what happened after that? You told me that we even kissed!"

All eyes turned on Joelle and with the instant heat on her face she was sure she was bright red.

"Sorry," Kaldar said with a small grin.

Joelle tried to ignore the stares. Something was coming together. A timeline of sorts, but she still couldn't grasp what it meant. She turned to Halsey and spoke. "And you? What do you remember, Councilor Halsey?"

"The attack on the school. Someone killed the headmaster. Then…then…the medallion…I remember you using it to try and heal him. Then things get a bit foggy."

"The medallion again," Joelle said. "Each of you remember the medallion. But I know Kyril didn't do this to you. He didn't attack the wizard school. He was fighting someone who did. Wizard Halsey, please, can't you remember anything else?"

Halsey shook her head. "After seeing the headmaster die, the council gathered together and…Marcus…"

Her words trailed off, but the rest of them strained to hear what she had to say.

"What about Marcus?" asked Joelle with a hand on Halsey's shoulder. She shook the wizard a few times when she didn't answer.

"Oh…what?" Halsey seemed to come out of a fog. "Nothing. I can't remember anything else until you woke me in that room."

"What does it all mean?" Maddox asked angrily. "What did you do to my father?"

"Nothing," Joelle said firmly. "I did nothing to your father. But someone did, and from what I can tell the problems seemed to have shifted from your father, to Kaldar, and then to Halsey—all centered around the medallion."

"A shifter?" Halsey's eyes went big and wide. "I thought they were only a myth. But that could explain it."

"What is a shifter?" asked Kaldar.

"It is said in myths and legends that one ability of wizards who used their magic for dark purposes is the ability to shift. Like a shadow they move in and out of other people's bodies. They take control, leaving the victim helpless at the time…but also physically unaltered so no one else around can tell the difference. They seemed to maintain their own thoughts, but also retain the knowledge of their victim."

"They didn't teach me that at the school," Joelle said, a little suspicious at the sudden information.

"No, we don't teach rumors," Halsey said, with a grim look on her face. "But as professors we do a lot of research. I've heard Marcus and the other wizards of the mind discuss their possibility before."

"Gamal," Joelle said softly. Could he have developed this power? Or did he hire someone? "It started on the ship, but now it could be anyone at the school. Anyone at all."

Halsey nodded her head. "And they'll be very hard to find."

"Unless we find the medallion," Joelle said as she jumped back out of her chair. "Each of you remembers the medallion. The shifter was after it and used each of you to get closer to it. I need to get back to the school. I need to find Kyril and warn him!"

"I can hire a carriage for us," said Sir Hughes. "But I don't understand why I can't remember things."

"I'm not sure," Joelle said, "but maybe the shifter inhabiting your body altered your memories in some way."

"Well, I want mine back," Kaldar growled. Halsey and Sir Hughes voiced their agreement.

Joelle nodded as they all stood and walked outside. "First we need to find the medallion. That is the key."

Soon all five of them were riding up the hill in a carriage and back to the school.

"What about the lockdown?" asked Kaldar. "How will we get into the school?"

"I will get us in as I got us out," said Halsey. "I'm not going to let any imposter ruin this school or harm anyone else."

They all rode in silence, deep in their own thoughts. It was now late afternoon and the breeze cooled the hot, humid air. Joelle leaned her head back and closed her eyes for a moment, wondering what Sylvie was up to and when she and Kyril would get back to Gildan. They were still no closer to finding the second medallion.

***

Sylvie and Bale had been stunned to find that Gamal was in Cyrene and in league with the young King Shafer.

Upon hearing the introduction they had both tried to turn and run but a wall of guards—most of which Sylvie surmised were wizards, stood in front of them. The king had beckoned them along with Gamal to his private audience chamber which now they were just entering.

Sylvie had rarely seen such overdone opulence. Gold and silver adorned everything in the room, with a large throne at one end. The tops of the walls were adorned with custom carved crown moldings made up of various creatures of magic. Four servants stood at attention as they entered awaiting their orders.

Sylvie wasn't sure of the amount of power Gamal had and with the addition of King Shafer's other wizards with them she decided to wait before fighting her way out.

"Nice to see you again, dear wizard Sylvonna Hickory." Gamal said his first words to her since being escorted away from the large throne room. "Please sit."

Sylvie moved forward but before she did Gamal's hand snaked out and grabbed a hold of her forearm.

"You don't have it yet, do you?" Gamal asked.

"Have what?" Sylvie answered with feigned ignorance.

"Don't play games with me," Gamal's voice rose louder. The servants eyes flinched but they stayed in their positions.

Black tendrils of power swirled around the black medallion hanging from his neck. Sylvie tried to pull away but he held her too tight.

"Leave her alone," Bale said trying to step in front of Gamal. "As a member of the Gildan nobility I place you, Gamal Turami under arrest for the attempted murder of our emperor and his son."

Sylvie almost groaned. Now was not the time for Bale to show his courage or loyalty to his kingdom.

Without any warning as to his intentions, and with only a small flick of his hand, Gamal threw Bale against the wall without missing a step.

"Bale!" Sylvie screamed and pulled herself away from Gamal. The ground underneath them shook with her fury.

"Get me some refreshments, boy," Gamal bellowed at the king.

King Shafer's eyes went wide at being called boy, but after a brief hesitation turned to his servants with orders. They all scrambled away but one hung back a bit as if wanting to help Bale and Sylvie.

"Now!" King Shafer ordered her to follow the others, "Unless you would like to clean the latrines."

With a brief glance back at Bale on the ground, she turned and followed the others while Sylvie leaned down to check on Bale. She was regretting her decision to not try and fight her way out early. She was fairly certain she could still get away from Gamal, and maybe even the other wizards, but she was worried what would happen to Bale.

Gamal picked up Bale by the scruff of his shirt and then hauled him back to his feet and pushed him onto a couch where Sylvie joined him a moment later.

"You and your pathetic friends have no idea what trouble you are in," Gamal said. He rubbed his bald head with his thick fingers. "I will have Kyril's medallion soon...very soon."

Sylvie tried not to gasp, but couldn't help her reaction. She hoped that Kyril was all right and that Gamal was just trying to scare them.

The servants returned and began setting out glasses of refreshments for them all when Gamal took a hold of his medallion in his hand and cocked his head to one side as if listening to or concentrating on something that the rest of them could not hear. His eyes closed briefly then quickly popped back open. He stood up and turned his attention back to the king.

"I have something I must attend to," Gamal said. Then turning to the four other wizards in the room continued, "I hold each of you responsible for keeping these two foreigners here while I am gone. I assume there will not be any problems."

The wizards nodded, a semblance of fear in their eyes, and resumed positions closer to Sylvie and Bale.

Gamal left the room and Sylvie gave Bale a quick look. This could be their chance to escape. She would have to act now and take the other wizards by surprise. But Bale shook his head at her with eyes that pleaded for her to wait. She couldn't understand why he would do that.

The servants resumed delivering their drinks to the king and the wizards.

"What about ours?" Bale said.

The king laughed out loud and once again Sylvie wondered what Bale was up to. He shouldn't goad them so. They needed to escape.

As if to emphasize his control over the two, King Shafer raised his glass high in the air and toasted with the four wizards. With long gulps they all drained the liquid.

"Would you like more, Your Highness?" said the servant who had lingered before.

The king and the four wizards pushed their glasses forward for her to refill them.

"Would you like food?" the servant asked.

"Yes, bring us some to eat in front of our guests," laughed the king, clearing enjoying his power over his guests.

With a nod of her head the servant sent the other three out of the room to fetch some food.

During a moment of silence one of the wizards sunk to the ground, followed quickly by the others. The king tried to stand up and had time to call out only once before he too fell to the ground.

"What happened?" Sylvie jumped to her feet, followed by Bale.

Bale turned to the servant. "Thank you. The emperor is in your debt."

The servant smiled.

Sylvie was confused, but Bale quickly cleared it up.

"She works for the spymaster," Bale said. "With a hand signal from me she knew what needed to be done."

"You didn't kill them did you?" Sylvie asked.

"No, but I should have," Bale said. "Arrogant wizards. All of them!"

He seemed to realize what he said and tried to stumble through an apology to Sylvie. She understood what he met.

"You need to go now," the servant pointed toward a back door. "Through the servant quarters and out to the back. Then you are on your own I'm afraid."

"What about you?" Bale asked with concern.

"I'll be fine," said the servant. "They'll never suspect me." She lifted a drink up to her own lips and drank.

Sylvie understood. "Let's go," she said to Bale.

CHAPTER THIRTY-NINE

Coming to the gate of the school, the carriage that Sir Hughes had hired for the group came to a stop. Where before there had been only two guards, now there stood at least a dozen, and Joelle knew that some of them were definitely wizards.

Something had happened. Something dangerous.

The group stepped out of the carriage and soon were surrounded by a half a dozen of them. One stepped out front; he held no sword, but looked ready to bring his power to bear. Joelle grasped her staff in her hand, but as good as a fighter as she was, her healing had always taken precedence, and looking around she knew they were outnumbered.

"Council member Wizard Halsey and Healer Joelle El'San, your presence is requested in the grand hall," said the man. "Who are these others?"

Joelle looked at Halsey, supposing she would take the lead, but once again she seemed to be momentarily confused. With a quick sigh Joelle stepped forward. "This is Kaldar, a friend, along with Sir Hughes and his son Maddox, merchants from Khazer. They are under my protection and have information about the recent activities here at the school." She stretched it a bit at that last part. They *might* have had information, but couldn't remember it if they did.

The guard raised his eyebrows as if deciding if what she said was true or not, but after a brief hesitation he shrugged his shoulders and turned to the other guards.

"Take them all in. The wizard council can figure this out."

As they stepped past the gate, Joelle heard a noise over toward the stables. Whinnies of Cremelinos were followed by an impressive dragon roar. The commotion actually comforted Joelle a bit. If the dragon was there, then that meant that Kyril was also there. Hopefully he had found the medallion and they could find who was behind this madness.

The five were escorted by six guards up the steps and into the foyer of the wizard school. Upon seeing the austere group, apprentice students walking down the hallway scrambled away, books in hand. However, two stood still as the group passed and gave a quick nod to Joelle before moving away themselves. They were Emory and Lisbeth, the two school wizards that she had met in the stable with Grantham, Liam, and the Battlemaster. Seeing them there signaled to Joelle that hopefully events were turning better.

"What was that?" growled Kaldar softly at her side. "Why are you smiling?"

"We'll be fine," she said. "Everything should be under control."

Kaldar grumbled a bit and pulled against the guard that held his hands behind his back. "Some control."

They soon reached two thick double doors where four other guards were stationed. With a nod of her head toward the guard that escorted the group, one of them turned and pulled on the gold handle. The room was ablaze with light both from candles and from magical globes of light. At the far end of the room sat a sturdy rectangular table, around which sat a multitude of people. Standing at one end was Dragon Rider Liam and the Realm's Battlemaster Kittoran. Both stood soberly listening to someone speaking at the table. They all looked up as soon as Joelle and her party entered.

Where was Kyril? Joelle looked around the room and thought that maybe things were not in control at all.

"Wizard Halsey," said Marcus, standing up from the table, "good of you to join us. Please come and take your place at the table and explain to us what you are doing in the presence of these troublemakers."

Halsey's eyes went wide and she glanced at Joelle, but Joelle barely paid her any attention. Instead she strode forward with as large of steps as she could muster. A guard jumped out to stop her, but Joelle waved her staff in the air and he went flying off to the side.

Battlemaster Kittoran's face went dark and she moved to intercept Joelle. However, Liam touched her arm softly, and though anger filled her face she relented and stayed where she was.

"Healer Joelle," said Liam, his face serious, but his eyes holding a glint of mirth as he watched her throw the guard to the side. "In light of circumstances here today, we thought you may want to add any thoughts to this proceeding."

"She escaped with Kaldar and helped Kyril lock me in the dungeon," Marcus said, spit flying from his lips, "and they have defied the rules of the school ever since they have arrived, bringing chaos with them everywhere they go."

"Chaos not of our doing, but yours," Joelle said as she stopped a few feet from the table.

Those on her side of the table twisted in their chairs to watch the exchange. Joelle recognized Fielding, Warren, and Amanda. On the other side of the table sat a scribe and Grantham the healer. He looked at her apologetically. He obviously was also there against his will.

"I am not your prisoner," Joelle continued. "I attended this school, graduated as a wizard, and have spent an honorable year serving at the Wizard Academy in Gildan."

"Where you aligned yourself with that evil man from there," Marcus said, "and travelled here with the intent to kill our headmaster and take over our school."

"I…" Joelle opened up her mouth to defend herself, but just then a side door opened. Ruthorford and Thane—the two wizard students she was sure had taken the medallion from Kyril—entered the room.

"Kyril!" Joelle called out upon seeing Kyril entering behind them.

He lifted his head and smiled at her. Hanging around his neck was the medallion once again. Joelle breathed out a sigh of relief.

"You!" Marcus pointed his finger at Kyril. "You have brought this trouble on us."

Fielding joined him on his feet and both appeared ready to pounce.

"Enough," Kittoran called out. "This will be a peaceful meeting. We will soon get to the bottom of this."

"Sit down, Marcus," said Amanda from beside him. "The Battlemaster is correct. This is a serious matter we are discussing here. Hot heads will not make things any better."

Joelle tried not to smile at Amanda's chiding. Both Marcus and Fielding sat down…but not before Marcus gazed hungrily at the medallion that Kyril wore.

"It's him," Joelle whispered to Kaldar who had stepped up to her side during the confrontation. "It's Marcus, I'm sure. He's been after us the entire time. He must be the shifter now."

She felt Kaldar stir next to her. His body was taut and ready to fight if needed. If the shifter had indeed taken control of Marcus, he could use the wizard's power, which was much greater than Joelle's own. She glanced at the Battlemaster and Dragon Rider Liam, but could not discern their thoughts on the matter.

Joelle sat down with the others. Kaldar, Sir Hughes, and Maddox stood off to the side. Kyril sat down at the head of the table in front of the Battlemaster, who along with Liam stayed standing.

"We have been sent by King Darius DarSan Williams to oversee the discussion of a new headmaster for the wizard school of the Realm," the Battlemaster began. "He gives his condolences about the death of Headmaster Penrose, whom he had appointed himself. Once the new headmaster is appointed we can continue on with the investigation into the attack. But leadership is needed at this time."

"And why are these others here for this formal occasion?" Marcus waved his hand around the room. "The constitution of the school is quite clear that a new headmaster is to be chosen by those remaining council members. Not all of these people."

"Do you deny my right to be here?" Liam said. His jaw was clenched hard and his eyes smoldered.

"Of course not…" Marcus struggled to find his words. "As a Dragon Rider you are above our laws, and as a prince of the Realm you are always entitled to be here; it's these others I have a problem with—some aren't even wizards."

"I'm not even sure why I am here either," Sir Hughes said. "I will be happy to leave."

At the end of the table, Kyril jumped out of his seat, almost knocking his chair into Liam, who had been standing behind him with Kittoran. He moved away from the table a few feet. "No one is leaving until we determine who the traitor is and a new headmaster is chosen."

Joelle was surprised by Kyril's outburst. His features were slightly twisted and his hand held onto the medallion that hung from his neck. It had been a hard few days and he must have finally reached the breaking point.

Sir Hughes stopped mid-step and looked around. "My son and I are not wizards," he said quietly, "and as such do not belong here."

"All will be made clear very soon, Sir Hughes," Kyril said, "and then you can get back to your merchant trade."

Now it was time for Marcus to stand up. With a red face, he pointed to Kyril, but spoke to the woman behind him.

"Battlemaster, this young wizard from Gildan has no authority here. In fact…"

He didn't get much further before a light shot out from the medallion around Kyril's neck and struck Marcus in the shoulder. Joelle gasped, unable to believe that Kyril had attacked him. Something wasn't right.

"As holder of the medallion I have all the authority I need," Kyril said. "And with that authority I declare that you, Wizard Marcus, are a traitor to this school and should be stripped of your council status and have no vote in these proceedings. From what I hear you have coveted the position of headmaster for many years, and now have orchestrated events to make that happen."

Oh no! Joelle thought to herself. She pushed her chair away from her table and grasped her staff.

"Kyril!" she shouted at him. "What are you doing? This is no way to find the truth."

CHAPTER FORTY

Everyone turned to Joelle. She didn't trust Marcus, but Kyril should not have attacked him.

"Everybody needs to sit down," Kittoran said, pulling her sword from her scabbard. "Or I'll have you all arrested. We will hear the accusations one at a time and evidence will be presented. If there is a traitor in our midst, then he or she will be taken and punished and a new headmaster will be appointed."

All sat down except for Kyril, who still stood a few feet away from the table with one hand clenched around the medallion. A crazed look covered his face. Joelle wondered what he was doing.

"We've taken long enough here," Kyril said with a wave of his hand. Off to the side of the table a shimmering filled the air and suddenly an apparition of Gamal's face appeared to float before them.

"My friend," Gamal said with a laugh. "So good to see you with the medallion. The others tried to do their part, but in the end were worthless in getting me what I really needed. Your abilities are really quite amazing."

All the wizards in the room were on their feet at once, pushing themselves away from the table. Joelle had her staff in front of her, and both the Battlemaster and Dragon Rider had stepped closer to the apparition.

"I told you he was in on it!" Marcus yelled while pointing at Kyril.

"It's not him," Joelle tried to explain. "It's not actually Kyril! It's a shifter that Gamal hired to do his bidding and to steal the medallion."

Gamal only smiled, his lips curling up over his teeth, then he laughed once again. "You pathetic wizards thought you could outsmart me. Your little friend from Arc will be next. I have her with me right now. Then I will find the other medallions and all will bow before the Shadow!"

Joelle hoped that Gamal was just making threats. He couldn't possibly have Sylvie. But before she could do anything, the Battlemaster ran toward Gamal and threw up a blazing wall of fire. Gamal's face dissolved, but moments later reappeared once more a few feet away. Amanda, Fielding, and Marcus all flung up their own hands, fire sizzling forth toward Gamal, but once again he disappeared and reappeared—now closer to Kyril.

"Give me the medallion, boy," Gamal called out, his hand reaching out of the shimmering light.

Joelle acted fast, racing toward Kyril with her staff in one hand. As Kyril lifted his hand, Joelle slammed her staff down on to his arm. Kyril bellowed in pain and turned to face her.

"Kyril, fight it," Joelle said. "This isn't you!"

Kyril snarled and leaped at her, wizard fire spewing forth from outstretched fingers. Joelle brought her staff up and met the attack. A blinding light surrounded Kyril and he disappeared. He transported behind Joelle and kicked her down, then began making his way closer to Gamal.

Marcus shot a wall of air at Kyril, distracting him for a moment as Joelle threw her whole body into Kyril. She knocked him to the ground, dropped her staff, and grabbed the sides of his head with her hands.

With no finesse and no permission she dove inside him with all the power she held, and both she and Kyril shrieked with pain. Joelle could feel the presence of another mind fighting against her. It really was a shifter! It was evil, slippery and dark. She used her healing powers to strengthen Kyril's soul and give him the energy to fight the shifter's presence. The two struggled for a moment and then his medallion lit up on his chest, and once more he transported away from her.

"No!" Joelle yelled as her hands were left holding nothing but air. She couldn't let Kyril hand Gamal the medallion.

Kyril reappeared closer to Gamal, but his movements were stiff. Kyril was fighting for control every step of the way and tried to keep the shifter from reaching Gamal with the medallion. But Joelle didn't know if he was strong enough to resist or not. Then Joelle had an idea. She ran to a spot directly in front of Gamal and stood ready.

"Attack him," she yelled to Marcus, who was the closest.

The wizard was more than happy to oblige and thrust his hands and ensuring fire toward Kyril. However, as Joelle had anticipated, his medallion turned bright and he transported, but this time it was right into Joelle.

Hating herself for doing so, but knowing there was no other way to keep it from Gamal, she pulled a short knife from her waistband and thrust it into Kyril's gut as he reappeared directly in front of her. A howl escaped Kyril's lips—a combination of both his voice and that of the shifter. A hollow echo of pain reverberated around the room.

Kyril slumped to the ground, but out of the corner of her eye Joelle caught a visage of a shape coming out of him and moving toward the closest person in the room--Liam. It had the look and form of a man from the ship. The one that had originally befriended Kaldar. The shifter had moved from person to person throughout the last few days and now was on the verge of taking control of another.

"Watch out!" Joelle yelled at Liam. "The shifter!"

Liam took a step back in surprise, but Joelle watched in horror as his visage changed. He appeared older and more harsh, his eyes going wild.

But Liam fought it. Thrusting his hands up high in the air, he opened his mouth. The roar of a dragon escaped his lips as an answering roar answered back from outside the building. Liam's body shook with tremors but the dual roars grew in pitch and strength until the glass windows in the room burst inward, shards of glass flying into the air.

When the air cleared, standing in the opening was Liam's red dragon, Ryker. A thin blade of fire flew from his lips toward Gamal's apparition and then snaked onward toward Liam himself. The flames grew wider and covered Liam's body. All stood transfixed watching the horrible scene. Through the flames the dark entity of the man emerged from Liam. Gamal appeared again and with outstretched hands beckoned the shadow of the shifter to him. Joelle jumped toward it trying to stop it but she couldn't get there in time. A dark shadow merged with Gamal's visage as a physical body suddenly materialized in front of them.

"I am the shadow master!" Gamal roared and then winked out of existence.

With a soft moan, the body of the shifter fell to the ground. It was scarred and singed from Ryker's dragon fire and in a few moments disintegrated into nothing, leaving only a few scattered ashes on the floor.

A dozen feet away Liam began to slump to the ground. The Battlemaster was at his side and cushioned the fall. Joelle was concerned for him, but more so for Kyril. She dropped down to her friend's side and placed a hand on him. She could barely discern the rise and fall of his chest. Placing her hands on his shoulders, she used her healing powers on him once again, this time stabilizing his vital organs where she had stabbed him. Soon his breath grew more steady.

Kyril opened up his eyes and turned his head slightly back and forth, surveying the scene around him.

"Where am I?" He tried to sit up, but Joelle kept him down for a few moments longer.

"In the council chambers," said Joelle. "Do you know who I am?"

Kyril's face screwed up a bit, then he laughed weakly, which turned into a cough. When he stopped, he tried to sit up again and this time Joelle helped him up.

"Well?" Joelle asked again, impatient for the answer. What if he turned out like Sir Hughes and Kaldar? She couldn't bear the thought of that.

He closed his eyes for a moment and his brow furrowed, then his hand went to the medallion. As it did, a small golden light encased it. Others in the room moved closer.

"Watch out," Marcus yelled—he looked like he was about to attack Kyril again.

Kyril opened his eyes and smiled. "Joelle?" The light receded from the medallion and Marcus backed up, but stayed at the ready.

"Oh, Kyril!" Joelle put her arms around him and hugged him tight. "I was so worried you'd end up like the others."

When she pulled back, Kyril looked around the room, still appearing a bit confused. His eye settled on Liam and Kittoran and he moved in their direction, the rest of the occupants following. Liam stood up, not a sign of dragon fire on his skin or clothes, but he clung to Kittoran to keep his balance.

"How?" Joelle voiced what they were all sure to be thinking.

"The fire from my own dragon does not hurt me," Liam said. The power of the dragon, along with the Cremelino is the power of the spirit. The power to bind all other powers. That binding was too much for the shifter, and he left my body."

"He is gone now?" asked Kaldar, his first words in a while.

Liam nodded his head.

"What about our memories?" Sir Hughes came forward. He and Maddox had retreated to the back of the room during the fighting.

Joelle looked at Kyril and his medallion. "In the short time that Kyril was possessed by the shifter I think that the medallion helped him to retain more of his memories" She reached a hand toward the medallion. "May I?" she asked Kyril.

Kyril took it off his neck and put it in Joelle's palm. Immediately she felt a throbbing of power. With one hand holding the medallion, she beckoned Halsey, Sir Hughes, and Kaldar to her one at a time. Placing her other hand on the side of their head she used the power of the medallion to delve into the far corners of their minds and now found the blockage caused by the shifter's presence.

One by one they pulled away from her with satisfaction on their faces. Kaldar chuckled and winked at Joelle.

"Ah, now I remember," he said. "I remember it all."

Joelle blushed profusely. They both knew what he was talking about. The kiss on the ship.

Kaldar stepped closer and gave her another one, this time on the cheek. Then he whispered in her ear. "Even though the shifter was trying to get information from you at the time, the kiss was from me."

"Kal…." Joelle didn't know what to say and blushed again—or maybe she was still blushing from before. She didn't know, but she laughed all the same and grabbed Kaldar into a fierce hug.

Sir Hughes and Halsey both offered their thanks. Then the room fell silent. They still had the reason for the meeting to attend to.

Marcus grunted, still glaring at Kyril and Joelle. "I had been trying to figure out what was happening. Ever since you two arrived the trouble started.

"The list," Joelle mumbled, remembering the four names on the desk in the office. "But what about the list in your office?"

"What list?" Marcus asked. "And when were you in my office?

Suddenly Joelle figured it out. "It was Halsey's office on the first floor. The list was made by the shifter as he took possession of each body—Sir Hughes, Kaldar, a student, and Halsey. There was a second list of wizards of the mind at the school. Those that I suppose Gamal was going to try and recruit."

"It seems we have discovered who was behind the attack," said Kittoran. "Now we must select the new headmaster."

As they walked back to the table, Joelle pulled Kyril aside. "I'm so sorry I stabbed you. I didn't know what else to do."

Kyril grinned. "You knew you could heal me. I understand."

"What about the other medallions?" Joelle asked. "We never found out anything else about them. We have failed."

Kyril didn't answer her right away but appeared to be thinking.

"Kyril?" Joelle elbowed him.

"I think I might know something," he said. "The shifter met us in Belor. He had been there searching for the other medallions. And in my vision of Gamal I saw the other two attackers mention Belor to him."

"Belor?" Joelle thought of home. With all the trouble she had met in the last few weeks, it would be great to see her family again. She missed them terribly. She reached forward to give the medallion back to Kyril. But before the transfer was complete, a bright light engulfed both of them.

"Joelle!" Kyril called out. "The medallion! What did you do?"

He grabbed her other hand and together they transported out of the wizard school on White Island.

CHAPTER FORTY-ONE

"Faster, Bale," Sylvie called out from behind. They were running across the courtyard and out of the king's palace.

"Stop them," shouted someone following them.

Sylvie didn't have to turn around to know it was a company of guards. They were nearly out of the palace gates. As they ran she used her powers to hinder their followers.

Cobblestone pavers were shaken loose, tree branches fell, and statues tumbled to the ground. All the while they were only able to put a short distance between them and the pursuing guards. Turning a corner they ducked behind some crates and waited for the guards to pass by. They waited enough time to catch their breath and then stepped back out.

"Where to now?" asked Sylvie.

But before Bale could answer a black shimmering appeared in the air around them and Gamal blocked their way. Shadows swirled around him as he raised his hand up, a ball of dark fire enveloping it.

"You are more trouble than you are worth to me," Gamal bellowed.

He was angrier than Sylvie had seen him before. But also appeared tired so she took her chance and struck at him before he could unleash his own attack.

He wavered on his feet for a moment but then transported a few yards away.

Sylvie didn't wait for another attack but went on the offense herself. As she did so a black shadow emerged from Gamal and headed toward Bale. It had the vague form of a man, but slithered and wavered as it moved. Sylvie jumped to intercede and felt an evil chill pass by her.

"Little Bale will be my shadow now," Gamal said, "and will do my bidding."

She had no idea what Gamal was talking about. He seemed out of sorts and didn't make any sense. However, before anything else could happen a lone guard who had doubled back showed up in the alleyway behind Bale. He drew his blade and brought it down on him. Bale jumped to the side, the blade drawing a deep gash down and across his shoulder, but in doing so the shadow passed by him and collided with the guard.

The man writhed on the ground for a moment as the shadow assimilated with him, but then stood back up and with teeth bared glared at both Bale and Sylvie.

"Take care of them," Gamal said. "I need to get back to Shafer. That boy will end up doing something stupid without me around."

"Yes, shadow master," said the guard, a dark gleam in his eye.

Gamal transported away and the guard lunged toward Bale who had no weapon and was now favoring his hurt shoulder. Sylvie pushed into the guard with a blast of air, but the man stayed standing and grabbed Bale around the neck.

"I'll kill him," snarled the guard.

Sylvie held off, trying to think of what to do. Blood soaked through Bale's shirt and his face grew pale.

"Go Sylvie," Bale moaned. "Get to Arc."

"No, Bale," Sylvie said. "I won't leave you."

"Don't worry about me," Bale said. "I have a few tricks up my sleeve."

As if on cue a group of three men showed up. They were winded and breathing hard but were prepared to fight. Sylvie prepared for battle as they came toward her.

"Get her to safety," Bale said to them, his voice growing tight as the guard now had his arm tightening around his neck.

Before she knew what was happening, two men grabbed Sylvie.

"You know the plan," Bale growled at them, still trying to get away from the possessed guard. "Do it."

A contingent of Shafer's guards now returned to the alley way and sprinted toward them, swords drawn and preparing to attack.

Sylvie tried to escape the clutches of the two men that held her, but someone pushed a bitter smelling towel over her mouth. She struggled for a moment and then grew light headed.

"Bale," Sylvie whispered, "what are you doing?"

"What I have to do, Sylvie," he said. "I am sorry."

The last thing she remembered before blacking out was Bale struggling to get away from the possessed guard that held him before the rest of the guards got there.

***

Sylvie sat up and glanced around the room she was in. It had a low wooden ceiling and wooden walls. There were three bunks, one of which she lay on. Sitting up, she moved slowly to put her feet on the floor. Her mind was foggy and she couldn't think clearly.

Where is Bale?

As she stood she wavered on her feet a bit, and then fell back on the bed. That was strange. She felt dizzy, as if…

"I'm on a ship!" she exclaimed as she stood up again. This time she held on to nailed-down furniture as she headed toward the door.

She reached her hand toward the door knob, but before she got there the door flew open. She jumped back with a yelp, bumping into a chair and then falling to the ground. Instantly she felt pain in her ankle.

"I'm sorry, miss," stammered a tall, thin man. He was wearing pants that went just down over his knees and had no shirt on. His skin was darker than hers, but not as dark as Bale's, and his muscles were toned. His dark hair was short and his brows furrowed with worry.

"Are you all right?" he asked.

"I think I hurt my ankle," Sylvie said. "I surmise you don't have a healer around?"

The man shook his head. "Afraid not. We're miles from shore already."

Sylvie thought about Joelle and wished her friend were there with her. She would have her ankle healed in no time.

"Where's Bale?" Sylvie asked.

"I'm not sure who that is, miss—I mean wizard," the man said, a bit confused. "My name is Rial, first mate."

"Bale," Sylvie repeated. "The man I was with in Hasari." She remembered they had been running from the palace guards and Gamal had appeared. Then three men had shown up and taken Sylvie on orders from Bale. Had he turned against her? She didn't think so. But now she was on a ship and having a hard time remembering what happened.

"Gamal?" said Sylvie. "Do you work for Gamal?"

Rial shook his head. "I'm not sure who Gamal is either, miss wizard. I'm just a sailor."

Rial helped Sylvie into the chair. He tenderly felt around her ankle and then stood up and pulled a long strip of cloth out of a drawer. He began to bind it around her foot and ankle and then smiled up at her.

"I'm Sylvie," she said, "and very confused."

Rial smiled up at her and continued wrapping her ankle. "It's not too bad. We have a few days out to sea. Should be good by the time we land."

"But how did I get here? Where am I going? What happened to my friend?" Sylvie said, suddenly feeling like Joelle in the amount of never-ending questions she had.

Just then, a well-built man came in. He wore longer pants and had on a thin shirt. His muscles were more bulging than toned, but he held a kind smile underneath a curled mustache. His skin tone matched those from Cyrene and Turg.

"I'm Captain Shalmanisar, but I go by Sar—or just Captain," said the man, giving her a small nod.

Sylvie stood up, trying not to wince as she did. The ankle did feel a bit better already, but the ship rocked and she fell back down in her seat.

"A rough storm is approaching from the northwest," said the captain. "It'll get a bit rocky and cold, but we'll get through it and get you where you are going."

"Do you know about Bale, my friend from Gildan?" Sylvie asked, becoming even more worried.

The captain shook his head. "I do not know your friend. Payment for your passage was set up two days ago. I was only told to be prepared to leave on a moment's notice as soon as you boarded." He frowned a bit before continuing. "You must be someone awfully special to pay for the entire ship."

"What?" Sylvie asked. "What do you mean?"

"You, Wizard Sylvie, are the only passenger we have on board," said Rial.

The captain gave him a dark look and Rial moved closer to the door.

A loud voice from above informed the captain that he was needed. The ship lurched again and Sylvie grabbed a hold of the table.

"But where are you taking me?" Sylvie cried out. This was all so confusing.

"We were hired to take you to Arc. Now stay here and you'll be fine," the captain said, and both he and the first mate closed the door and left.

At least she was going in the right direction. But she was concerned about Bale. Though, he likely had somehow arranged for her to get to Arc ahead of time. With that and them being able to escape the palace, maybe he was a better spymaster than she had given him credit for. But he did have a way of getting into trouble and she worried about if he had been able to get away from the guards in the alley.

Sylvie had only been on a boat once before, and that was a small pleasure ride on the Saar River in her home kingdom of Arc. She had traveled over land when first coming to Gildan. Looking around the cabin she spied a small portal window behind one of the bunks. She carefully walked over and brought her face up close to the thick glass. Dark clouds and approaching rain filled her vision. The sea churned and she felt her stomach drop again.

Once again, she wished that Joelle was with her. This wasn't going to be good for her stomach.

CHAPTER FORTY- TWO

In an instant Joelle and Kyril found themselves transported from the meeting room in the wizard academy on White Island to a small garden. Summer flowers of purples, reds, and yellows circled around a tall tree. Its broad branches and bright green leaves reached all the way to a small domed building in front of them.

Before either one could say anything, a woman with wide green eyes and long red hair came bursting out of a nearby door toward them.

"Mother!" Joelle said as she rushed into her arms.

It had been over a year since she had seen her.

"So we are in Belor?" Kyril grinned back at Joelle.

"Yes," Joelle squeaked. "That was where you said we should go, right?"

Kyril rolled his eyes at her but didn't seem too angry with her. "I just didn't think it would be right *now*. What will the others think of us?"

Joelle cringed at the thought of leaving the school so quickly and hoped they hadn't made too big of a mess. Her thoughts turned to Kaldar and her face fell a bit. She knew she would probably never see him again. They had different lives to live. He really had only been an innocent traveler in all this.

"Joelle, are you all right?" her mother, Celia, said. "How did you get here?"

Joelle glanced at Kyril and he gave a short nod, holding out the medallion that once more was in his possession.

"We transported here," Joelle said. She knew it would be a surprise, but she wasn't prepared for her mother's reaction.

"Trey!" Joelle yelled out and ran and hugged a younger boy that Kyril surmised was her brother.

"Go find your father," her mother said with a curt voice to Trey. "Now!"

Her brother's eyes went wide at their mother's stern words, but he obeyed nonetheless.

"Mother, what's the matter?" Joelle said.

Her mother's face went pale and she couldn't keep her eyes off of the medallion. They followed her inside and Joelle watched as her mother lowered herself slowly into a chair.

"Why are you here?" Celia asked. "Why now?"

"We traveled to White Island," Joelle answered, still wondering why her mother was acting so strangely. This wasn't like her at all. In light of her reaction, she didn't want to say much more. "We were doing some research at the school."

They sat strangely quiet for a few moments. Kyril kept glancing at Joelle as if he was wondering what was going on. Joelle would have liked to know herself. For the past five years she had been attending the wizard school most of the year, but when she was able to come home on holidays she had been greeted warmly. Her parents had always been kind to her and her brother. Something wasn't right.

"Mother." Joelle opened her mouth to speak.

"Not yet," said her mother firmly, but then her eyes grew a bit moist and she continued in a softer voice. "Just wait until they get here."

"They?" asked Joelle.

But her mother said nothing else.

"I'm going to get something for Kyril and I to eat," Joelle said as she stood up and walked to the kitchen. The front room and kitchen were connected by a small archway. The rest of the downstairs had a library and a bedroom, while upstairs had three other bedrooms.

"Quite a home," Kyril whispered as he followed her into the kitchen. "You never mentioned you were rich."

"It's nothing," she said in an effort to play it off.

"Nothing?" Kyril began.

But she cut him off before he could continue. Joelle actually hated people finding out about her family's finances. It always separated her from others. "My father inherited a large sum of money early in my life—when I was a baby. He works as an advisor to Governor El'Han. It doesn't make me any different from you."

She could tell Kyril didn't agree. She knew of his humble upbringing and the loss of his family. She had never experienced that. He had the good graces to change the subject.

"What's going on here?" Kyril asked.

Joelle grabbed a loaf of bread and began slicing a few pieces for them to eat. She pointed toward a pot of honey and Kyril brought it closer.

"I don't know," Joelle said. "Something's not right."

"Maybe we should just leave," Kyril said. "We need to find the medallion."

"Not until my father comes," Joelle said. "Then we can leave."

They stood for a few moments taking bites from their bread, and then the front door opened.

"Celia," called out her father's voice.

Joelle's mother stayed sitting, but turned her head toward the door. In walked Joelle's father. He had very short auburn hair with a hairline that had receded since she had last seen him. He was slender and about six inches taller than her. He wore green silk robes over loose-fitting pants and shirt. But it was the man behind him that quickly caught Joelle's attention.

"The governor," she whispered to no one in particular, but Kyril nodded his head in acknowledgement beside her.

"Joelle!" Her father's voice was deep and carried across the room. His mouth opened into a wide smile but there were lines of worry around his eyes. He stepped up and gave her a hug, but then she felt him stiffen and he moved away.

"Governor." Joelle bowed her head to the man behind her father. He had unruly red hair, graying just a bit at the temples. He was shorter than her father, and freckles covered his face. He carried himself in a youthful manner despite his being the same age as her father. His warm smile carried to his eyes.

"Healer Joelle," he said. "It is always wonderful to see you. I hear good things about you in Gildan."

Joelle felt her cheeks redden, knowing that the Governor of Belor was keeping tabs on her. "Thank you, sir."

"And who might your traveling companion be?" the governor asked.

"I'm Kyril Siravan from Gildan, sir," Kyril said.

"Well met, Kyril. I'm Kelln El'Han, the governor of Belor."

Kelln's eyes lingered for a moment on Kyril's medallion, but with a quick shake of his head he turned back to Joelle's father with raised eyebrows.

"I'm Joelle's father, Royce El'San," he said to Kyril. His eyes also lingered on the medallion before he motioned Joelle and Kyril to sit down.

"Trey, go and play," said Celia.

Trey appeared about to argue, but with a shake of his father's head he reluctantly obeyed. Once everyone was seated, Joelle's father cleared his throat. With a quick glance at his wife and then the governor, he began to speak.

"Joelle, I must share something with you today that I never thought to do…well at least not in this circumstance."

Joelle moved to the edge of her seat. The side of her leg was touching Kyril's on the small sofa. He appeared anxious to hear what was to be said.

"I'm not sure there is any easy way to say this, my dear daughter." Joelle's father shifted in his seat, and he looked down for a moment before turning back up and looking Joelle in the eyes. "And you will always be my daughter."

"Father," Joelle cried out, tears springing to her eyes. "What is this all about? Please tell me. You're scaring me."
"Your mother and I adopted you, Joelle," her father said.

CHAPTER FORTY-THREE

Joelle's breath quickened and tears instantly flooded her eyes. She sat back hard against the cushion and tried to breathe. This wasn't supposed to happen. Maybe this was another of Gamal's cruel jokes. She thought back on her sixteen years and couldn't remember anyone but Royce and Celia as her parents. They were good people, hardworking, and they loved her. And she loved them. But now…

"Adopted?" Joelle's voice caught in her throat. "What do you mean?"

The governor cleared his voice and with compassion for Joelle tried to continue for her father. "Let me try and explain. Before I was governor, and back in the early days after the last rebellion of Belor, there were bad men in the city that went into hiding. They were trying to avoid being put on trial for crimes they had been involved with during the rebellion. Back then, wizards in the Realm were just beginning to be recognized and accepted again. Belor had almost been destroyed by one—a man who referred to himself as only the Preacher. If you remember our history our new king, Darius DarSan Williams, had only recently declared himself as a wizard."

Joelle had known most of this already. The King's children, Dragon Rider Liam and his sister Breanna had been students at the wizard school with her. "But what does this have to do with me? I can't be adopted!"

"During those difficult years there were many who vied for power in Belor," the governor continued. "One man, Duvall, a minor wizard, infiltrated the ranks of the city council and became a close friend to the governor at the time. But behind the scenes he was a horrible man. He was greedy and vicious, and through the use of various artifacts tried to teach himself magic of an evil nature. The governor's counselors finally built up enough evidence against him. I was the king's ambassador at the time and had the responsibility of making the arrest. Late in the evening we went to his home to capture him. A fight ensued and he held his wife…your birth mother, Cherise and you, as hostages."

Joelle realized that tears streaming down her face. "My father was this Duvall?" She felt ashamed to be related to such a man. But now she knew where she had gotten her wizard powers.

"I was a young guard at the time," Joelle's father said. "We stayed outside of your home so as not to harm you or Cherise. Duvall kept shouting for her to bring him something but she wouldn't tell him where it was. Finally an explosion rocked the house and he fled out the back door. A group of guards chased him while I went into the house. The explosion had caused a fire and the flames grew quickly. The smoke made it hard to breathe, but we made our way to you and your mother. Your mother was crawling on the floor toward a small table. She pushed it over, and in the floorboard was a small crack. She pried a hidden compartment open."

Joelle grabbed Kyril's hand. She felt him stiffen for a moment, but then she smiled, and with a bit of her magic he relaxed and turned back to her father.

"I found you in the house lying in a corner on a blanket," her father said, tears coming to his own eyes. "You were so small. Hardly more than six or seven months. You weren't crying, but your bright green eyes were taking in everything around you. I reached down and picked you up and held you. I remember the moment your little hand reached over and grasped one of my fingers."

Her father stopped for a moment, trying to gather his emotions. Joelle's mother was also crying. Why had they never told her? A slow underlying anger began to build deep inside her. She knew they loved her, but they didn't have a right to keep this from her.

"But what happened to my birth-mother?" Joelle blurted out, more loudly than she intended. All in the room reeled back as if a force had knocked into them. She realized her powers of the heart—a heart that was now being torn—had fed on her anger. But she didn't care much at the moment.

"While I was looking down at you in my arms, a portion of the wall fell on top of Cherise," said Joelle's father. "I cried out for help but the others were chasing your father. I tried to find a place to put you down, but the smoke was getting too thick and you were crying. I tried with one hand to help your mother…but I couldn't…I just couldn't do anything."

"You let my mother die?" Joelle cried. "You killed her."

"No. No, Joelle," her father said, tears streaming down his face. "Duvall started the fire that killed Cherise. I tried to help her, but I couldn't without hurting you. Your little lungs couldn't take much more smoke. Her legs were pinned by the wall. She stuck her hand into the hole in the wooden floor and brought something out. With her last ounce of energy she pushed it into my hands and told me to get you to safety and keep you away from your father. And when you were older to give it to you."

Joelle sobbed and couldn't stop. Her entire life had just been turned upside down.

"I really tried to help her, Joelle," her father said. "I put you down outside where it was safe and ran back to help. But the fire it was…it was just too hot."

After more tears were shed an uncomfortable silence followed. Joelle didn't know what to do. She felt lost.

"Did they catch him?" Kyril asked after a moment of silence. "Did they catch Duvall?"

"Yes, they did," the governor said. "They tried him and found him guilty of stealing from the governor, inciting riots, using magic unlawfully, and many other things. Due to the new king and his benevolent nature, it was decided to not have him executed, but instead confined to prison for the rest of his life. But…"

The governor looked at Joelle's parents for a moment before speaking again. All of a sudden he appeared older than he had when he had first come in.

"But," he said, "he escaped last week and came here with another man, looking for you and the object that Cherise left. There have been guards outside since, but we don't know where he is at the moment."

Joelle got her sobbing under control. "What was it? What did she leave me?" She couldn't believe that there might be something after all these years that she could have as a keepsake of her birth mother.

Her father put his hands in his robe and brought out a small wooden box. It was a simple box with no markings on it and only a small latch on one side. He stood up and held his hand out. Kyril jumped up, took it from him, and brought it back to Joelle. Holding it in her lap for a moment, she glanced up and saw everyone watching her with a mixture of fascination and sadness.

"Open it, Joelle," Kyril said, leaning in from the side.

Slowly she lifted the latch, and then the lid. She didn't know what to expect, but this was not it.

"A medallion!" Joelle exclaimed with tears streaming down her face once more. "It's the bronze medallion!"

CHAPTER FORTY-FOUR

Kyril's mouth fell open as he peered down at the bronze medallion. It had an identical pattern to his own gold one. He stifled a small laugh about all they had just been through at the wizard school, only to find that the medallion was here with Joelle's family all that time. He wondered briefly if it would be the same with Sylvie…but then dismissed the thought, thinking that it would be too much of a coincidence.

Joelle brought her fingers to the medallion, but then glanced up at Kyril as if asking permission to touch it.

"Go ahead," Kyril said.

Joelle gently lifted the medallion out of the small wooden box by its chain with one hand, and then carefully slipped it over her neck. As soon as she did so, a flare of bright bronze light spread out from the edges of the medallion. Kyril leaned forward, and a portion of the light snaked toward him and caressed his own gold medallion that was once again hanging around his neck.

In that instant, he found himself, as he had before when he had first touched his medallion, on a hillside overlooking a large city—one he now knew as Anikari, the capital of the Realm; only 400 years ago. Hearing a gasp beside him, he turned and saw Joelle standing there with him. Her mouth was open and her green eyes were wide. The wind ruffled her long red hair around her shoulders.

"This is where I saw King Anikari give the medallions to the others," Kyril said softly. "But they are not here now. I don't understand."

Hearing the sound of voices, Kyril took a few steps down the hill. A man dressed in black robes walked out from behind a tree and a pretty middle aged woman joined him. Kyril crooked his finger for Joelle to join him and they both crouched down low, even though Kyril figured they probably wouldn't be seen anyway. They were watching something from the past unfold.

Where was the king and who were these two people?

The man turned and Kyril saw a black medallion swaying in front of his broad chest. It appeared similar to the one that his old master Targon had owned and that Gamal had taken.

Without warning another man materialized in front of the other two, obviously using the power of transportation.

"He is coming." The newcomer spoke in a low whisper, but his voice carried on the breeze to where Kyril and Joelle crouched. "Anikari is coming."

"My friends, we have lost today," said the man wearing the medallion, spreading his arms wide, "and so I must leave and prepare for the future."

"Where will we go, shadow master?" asked the woman.

Shadow master? thought Kyril. That's what Gamal called himself.

The man in black laughed and sparks swirled around his fingertips. "Oh, Lyana, you will not be going anywhere."

"He's going to kill her," Joelle whispered into Kyril's ear.

Kyril said nothing back and just watched. Why would he kill his friends?

The man reached his hands out, one toward the man who had brought the news and the other toward the woman. A black fire sizzled from his medallion to his fingertips and then snaked out toward the two of them.

"Sire," said Lyana, her voice growing in panic and volume. "What are you doing? Haven't we served you faithfully?"

"Yes, my dear, you and Roeth have done well," said the man. "You have done all I have asked of you. The artifacts of darkness are now safe, and with this medallion I'll soon control them all."

"We can go with you and help you." Roeth rose up on his tiptoes in obvious pain, his teeth clenched tight and the muscles in his neck throbbing.

The shadow master cocked his head to one side. "In a way yes, you both will always be with me. Your powers will live on for centuries and anytime chaos is needed, anytime there is one worthy to assume the mantle of Shadow master, he will use you…as I have."

Kyril and Joelle watched as the man pulled upon greater power. Roeth collapsed to the ground and his eyes rolled up into the back of his head.

"Ah, Roeth, always the weaker one," the shadow master said, "but now I have stolen your ability to transport. It will serve me well in my escape."

In an instant he had moved closer to the woman and now stood mere inches from her. The woman's face held firm, but her blue eyes bulged and her knees were beginning to collapse.

"She's going to stab him," whispered Joelle.

Then before Kyril could say anything, the man attacked her with his wizard powers.

"Now I will steal your ability."

A shadow began moving out from the woman and into the man. He breathed in deeply as a satisfied look spread across his face.

"Ah, now I have your ability to shift and possess the bodies of others," the man said.

Then the woman flicked a small dirk out from the sleeve of her dress and sank it deeply into the chest of the man. A surprised look spread across the man's face, but no more surprised than the look Kyril was sure was on his own face. How had Joelle known?

However, before the man fell, a dark shadowed shape moved back out of him and entered back into the body of Lyana instead. She threw her head back and let out a loud cackle.

"Ah, Lyana," came the voice, a combination of both her and the shadow master. "With your own ability I will now shift my soul into your body and will control you forever."

"She was a shifter," Kyril said.

"We should do something," Joelle said. "We should stop him."

Kyril shook his head. "It doesn't work like that here. They can't see us."

"Then why are we hiding?" asked Joelle as she stood up and began walking toward Lyana, who the shadow master now possessed.

"Joelle!" Kyril called out.

Joelle brought her staff out in front of her and marched forward, but as Kyril had thought, the shadow master paid her no attention.

As the body of the man in black stilled, Lyana—now the shadow master—reached down and grabbed the dark medallion off his neck and placed it around her own. Then, at the sound of others approaching, and with a quick bolt of lightning from her fingertips, she completely disintegrated the two male bodies on the ground.

"Malek!" came a booming voice.

Up over the hill came King Anikari. His stormy gray eyes took in the scene around him, and he looked in the direction of Kyril and Joelle for a moment. He tilted his head and a small grin flickered over his face—could it have been in acknowledgement? A gold-lined blue cloak sat royally across his broad shoulders and a gold crown sat on his head of brown hair.

Seeing only the presence of Lyana standing before him, the king appeared confused for a moment…but then he nodded. "It is you, isn't it?"

"It is."

"And what will you do now?" Anikari asked, his eyes growing sad. "It didn't have to end this way, Malek. You were my friend."

Lyana spat on the ground, a sight that contrasted with the beautiful woman standing before them. "I was never your friend, Anikari. I was just someone to do your bidding."

"That's not true," Anikari said. "I have united the cities and the Realm will be as strong as any kingdom. You could have been a part of that. But you always wanted more. More power. The wrong power. That was your downfall."

Coming up behind Anikari came three others and fear flashed across the face of Lyana-Malek.

"It's time for me to go, Anikari," she said. "But beware, I will sow chaos around you, I will pass it on to others. There will never be peace again. You will watch loved ones die and be destroyed, and each time you do, you will think of me, the shadow master."

"I will stop you, Malek," Anikari said.

"You will not live long enough to stop me," Lyana said as a glow began to develop around her.

"Then others will," Anikari said as he glanced in the direction of Kyril and Joelle.

Kyril took a step back in response to the attention.

With a bright flash of light around them, The shadow master, in the form of Lyna disappeared and Kyril found himself back in Joelle's house, standing next to her.

"Was that real?" she asked him.

"Was what real?" asked her mother. "Joelle you are in danger. You need to lea—"

Her voice was cut short by their back door crashing open. Joelle brought her staff out in front of her and Kyril followed her toward the door.

A frail man entered with two other bigger men behind him. They all held swords and one held an additional club in the opposite hand. They appeared vicious and ready to kill.

"That medallion belongs to me," said the man in front. "Give it to me."

"Father?" Joelle asked, a combination of loathing and longing flickering across her face.

"Duvall?" whispered Royce.

The man stopped for a moment and his face dropped as he looked Joelle up and down. Then his eyes grew hard and he moved forward. The other two men spread out to the sides.

"I knew your mother had it along," said Duvall. "And it cost her her life."

Joelle's back stiffened and Kyril moved up next to her. He couldn't know what she was feeling at the moment. Facing the man who had caused her birth mother to die and had never reached out to her.

"Kyril, take the man on the left," Joelle said. "He favors his left leg."

"How…?" Kyril shook his head.

"Just do it."

Kyril did as he was told and leaped toward a man as he came at him from behind Duvall. Kyril ducked under a swinging sword and kicked out at the man's left leg. He bellowed out in pain and his sword arm dropped. With that opening, Kyril lashed out at him with a blast of wizard's fire and the man went down.

Both Royce and the governor joined them in the attack. As Duvall and the other man came forward, Joelle gave the governor and Royce instructions. With each attack, they advanced a bit more against the assailants. Shortly, the fight was over and Joelle stood over her birth father. He had his hands up in the air and she stood with her staff just above his face. It crackled with power and grew brighter and brighter.

"Joelle," Kyril tried to bring her back down. He knew too well the amount of power that could come from the medallion. And as a wizard of the heart she fueled it with her anger right now.

"Please," the man wailed. "I'm your father."

"My father would never attack me," Joelle said.

"But, he…," Duvall said, his voice cracking and pleading, "he is too powerful. You don't understand, daughter."

"Don't call me your daughter," Joelle said. "And I know who you work for. A man who is selfish and evil, just like you. Gamal. Gamal Turomi."

The man gasped. "He is stronger than all of us. He is the shadow master."

Joelle glanced at Kyril. They had seen a man referred to as the shadow master in their vision. Knowing that Gamal may have descended from that man, or have inherited his powers, was worrisome.

"Please…" the man said once more. "Don't kill me."

Joelle hesitated for a moment and appeared to let her guard down. Without any warning, Kyril saw her leap up in the air as if to kick something, but at first there was nothing there. However, at the moment her foot hit its peak, her father had tried to get up—and his head was at that exact spot and it collided with her foot with a *thud.* His body fell back to the ground unconscious.

Joelle turned to him with the answer to Kyril's unasked question. "I knew what he was going to do ahead of time. It's the medallion. I can discern the intents of others, as well as some of their thoughts."

"That could be dangerous," said the governor.

Joelle nodded her head. "Yes, it could; but you don't have to worry about me, I won't be staying around here, Governor."

The governor's eyebrows lifted high.

"Joelle!" her mother said with a worried face. "What are you talking about?"

"Kyril and I are on an urgent mission. A mission that started hundreds of years ago. These medallions were made by King Anikari for just this time. Gamal is spreading chaos and is the new shadow master of our day, it appears. His reach is longer than we suspected. He's been in both the wizard academy in Gildan, the wizard school on White Island, and who knows where else his followers are. I'm afraid he is going to the Wizard Conclave in the kingdom of Arc now if I had to would guess."

Joelle glanced at Kyril for confirmation and he agreed with her assessment.

"His plans have been in motion for years," Kyril said. "He must be stopped. But we need the power of the medallions to do it. "

"And you must do this?" her father asked.

"Yes, we must do this." She grabbed hold of Kyril's hand and spoke to him. "We need to get back to Sylvie in Gildan. She must be warned before we go to Arc."

Kyril nodded. Bringing up the power of his medallion he thought about the wizard school in Gildan and prepared to transport. There would be no mistakes this time.

"Goodbye, Mother and Father," said Joelle. "Tell Trey goodbye for me. I'll come back after this is done. I promise."

And with a flash of light they were gone.

CHAPTER FORTY-FIVE

It had been four days since Joelle and Kyril had returned to Gildan. They had met with the emperor each day since. He had informed them that Bale had escorted Sylvie to the coast and that she would take a ship to Arc and begin searching for the other medallion by doing research at the Wizard Conclave there.

They had both been surprised to find that she had left, and Joelle was sad to have missed her friend. But Sylvie never did like to sit still for long.

"Now we don't have a good way of getting there quickly," Joelle said to the emperor and Kyril during another meeting.

The emperor didn't seem to understand.

"She means that I or someone with me still has to have been to where we are going in order for me to transport there. Since Sylvie attended the Wizard Conclave, she was our way there. I wish she would have waited. We should have heard something by now from Bale."

The emperor sat thinking for a moment.

"You are worried, my lord," Joelle said to the emperor. She could *feel* it.

Ever since returning from Belor with the medallion, she had heard many thoughts and seen many intentions. It was quite overwhelming, and she was having a hard time thinking about anything on her own. The only person she didn't get anything from was Kyril—most likely because of the medallion.

"Be careful, young healer," the emperor chided her. "You need to learn to control your newfound skill. It is a dangerous ability you have."

"But one that could be helpful in the fight to come," Joelle said a bit too defensively.

Mezar Alrishitar smiled broadly and didn't appear offended at her response. "Yes, it might at that. As emperor, it would be a valuable thing to be able to discern the intentions and thoughts of others."

Joelle's heart skipped a beat. He wouldn't try to use her, would he? Before she could voice her concern, he continued.

"But that would not be right," the emperor said. "And I'm not quite sure if we should judge people for their thoughts or intentions. You must be very careful, Wizard Joelle. I must warn you that an intention of evil or even a negative thought may not necessarily mean that intention or action will follow.

"But…" Joelle started to argue.

"Have you ever been angry or thought badly of someone?" the emperor asked. "And were there times when you wished some harm to them, but you never did carry it out?"

Joelle felt herself turn red.

"Don't feel bad," Emperor Alrishitar said. "These are normal human feelings. Your control over those thoughts and feelings is what's important."

"So you are saying that the intentions or thoughts of someone that come to me because of the medallion may not be accurate?" Joelle asked with concern. "How am I to know? What if I make a mistake?"

"I've made plenty of those," mumbled Kyril from beside her.

The emperor chuckled. "As have I, young wizards. As have I."

Kyril and Joelle stood in silence for a moment when the door burst open. Falling through the door was Bale, with Prince Zaidan close behind.

"Father," the prince spoke in a rush. "We have a problem."

All eyes turned to the prince—though Joelle glanced over at Bale first. His shirt was torn, there were bruises on his face, and one of his eyes was swollen shut. He was dirty and appeared exhausted.

The emperor had the door closed by a guard and ushered them all over to a small sitting area. Bale all but fell onto a sofa and Joelle took the opportunity to sit down next to him. She placed one hand on his upper back and sent a small trickle of healing into him. He stiffened for a moment, glanced at her, and then looked down. His eyes held pain and disappointment.

"She's lost, Sire," Bale said without any other explanation, "and he's there."

"Slow down, Bale," said the emperor, "and tell me what happened. Who is lost and who is where?"

"We were taken in by King Shafer," Bale began, "and I was treated badly. Sylvie had a plan for us to get away, but…Gamal was there. He was *there*."

"Gamal in Cyrene?" Kyril asked. "What is he doing there now?" His face grew pale and he glanced at Joelle before turning back to Bale.

Gamal always seemed to be ahead of them. But he didn't have any of the medallions yet. As if to make sure, Joelle wrapped her right hand around her own, still hanging by a chain from her neck.

"He was invited there by King Shafer," Bale explained.

"Shafer's formed an alliance with Gamal Turomi?" the emperor said loudly. "He is a young fool, but I would not have believed that. But what about Sylvie?"

Bale shook his head for a moment, his eyes haunted by something. "We escaped the palace and ran from the guards. Gamal attacked us, but then left some kind of shadow to do his bidding. It possessed one of the guards and tried to attack me.

"A shifter," Kyril whispered. "Just like in our vision. Gamal now has the ability to shift."

"Then others came," Bale continued without responding to Kyril's words. "I had to get her to safety, Sir. I had arranged passage in case anything happened and used the spymasters organization there to get her to a ship."

"Then she is safe," Joelle said,"and on her way to Arc. We can go overland and meet her there."

Bale shook his head multiple times and put his head down into his hands before raising it back up slowly. Tears came to his haunted eyes. "I've failed you, Your Highness. I've failed us all."

"But she got to the ship," Kyril said. "You did what you could, Bale. She can take care of herself. You know that."

Bale looked at the prince for a moment.

His eyes were moist also and he nodded his head toward Bale. "Tell them."

Everyone leaned in closer and Bale opened his mouth and spoke slowly and softly. "There was a storm…a terrible, horrible storm. Word came back that parts of a ship were found at sea. One of the men—the first mate—was clinging to a board, barely alive. He knew who Sylvie was, but…but…he was the only survivor. The only one!"

Joelle gasped out loud and jumped up. She couldn't believe the news. It couldn't be true. Sylvie couldn't be dead.

"She could have survived," she said softly as she fell back onto her seat.

"It was a horrible storm. Lots of ships were lost and hers was in pieces," Bale said. "I know she's powerful. But no one could have lived through that."

Joelle glared at Bale and felt his raw emotional thoughts and intentions. It was hard not to become overwhelmed with his pain. The man surely believed her dead.

"This is grave news indeed," the emperor finally spoke. He then turned to Joelle and Kyril. "What will you do?"

Both of the young medallion holders sat quietly for a moment, then Kyril stood up. Joelle tried to feel what Kyril intended to do, but she couldn't get past the medallion.

"We must go on," Kyril said bravely, though his eyes were moist. "We've seen too much of what Gamal can do with the powers he is amassing. The darkness and chaos are growing. We must find the other medallion. The powers of the medallion are the only thing that can save us now. We must go to Arc."

Bale jumped from his seat. "I will go with you."

The emperor put his hand out in front of him. "That is not necessary or maybe even wise, Bale Nabhani. You are injured and grieving, and we may need your services here."

"I will resign my position and go with Kyril and Joelle," Bale said firmly. "Sylvie was my responsibility, and I will avenge her. I will not stop until Gamal and his darkness is destroyed."

Everyone else stood and awaited the emperor's words. He then nodded his head once.

"You were a good friend to Sylvie, and good friends are hard to come by," Emperor Alrishitar said. "I honor your request but do not release you from your position. Go with Joelle and Kyril and bring justice to Gamal. Bring honor to your kingdom, Bale Nabhani." Then he turned to them all. "Many kingdoms rest on the shoulders of all three of you."

"Four shoulders, my Lord, four," said Joelle with firmness. "I will not believe Sylvie is dead until I see proof with my own eyes."

The Emperor smiled. "My blessing go with your journey. Let me know what I can do to help. All I have is at your disposal."

"Thank you, Sire," said Kyril. "We will not let you down."

CHAPTER FORTY-SIX

Sylvie rolled to her side and was met with stabbing pain. Her entire body hurt so badly that she wondered if she was actually dead. But if this was death it looked an awful lot like the inside of a large tent. She lay on a cot, similar to three more in the tent. Multiple large chests, a table and chairs, and other belongings were neatly arranged throughout.

The storm had been fiercer than the captain had thought and the ship had been blown off-course. She remembered sitting in her room, terrified at the sounds going on around her. Then suddenly, like a crack of lightning, the ship had hit something and split in two.

She remembered water coming into her room and enveloping her before she could think to do anything about it. She had swum, trying to keep afloat, and grabbed onto a piece of wood. Sounds of screams and cries had filled her ears—even now she put her hands over them to stop the pain. How could she still be alive? Surely everyone else had perished.

After a moment a shadow moved over her and she turned and looked up. Two women, both scarcely older than her, stood above her. Relief spread across their faces.

"Miss, how are you feeling?" One of them said, her voice musical and light.

"I'm…I'm…" Sylvie tried to think of how to answer. "I'm sore and hungry. How long have I been here?"

"You've been asleep for five days," said the other.

"How?" was all Sylvie could say. It was all so fuzzy. She knew she had been on a ship, but couldn't remember why or where she had been going. The horror of watching many of the crewmen drown before her eyes kept replaying itself in her mind. But nothing after that.

"One of our small fishing boats found you at sea, lying across a board after the storm, and they brought you in to us."

"Who are you?"

The first one to speak answered with a soft smile. "I am Eva, and this is my sister Elise."

Elise helped her to sit up and Sylvie got a better look at them. They both had long dark hair but light skin. Eva appeared a bit older and had a more angular face, while Elise, closer to Sylvie's age had more ample cheeks, but the fact that surprised her the most was that they both had somewhat pointed ears.

Sylvie had seen elves before; a few came to Gildan to the school there to visit or trade from time to time, and two had come to Arc to meet with leaders at the Wizard Conclave, but these appeared a bit different. She couldn't quite place it, but maybe they weren't full blooded elves.

Where am I? The thought kept echoing in her mind. Her head hurt horribly and she put her hand on it to try and feel what the problem was.

"What is your name?" Elise asked as she helped Sylvie back down. "Do you remember who you are?"

"Sylvie." She knew that much about herself, but not much more.

"Well Sylvie, that's a beautiful name," Elise smiled at her. "You need to rest a bit more. Your body is still quite weak."

Sylvie nodded her head in agreement. She didn't feel good at all.

"We'll get some food," Eva said, her face more serious than Elise's, "and leave it for you to eat when you wake up."

"Mmm," Sylvie mumbled, feeling very tired again. But before the two sisters left the tent, she turned her head and asked, "But where am I?"

A brief silence followed until Eva spoke up. Her voice was softer than before. "You're someplace safe, my dear. Someplace safe. Don't worry. This is a very special place. You'll never be in danger again. Never."

Eva's voice was so calming and musical that it lulled Sylvie back toward sleep. She would stay there for a while and relax. As far as she knew she didn't have any other pressing matters to attend to, did she?

It would be good to always feel safe.

***

To continue the adventures of Kyril, Sylvie, and Joelle and their quest to find the remaining medallion and stop Gamal, read Power of the Medallion, Book 3 in The Wizard Academies.

Other Series By Mike Shelton

The Alaris Chronicles

For 100 years it protected them…
…and now the magical barrier is about to fail.

What waits on the other side?

Bakari is nerdy and awkward. At 15, he's lived at the Wizard Citadel for most of his life. Everything seems to be working out like he'd hoped. He just got promoted to Level 1 and despite being painfully shy, he has a friend.

Kharlia knows medicine. And he really likes her.

When Bakari finds an ancient map that marks a source of power, he must check it out. With Kharlia by his side, they wander through the Kingdom toward the spot on the map. The trip isn't what they expect.

Magical creatures have made it through the barrier. Should they fight or flee?

Bakari knows they are in trouble. He isn't a battle wizard. As they struggle against the beasts, the worst thing Bakari can imagine happens.

Will they survive?

You'll love this first book in *The Alaris Chronicles,* because of the beautifully woven story with diverse characters, great adventure, and political intrigue.

Sign up on Mike's website at www.MichaelSheltonBooks.com and get a copy of the prequel novella e-book to The Alaris Chronicles, Prophecy of the Dragon.

Protect the youngest heir of the Dragon King. That is the mission given to Imari in this prequel novella to The Alaris Chronicles.

The Cremelino Prophecy

About 15 years prior to The Alaris Chronicles and a few kingdoms to the north.

A Prophecy. A Powerful Sword. A reluctant wizard.

Darius San Williams, son of one of King Edward's councilors, cares little for his father's politics and vows to leave the city of Anikari to protect and bring glory to the Realm.

When a new-found and ancient magic emerges within him, he and his friends Christine and Kelln are faced with decisions that could shatter or fulfill the prophecy and the lives of all those they know.

Wizards and magic have long been looked down upon in the Realm, but Darius learns that no matter where he goes, prophecy and destiny are waiting to find him.

Sign up on Mike's website at www.MichaelSheltonBooks.com and get a copy of the prequel novella e-book to The Cremelino Prophecy, The Blade and The Bow.

Follow Darius and Kelln in one of their more fantastic adventures prior to The Path Of Destiny.

The TruthSeer Archives

On an island far out in the Eastern Sea join a new adventure of magic through the stones of power.

Everyone lies.
What if you could tell when they did?
What if this knowledge caused you immense physical pain?

Given a rare TruthStone, Shaeleen suffers immense agony with every lie she hears or tells. While struggling to control her new power and curb the pain she learns a powerful truth that could thrust an entire continent into civil war.

The stones of power protect the five kingdoms of Wayland - and have done so for two hundred years. Now those stones are failing and a dark power threatens to take control. With the help of her brother, and a young thief, Shaeleen sets out on a dangerous journey to gather and restore the power of all the stones.

The lies could kill her, but the truth could destroy a kingdom.

Will she succeed before the endless lies destroy her?

About the Author

Mike was born in California and has lived in multiple states from the west coast to the east coast. He cannot remember a time when he wasn't reading a book. At school, home, on vacation, at work at lunch time, and yes even a few pages in the car (at times when he just couldn't put that great book down). Though he has read all sorts of genres he has always been drawn to fantasy. It is his way of escaping to a simpler time filled with magic, wonders and heroics of young men and women.

Other than reading, Mike has always enjoyed the outdoors. From the beaches in Southern California to the warm waters of North Carolina. From the waterfalls in the Northwest to the Rocky Mountains in Utah. Mike has appreciated the beauty that God provides for us. He also enjoys hiking, discovering nature, playing a little basketball or volleyball, and most recently disc golf. He has a lovely wife who has always supported him, and three beautiful children who have been the center of his life.

Mike began writing stories in elementary school and moved on to larger novels in his early adult years. He has worked in corporate finance for most of his career. That, along with spending time with his wonderful family and obligations at church has made it difficult to find the time to truly dedicate to writing. In the last few years as his children have become older he has returned to doing what he truly enjoys – writing!

mikesheltonbooks@gmail.com
www.MichaelSheltonBooks.com
https://www.facebook.com/groups/MikeSheltonAuthor/
http://www.Twitter.com/msheltonbooks
http://www.Instagram.com/mikesheltonbooks

www.ingramcontent.com/pod-product-compliance
Lightning Source LLC
Chambersburg PA
CBHW020919110726
47900CB00001B/213

* 9 7 8 1 7 3 3 5 1 0 4 6 2 *